THE FIRST MURDER

a novel

CAROL GOODMAN KAUFMAN

THE FIRST MURDER
By Carol Goodman Kaufman

Copyright © 2024 Carol Goodman Kaufman
All rights reserved.

Published by TouchPoint Press
www.touchpointpress.com

Softcover ISBN: 978-1-956851-75-5

Permissions and review inquiries: media@touchpointpress.com.
Rights: info@touchpointpress.com

Editor: Eleonora Masala
Cover Design: Sheri Williams
Cover images: Adobe Stock

Connect with Carol Goodman Kaufman online:
carolgoodmankaufman.com

First Edition

Printed in the United States of America.

For Joel, who throughout our years together, has supported my writing and every other project with which I've become involved.

They say that plans themselves are of little importance, but planning is vital. Ha. Did you get that? Vital?

"Concerned with or necessary to the maintenance of life." Good one, Merriam-Webster. You really know how to make a person laugh. You kill. Got that one, too? I'm really on a roll. Sometimes I'm so clever I amaze myself.

So, to planning. Every element of my project needs to be in place for it to work, and I must practice to make sure there are no glitches. Practice makes perfect. The key to it all is timing.

No need for a flashlight. A full moon will provide enough light to guide the way.

Into the house I'll go, up the stairs, and down the hall, past the closet door and the bathroom. Until I arrive at the master bedroom.

I do the job. I let myself out.

Easy peasy.

Then it's back to our regularly scheduled life.

CHAPTER ONE

Chief of Police Caleb Crane emerged from the pre-dawn fog into the Queen Bee Diner, causing the bell over the door to jingle. Droplets of mist on his wavy black hair sparkled in the eatery's bright lights. He greeted the regulars at the counter, seekers of coffee and sustenance before heading off to work at the local quarry or paper plant.

"Ah, the cop who came in from the cold," one said.

"Good one, Earl," he replied.

Caleb settled into his favorite perch by the bay window overlooking the village square. A pony-tailed waitress hustled past him and pushed through the swinging door into the kitchen. It made a soft swishing sound followed by a bang as it hit the tiled wall.

He looked out onto the peaceful scene. Three antique gaslights, one on each block of Queensbridge's Main Street, cast circles of pale yellow into the pre-dawn gray, their glow diffused by a haze so thick that every store, every tree was shrouded. He wondered what else the fog might obscure. Every person?

You're getting jaded, Caleb. You're not in New York anymore.

His stomach grumbled as he inhaled the aroma of frying bacon. He'd been up since 4:00 a.m., when Jonas Summers had called him at home, panicked that someone was trying

I

to break into his house. Caleb had rushed out, only to find a mother bear trying to pull an air conditioning unit out of a window. After calling animal control, he told Jonas that if he insisted on keeping bird feeders, he shouldn't be surprised if a bear showed up, and then warned him that this would be the last time he came out to run one off.

An apron-clad waitress approached the table and poured coffee into a bright red Fiestaware mug. Caleb took a big gulp, savoring the chicory overtones of the scalding liquid, added in honor of the owner's New Orleans roots. As he drank, he mulled over his decision to take the chief's position in Queensbridge, perhaps the hundredth time he had done so. The tiny Berkshire village was beautiful, and a hell of a lot quieter than his Brooklyn beat. But were quiet and peaceful what he had signed up for when he applied to the police academy?

Then again, for Rachel there would never be enough peace. Not after New York. Not after Manny.

He picked up the *Berkshire Eagle* and scanned the headlines. Drug bust in Pittsfield. Domestic violence in North Adams. And an article citing a study showing the state had the third highest number of deaths from out-of-state air pollution.

As the sun began to peek over the hills, he decided to try the crossword puzzle, and plucked a pencil from a mug. Only at the Bee could you find sharpened pencils with good erasers on every table.

He had just filled in the first few squares of the grid when Elliot Freund entered the diner. He crossed the wide-plank pine floor with long strides and plopped down in the opposite seat.

"Hey. Have you eaten?" Elliot asked.

"Not yet."

Caleb signaled to the waitress and the two friends ordered.

Elliot pointed to the newspaper. "Isn't that something about death in the state from pollution? It's also killing our trees."

"How's that?" Caleb asked.

"Air pollutants predispose them to damage by insects and disease. Between that and the Asian long-horned beetle, gypsy moths, and ash borers, we've got a real problem on our hands."

Earl Bennett jumped off his stool at the counter and into the conversation. "Freud, you're such a wingnut. Is this some more of your cockamamie global warming theory again?"

"First of all, it's Freund, and you know it. But you think I'm a wingnut because I'm concerned about the environment? All this has an effect on real people, Earl. Your grandchildren will be breathing polluted air and drinking dirty water."

"You leave my grandchildren out of this," shouted Earl, his chin jutting out, his hands balled into fists, his face flushed. His silver-gray brush cut seemed to bristle with anger.

Elliot stood up. "No, I won't. I don't want my legacy to be a world with filthy air and water. And neither does Mary Jane."

Suddenly, Earl lunged at Elliot and punched him. Elliot, with a good four inches and thirty pounds on the older man, stepped back, stunned, and rubbed his jaw.

Caleb jumped in to separate the two men. "Hey, back off, Earl. There's no need for violence."

"He's asking for it." Earl sneered the words. "I could kill him for what he's done, the son of a bitch." Then, turning away from Caleb, he spat, a wad of frothy saliva landing squarely on Elliot's cheek. "And I could wring her neck."

Caleb grabbed him by the shoulders and pushed him against a wood paneled wall while Elliot grabbed a napkin from the table to wipe off the spit.

"Nobody's asking for anything. And Earl, stop. Think. You have a business here. You of all people should know how many people here depend on tourism. If we don't have nice foliage come fall, people won't be flocking into town, eating and drinking in our restaurants, and staying in our inns. They won't buy art or tickets to theater and concerts. And, if we're not attractive as a destination, your property values will fall. Do you want to lose money on your biggest investment?"

Earl turned toward Caleb and jabbed a finger at his chest. "You're really under that lefty's influence, aren't you? Damn New Yorkers think they know everything. It's people like that who're going to destroy what we have here."

"Earl, it's time to leave. Now."

Earl pulled out his wallet, slapped some bills down on the counter, and slammed out the door, clanging the bell as he did. Dead silence filled the room.

The two friends returned to their booth. Caleb shook his head, trying to work out what had just transpired in the diner. "What's up with Earl today? He's not usually this bad."

"Caleb, you give him too much credit. Earl's an intolerant, bigoted son of a bitch. He's suspicious of anybody who hasn't lived here for at least four generations. And he especially hates anybody from a big city. One of these days he's gonna offend the wrong person and that person's gonna pop him one."

4

"He's always been very good to Rachel."

"But snotty to you, right? Rachel is probably the only non-native he'll tolerate, and that's only because she and Mary Jane are best friends." Elliot hesitated for a moment, then lowered his normally booming baritone. "And he may be worse than usual for a reason. He just found out Mary Jane is pregnant."

Caleb's jaw dropped open. "What? Congratulations! When were you going to tell us?"

"Mary Jane wanted to wait to tell anybody until she was sure she was safe, but then Earl showed up at the house while she was losing her breakfast and figured things out."

"So, his behavior just now is his reaction to the news he's going to be a grandpa?"

"Oh yeah. He went ballistic. Mary Jane was actually shaking after he left. She said she's never seen him like that before. We all know Earl hates me and my liberal politics. But he hates it even more that his precious daughter not only agrees with me, she lives with me. Of course, the thing that really burns him is that we're not married. Rather, that she's not married. The last thing he wants is me as a son-in-law. And now she's gonna have my baby."

"Ell, how are you feeling about this? I thought you didn't want kids."

Elliot frowned, accentuating the wrinkles in his forehead. "Mary Jane says it was an accident, but she's really happy about it. Hey, I like kids, but look, I'm forty-five years old. By the time this kid graduates college, I'll be sixty-eight. I'll be working 'til I drop. If we had started ten years ago, that would be one thing, but . . ."

"You didn't know Mary Jane ten years ago. You'll be a great dad."

"Caleb, you'll be a great dad. I'll be this kid's grandfather." Elliot sighed. "So, Plan B is that she'll tell Rachel and Zoe first, and then we'll all celebrate at the dinner we'd already planned for Thursday. Just pretend you haven't heard anything and let Rachel tell you."

"Your secret is safe with me. What about Earl?"

"Earl? He's so pissed off there's no way he's gonna tell anybody."

"So, we're good to go."

Elliot looked around to make sure nobody was in earshot, then leaned forward to ask, "Is Mary Jane's pregnancy going to upset Rachel?"

Caleb coughed. This was a difficult question. How to answer?

"They're best friends. I'm sure she'll be thrilled for both of you."

"I hope you're right. I know how hard it's been for her. And for you."

The waitress arrived with their orders, and the two men dug in.

Twenty minutes later, Elliot pushed himself up from the table. "I've gotta go. I need to get ready for court."

"Okay. We'll see you Thursday night."

"And remember, don't say a word to anybody," Elliot said.

"You got it."

The minute he was out the door, the smile left Caleb's face. After three miscarriages, Rachel was frustrated and beginning to panic. Would she be able to find it within herself to be happy for her best friend when Mary Jane had what she wanted so badly?

Elliot said I'd be a great dad. I'm not so sure I want to be one at all. Especially if I turned out like my own father. He was no Dad.

He picked up his mug to finish off the remaining coffee. It had gone cold.

CHAPTER TWO

The sun was just beginning its descent into the western hills when Caleb walked through the back door into the kitchen. His mouth watered at the aroma of sautéed garlic and onions filling the air, and he headed straight to the stove. He picked up the cover on a large stockpot and saw what looked like Rachel's sausage minestrone.

"Damn, that smells good," he said, and his stomach grumbled in agreement.

He pushed through the swinging door to the dining room to find Rachel sitting at the long white oak table, books and papers spread out along its length and breadth. Her full auburn hair was pulled back into a ponytail, and she sat, legs curled under her, on a large Craftsman armchair.

"Hey."

"Hey you." Rachel looked up and flashed a wide smile. Caleb's heart skipped a beat. Even after twelve years of marriage, he still responded the same way.

"What's all this?"

"Today was my first staff meeting for the Sunday school, remember?"

Caleb slapped his forehead. "Oh, right. I did forget. How did that go?"

"Really well. They've got a great team there. Everybody was so nice, I felt right at home."

"So, is this for next year already?" he asked indicating the mess on the table.

"Yes. Judy, the principal, assigned each of the teachers a holiday. We're to design a school-wide program. Since I'm new, mine is Purim, so I have until March to get ready."

"You certainly do plan ahead."

"Yeah, well I wanted to get a head start over the summer before I get too busy in the fall with both school and Sunday school. I'm also realizing now that there's a lot more to the holiday than I learned in Hebrew School."

"Even though you grew up Jewish?"

"Even though."

"You sure this won't be too much, doing two jobs?"

"Babe, I'm young and child-free. I have plenty of time, and it's only Sunday mornings for half the year."

Caleb fell silent at the mention of their childless status. *I hope we're not going to have that conversation right now. Not again.*

Rachel changed the subject. "Mary Jane finally walked with us this morning."

"Oh, she's over that stomach bug?" Caleb hoped he could do a good imitation of being clueless.

"Turns out she never had a bug. She's pregnant. Isn't that wonderful?"

Her mouth is smiling, but her eyes are not.

"Wow. How did that happen?"

Rachel squinted at him. "Probably the usual way."

"I mean, did you know they were planning on this?"

"I knew she wanted a baby, but I thought she was waiting for me to have a pregnancy that actually stuck." She got up from her chair and began to pace around the table. "I guess she couldn't wait any longer. But that's all academic now, isn't it?" She stood up and began to straighten papers.

"Well, at least now you know why she's been canceling your morning walks."

"I'm glad her morning sickness is over. I've missed being with her."

"Zoe's good company, isn't she?"

"Of course, but Mary Jane and I have been walking together for years. And now that I know she's going be really busy next year, I want to get as much time with her as I can. Besides," she continued, "without Mary Jane, I'll have way too much free time, especially with Zoe back in New York after the summer."

Her face suddenly crumpled, and her body heaved with sobs.

"We were supposed to have our babies together. That sure worked out well." Her voice was loaded with sarcasm.

Caleb froze, his throat constricting. He straightened up and held Rachel by her shoulders. His mouth was so dry he had trouble croaking out the words. "Maybe she got pregnant by accident."

"That's what she said." Rachel coughed. "So much for plans. Who knew how hard it could be to make a baby?"

Rachel's bitterness struck Caleb hard. He could hardly blame her, but he had never once heard her doubt her friendship with Mary Jane. He lifted her chin and looked into her eyes, their irises the color of sea foam through the prism of her tears. He marveled at the many shades of green they could turn.

He pulled her toward him and put his arms around her. Rachel rested her head on his chest.

"Talk to me."

She croaked out an answer between tears. "Mary Jane and I have been best friends since we were ten, at summer camp. I love her like a sister, but . . ."

Caleb hugged her even more tightly.

She sniffled and blew her nose. "But we'll all celebrate at dinner Thursday night."

"You sure?"

"Yes. She's my best friend and I'll be happy for her."

"If you're okay, then I'm okay."

Caleb cleared his throat and changed the subject.

"So, what is Purim, anyway?"

Rachel shook her head as if ridding it of bad thoughts before sitting back down. "Well, the executive summary would be this: It's the story of a young, beautiful woman— a girl, really— named Esther, who becomes queen in ancient Persia. Her uncle, Mordechai, refuses to bow down to the evil vizier Haman. Only to God will he bow. Haman can't stand that and, in revenge, plots to murder all the Jews in the empire. Esther pleads with the king to save the lives of her people. She exposes Haman's plot, and he and his sons are hanged from the gallows he had built to hang Mordechai."

"This is a story for kids?"

"It's a story for everybody. Parts of it are very violent, but the main point is that due to her courage, Esther saves the day, so we rejoice. Everything is upside down. The intended genocide victims are saved while the killers are condemned. Another theme of the holiday is that nothing is as it seems. So much is hidden. Today, we wear masks and costumes when we celebrate the holiday."

"We're not who we seem to be. That's pretty sophisticated for an old text."

"You're right, it is. There are all sorts of lessons to be learned from the ancients."

"Hmmm. So, what do you plan to do with the kids?"

"That's just what I was sitting here trying to figure out. I'm thinking of doing something with food."

"I'm in. Speaking of food, I'm famished."

"Then we must feed you. Soup is simmering on the stove. If you'll make a salad, I'll set the table. I also have a loaf of whole wheat bread that came out of the oven only an hour ago."

As she headed toward the kitchen, Rachel reached out to stroke her husband's belly, feeling the hard muscles beneath his uniform shirt.

"You're amazing," Caleb said as he picked up a carrot and a vegetable peeler.

"Yes, I am," she said with an impish grin. She eased past Caleb with an armful of dishes and flatware and bumped her hip into his. He reached out a hand to stroke her cheek, leaving a speck of carrot. He leaned in to wipe it off with his thumb.

— • • • —

After dinner, the two stood side-by-side, washing and drying the dishes.

"Caleb, has Elliot said anything to you about Earl lately?" Rachel asked.

"Regarding?"

"His behavior."

"Why are you asking?"

"In the teachers' lounge today, there was some talk about how he was in the Queen Bee this morning, ranting about New Yorkers and evil left wingers, and . . ."

He blew out a breath. "That's pretty accurate, and let me tell you, it was not a pretty scene."

"Harriet Jablow said he was really on a roll."

"That's putting it mildly. He physically assaulted Elliot."

"He just doesn't let up on them. Did you know that Earl actually called his own daughter a slut?"

"Elliot thinks he'd probably say that even if they were married, Earl hates him so much."

Rachel was quiet for a moment, then took a deep breath and shrugged her shoulders. "Do you think the cancer treatments could be affecting his brain?"

"I suppose that could explain it."

Sick or not, Earl might just be a problem waiting to happen. His attack on Elliot was disturbing.

"So, tell me about the rest of your day," Rachel said as Caleb picked up the soup ladle to dry. "After the bear burglary."

Caleb laughed. "Pretty quiet at work. Not one crime, although Jack had to go up to the Jordan house. Matt locked himself out of the house."

"Again?"

"Again. Maybe we should get him one of those high-tech fingerprint scanners. He'd never need a key again."

Rachel turned to face him. "Caleb, do you ever miss New York?"

He bristled. "You mean real police work?"

Rachel pressed her lips together. "No, I meant the electricity, the energy."

"Hey, I'm sorry." Caleb poured water into a glass and gulped it down. "I sometimes feel like the Andy Taylor of the Berkshires."

"Honey, you're a damn good police chief. That's why there's so little crime here."

"Yeah, good for a town where the most exciting thing to happen is a bear B&E."

"Be careful what you wish for," Rachel said.

Caleb knew she was right, but he had to admit to himself that he almost wanted some crime in this pastoral little village. He missed the adrenaline surge of police work in New York.

And he needed the challenge, if for no other reason than to prove to his father that he had what it took to be a cop, not a lawyer in his father's white-shoe firm. He needed something that would test his mettle.

They had made the move to Queensbridge to ease Rachel's concern for his safety in the city, but Caleb sometimes worried that he was simply using her fear as an excuse to run away from bad memories.

Were ursine birdhouse intruders really what he had trained for?

CHAPTER THREE

The Queen Bee was busy with the breakfast crowd when the jingle of a bell drew everyone's attention to the door. Local real estate agent Dennis Hendrikson entered with Zoe Bouvier.

"Good thing Earl's not here today," Elliot said, setting down his coffee mug. "In the mood he's been in, he would've had Zoe running for her life. She's nothing if not the quintessential New Yorker."

Caleb grunted through a mouthful of eggs. Rachel and Mary Jane had met the newly widowed Zoe at the farmers' market a few years ago and bonded over Death by Chocolate from the Pittsfield Rye Bakery. The three had become inseparable, at least during the summer.

Zoe was slim and elegant, with a long French braid the color of honey. She looked stylish in black leggings over which flowed a coral tunic that appeared to have been fashioned from a silk one might see on an Indian rani's sari. Black ballet flats on her feet prevented her from towering over Dennis. She spotted Caleb and Elliot and pulled Dennis over, her smile showing a slight gap between her two front teeth.

"Hi, guys."

"Hey, Zoe."

"So, what are you doing slumming with Dennis, Zoe?" Elliot asked.

"Hey, how do you know I'm not the one slumming?" Dennis said.

"Look at you. Look at her."

"You're such a charmer, Elliot," Zoe said, swiping his shoulder with her hand. "I'm actually working with Dennis." She glanced down with a puzzled frown to see a blob of shaving foam on her fingers.

Caleb passed her a napkin that she used to wipe her hands. "I guess we should be thankful that he shaved."

Dennis interrupted, "Come on, Zoe. Enough of these lowbrows. I'm famished. Let's eat and get to work."

Zoe rolled her eyes and said, "Bye!"

A waitress came over with the coffee pot and refilled the men's mugs. Caleb took a sip of his, then said, "Rachel's bound and determined to fix Zoe up. She thinks she depends too much on Dennis."

"Yeah, I know. I think Rachel and Mary Jane have a list of every single guy in the county. Mary Jane keeps saying, 'Every pot has a lid.'"

"No, I think what Mary Jane really said was that you're getting a big pot and that she has to put a lid on it."

"And you call yourself my friend?"

— • • • —

Thursday evening, the six friends settled into a booth at the Little Szechuan restaurant. After a few minutes of debating the menu options, they decided on spicy eggplant in garlic sauce, General Tso's chicken, vegetable lo mein, and both plain and fried rice. While everybody else ordered Tsingtao beer, Mary Jane asked for a Saratoga water.

"I think we need to toast the health of the mother-to-be and her baby," Zoe said, lifting her glass.

Mary Jane smiled and a flush rose in her cheeks. She looked at Elliot, beaming.

Caleb shot a look in Elliot's direction. Completely inscrutable.

"I'm so thrilled for you," Rachel said.

Caleb noted that his wife's normally sparkling emerald eyes were now a dark jade. There was a little mist in there, as well.

"How far along are you?" Dennis asked.

"Sixteen weeks. Almost halfway there."

"I'm totally ignorant about this stuff," he said. "How long is the morning sickness supposed to last?"

"It couldn't stop soon enough for me. Thank goodness it's summer and I haven't had to worry about getting to school by eight o'clock."

"Are you sleeping okay?" asked Caleb.

Elliot chuckled. "Mary Jane sleeps like a log. It would take an earthquake to wake her."

Caleb saw Zoe move her hand to Rachel's back in a show of support. This had to be so hard for his wife, but Zoe would be there for her. Two childless friends.

He glanced over at Elliot, who had a tight smile on his face.

"How did Earl react to finding out he'll be a grandfather?" Dennis asked.

Mary Jane shrugged.

Dennis raised his eyebrows. "You have told him, right?"

"He kind of accidentally found out," she said. "I was throwing up when he came by the house. He went into a real rage."

17

"I was afraid he might actually hurt her," Elliot said.

Zoe gasped and her hand flew to her mouth.

"According to Earl, we're gonna have a version of Rosemary's baby 'cause I'm the devil incarnate," Elliot said.

Mary Jane sighed. "I can't understand why he's so angry. Elliot and I have been together for a long time. It's not as if my pregnancy is the result of a one-night stand."

"How's Earl feeling health-wise?" Zoe asked.

"The doctor says his cancer is in remission, so that's great news," Mary Jane said.

"Mary Jane, he's sure to come around when the baby is born," Rachel said. "After all, the baby will be his grandchild. And you've been such a good daughter."

"I hope you're right."

"It's not as if you did this to hurt him," Zoe said.

"No, but he sees it that way. He can barely look at me these days and he won't talk to Elliot at all. I swear, he looks like he wants to kill me."

"So, you're sixteen weeks along. That means the baby is due—help me with the math here," Dennis said.

"February 14th."

"Valentine's Day!"

"I can't wait to go shopping with you for baby things. Won't this be fun?" Zoe said. She turned to Elliot. "So, how does it feel to know you're going to be a dad?"

"Well, mornings are awful, but by about noontime I start to feel better."

Everybody laughed.

Mary Jane's eyes twinkled. "Elliot conveniently scheduled a conference in Chicago next weekend. D'ya think he wanted to be out of earshot of my retching?"

"In my defense, that conference has been scheduled for months." He put a beefy arm around Mary Jane's shoulders, dwarfing her petite body. He kissed her on the cheek.

Watching Elliot, Caleb noticed the tight smile return. Rachel was quiet as Mary Jane and Zoe began to chat with animation about quilts and toys and educational videos.

Elliot turned to Caleb and lowered his voice. "Mary Jane is really taking the brunt of Earl's anger."

"Have you spoken to him?"

"Are you kidding? I get it that he hates me, but it really grates on me that he claims to love Mary Jane at the same time he makes her miserable. I could really kill the bastard."

Caleb frowned. "Be careful what you say, Elliot. It could come back to bite you in the ass. Remember, I *am* the Chief of Police."

"Okay then, let's change the subject." He raised his voice. "How's the real estate market doing, Dennis?"

"Actually, things are pretty busy. Zoe? Ready to tell them?"

She coughed. "Dennis has been helping me buy a house. After so many summers as a renter, I've decided to make Queensbridge my full-time home. The Turners want to sell, and I love the house. And now that I know about the baby coming, I'd miss out on way too much if I'm in New York. You guys have become my family, something I've never found there. But Queensbridge is perfect, just like a picture postcard."

Rachel's words about things not always being what they appear to be echoed in Caleb's mind. While he often wished for more action in his little village, he hoped that Zoe wasn't being naïve. People were still people, with all their faults and secrets. A picture postcard was all about image.

"What about work?" asked Elliot.

"New York's only a few hours away. But," she said, turning towards Dennis, "I think I'll have enough business here to keep me busy. With all the technology in my office, I can do just about everything from here. And I can even shop here for the antique lovers. There are plenty of stores—and auctions—in the Berkshires."

"I can't wait to hear your plans," Rachel said.

"The house has good bones, but it does need some major renovation. I like clean lines. And organization. You probably think I'm all about the décor, but I'm really very practical. One of the first things I'll do is install closet organizing systems everywhere."

Mary Jane straightened up. "Then you should come and see the closet Elliot built for me. It's fantastic. I think it's his best project ever."

"Closet?"

"Yeah, Elliot's really good with his hands," Caleb said.

"Indeed, he is," Mary Jane said, and arched an eyebrow.

Zoe blushed. Elliot coughed.

"There's a place for everything, and everything in its place," Mary Jane said.

"That's exactly my philosophy," Zoe said.

"There's a special cabinet for her jewelry, one for her sweaters, and even one for her scarves," Elliot said.

"Why don't you come over tomorrow?" Mary Jane said.

"Excellent. I'll be there. Now, back to babies. This is going to be a big change for you. Having one after so much freedom for so long."

"That's fine with me," Mary Jane said with a serene smile. "I love kids."

Caleb saw Elliot's hand tighten around his beer glass and tried to catch his eye.

When they had all finished their meals, the waitress brought over a little tray with fortune cookies and the check.

Caleb read his fortune aloud first. "Fortune favors the bold.'"

"In your line of work, that sure is true," Mary Jane said. "What does yours say, Ell?"

"'You will travel to many exotic places in your lifetime.' That's already been true, and I hope it will be again."

"With the baby?" Dennis asked.

"Sure. Why not?" said Mary Jane. "That's what backpacks are for. Rachel, what's yours?"

Rachel read hers. "'A dream you have will come true.'" She winced, a forced smile on her lips.

Caleb clenched his jaw.

Zoe turned to Mary Jane and asked, "So, what does your cookie predict?"

Mary Jane's face turned ashen as she read her fortune. "It says, 'Russian proverb: Jealousy and love are sisters.'"

Zoe gasped. "That sounds ominous."

Caleb saw Rachel stiffen. He took her hand under the table. It was clammy.

CHAPTER FOUR

Caleb had just taken a seat at the counter in the Queen Bee, watching owner Sally Bartlett pour his coffee, when his phone rang. Rachel's number was displayed on the screen. He got up and moved to a quiet spot in the diner's back hallway.

"Mary Jane didn't show up for our walk," she said, her voice tight with anxiety. "Where could she be? She's not answering her phone."

"Calm down. Maybe she had to take Earl to a doctor's appointment."

"An appointment at 6:30 a.m.?"

"Doesn't Earl see an oncologist in Albany? Maybe she had to take him there. That would be a long drive. And medical offices often ask people to turn off their phones."

"Then why didn't she call me? We meet every day for our walk. She wouldn't have missed it without telling me."

"I'm sure she's okay. Maybe she's in the bathroom. Maybe she's having morning sickness again. Wait a while and try calling her again."

"She hasn't been sick for a while," Rachel said. "Oh, God, what if she's having a miscarriage?"

"Honey, why don't you go on up to the house? Maybe she got a phone call that took a lot of time."

"Good idea. I'll do that."

He returned to his seat to find his breakfast waiting. He took a bite of his spinach and feta omelet, thinking about Rachel's call, when a thumping sound interrupted his thoughts. He looked up to see Zoe hobbling across the floor on crutches. She grimaced in pain with every step.

"Zoe!" he said. "What's with the crutches?"

"Oh, Caleb. I'm such an idiot. I tripped on the cat on the way to the bathroom and sprained my ankle."

"You really did some damage, didn't you? You're completely covered with scratches."

"I know I look like hell. I fell onto a wicker basket filled with pinecones and branches."

"When did all this happen?" He rose to help her into a booth, then retrieved his breakfast and sat down to join her.

"Friday night." She scrunched her nose in embarrassment. "I really should have bought a night light for the hall. I keep meaning to."

Caleb frowned. "Why didn't you call us?"

"There was no need to bother you. Dennis drove me to the emergency room."

"That's me," Dennis said, coming up behind Zoe with a newspaper under his arm. "Saint Dennis of Queensbridge."

"The worst part is that I won't be able to walk with the girls for a few weeks." She shook her head.

"And just when Mary Jane's feeling better," Caleb said.

Except for the Earl factor.

"Her morning sickness has finally passed, and she wants to get out and enjoy the rest of whatever summer we have left. By the way, I have to get that recipe for the lentil stew you made Friday night, Caleb. It was fabulous."

"Thanks. It was the least I could do with you all working so hard on the library book sale. Rachel told me you donated so many books that they're sure to make a lot of money."

"Believe me, I was happy to get rid of the Turners' books. I have my own that need shelf space."

"Hey, back up there!" Dennis said. "You served lentils to the carnivorous Elliot?"

"Elliot wasn't there. He had a conference in Chicago this weekend," Caleb said.

"Oh, right. Remind me, what was he doing there?"

"He presented a paper on race issues in legal aid," Caleb said.

"Didn't Mary Jane go with him?"

"No. She has students to tutor over the summer," Zoe said. "Besides, there was another reason she wanted to stay."

"Oh?" Dennis raised an eyebrow.

"She wanted to redecorate the master bedroom and prepare the nursery while he was away. Rachel and I didn't want her pushing furniture around, so we volunteered to help. The three of us painted and sewed our little butts off all day."

Just then, the bell over the door jingled, and the group looked up to see Sandy True wheeling herself into the diner, the door held by a man with dirty blond hair and beard. He was dressed in jeans and a denim work shirt. The sleeves rolled up to his elbows, exposed a nautical star tattoo on his forearm.

"Who's that with Sandy?" Dennis whispered, lifting the napkin dispenser to use as a mirror to check his hair. "He's cute, in a rugged, outdoorsy kind of way. I'm impressed."

Zoe shrugged. "He's not my type. More yours."

"What d'ya mean? You love a good fixer upper."

Sandy looked around the diner and, seeing the group, headed toward them. The man followed right behind her. As she reached the booth, she said, "This is the handicapped dining spot. I hope you have a special plate, or we'll have to ticket you. And I know a cop or two who would be happy to do it."

"Come on, roll up a chair," Dennis said, "and she'll tell you the whole, sorry tale of how she sprained her ankle."

"I don't think we need to hear it," said the tattooed man.

Sandy blanched. "Guys, this is my brother Hollis. You'll have to excuse him. He's not house-trained. Hollis, this is Zoe Bouvier and Dennis Hendrikson. And, of course, you already know the Chief."

"Sure. He's your boss." The two shook hands.

Zoe extended her hand to Hollis.

"Sandy's been keeping you a secret," she said.

"Yeah, well I haven't been back to Queensbridge for a long time. The family prefers it that way. The scene of my downfall and all that."

Sandy straightened in her chair and forced a smile to her lips. "But now he's the reincarnation of the prodigal son, come home to the welcoming arms of his family."

Hollis coughed.

Dennis jumped in to rescue the situation. "So, Hollis, what do you do?"

"I'm in the Merchant Marine."

"You travel all over the world?" Dennis asked.

"Yeah. From tiny little Queensbridge to ports around the globe." He opened his arms wide to indicate the extent of his travels.

Zoe's eyes opened wide. She dived into her purse, pulled out a business card, and handed it to him. "We should talk," she said, "I want to hear about all the fabulous places you travel to. You might be able to help me with my business. Maybe we could partner up to get some really good *objets d'art*."

"Um, okay. I guess so." Hollis turned the card over in his hands, then tucked it into his shirt pocket.

"Sooner is better. Come to my house tomorrow. I can show you the kind of things I'm looking for. I'm just up on Swift Road."

Dennis turned toward Caleb and grinned. "Nothing gets in the way of business, even a sprained ankle."

"Be careful, Hollis," Caleb said. "Soon you'll be out shopping more than working on the ship."

"Actually, I was just thinking he could pick up something special for Mary Jane's baby," Zoe said.

"Baby?" Hollis's eyebrows went up.

"A new business for you, Hollis," Sandy said with a laugh, punching her brother in the arm.

"Yeah," he grumbled. "Who thought I'd ever be buying something for a pregnant Mary Jane Bennett?"

Caleb pushed his chair back and stood. "Time to get going. Good to see you, Hollis. Take care of yourself, Zoe. If you need anything, just call."

He headed out, carrying a to-go cup of coffee. He heard Zoe talking with excitement about scouring the world's ports for exotic items, but he couldn't hear Hollis True's responses. He crossed the street and went straight to his office, where he attacked a pile of paperwork. Barely five minutes passed when his phone rang.

Officer Jack Corwin's voice was low and tense. "Chief, it's not good."

"What's not good?"

"I'm up on Pine Mountain Road."

Caleb's stomach tightened. Straightening up, he set his coffee mug down onto his blotter, precisely within the boundaries of a brown circle formed by hundreds of cups consumed at this desk.

"What's going on?" he asked.

"Chief, Mary Jane Bennett is dead."

CHAPTER FIVE

"Be careful what you wish for." Rachel's words echoed in Caleb's head. Now he had something serious on his hands.

"It looks like she was strangled by her own scarf, but it's weird," Jack said.

"What do you mean, weird?" As he said the words, scenes from an old movie about the dancer Isadora Duncan flashed through his mind. Her long scarf had caught on an automobile wheel and strangled her. Mary Jane did love her long, flowing scarves. She'd been collecting them for years.

"Chief, you there?"

"Yeah. I'm coming. Don't let anyone in."

Caleb jumped up and headed out of the station. He climbed into the Ford Explorer but didn't start the ignition right away. He took a few deep breaths to steady his nerves and focus on the task at hand. No sense in putting on the lights or the siren. Too late for that.

Heading up the mountain, he took each sharp curve at a speed that would have earned him a citation had he been watching from a cruiser with a radar gun. As he drove, he thought about how he would tell Elliot. How would his best friend react to losing the love of his life? He snorted, thinking about his father's response when his wife, Caleb's mother, had died. Stoic. As if he were in court. And cold. As an iceberg.

Where did that memory come from? Why am I thinking about that now?

He pulled into the driveway of the log cabin nestled in the woods. As he set the parking brake, he saw that his fingers were white from clutching the steering wheel. He shook his hands out and rolled his shoulders, taking deep, measured breaths until he felt ready to approach the house.

Officer Jack Corwin was slouching in the open doorway, his paunch hanging over his belt and his uniform shirt hanging out.

Jesus, when did Jack get so out of shape?

He took a deep breath and swung his long legs out of the Explorer. From the back of the cruiser he pulled an evidence kit, then headed toward the house. He was at the front door in six long strides. Up close he could see that Jack was gray and clammy. He reminded himself that the officer probably hadn't seen too many dead bodies in Queensbridge.

"Talk to me, Jack. What made you come up here?"

With a uniform sleeve Jack wiped sweat from his balding head. "Rachel flagged me down by the side of the road. I picked her up and brought her to your house to get the house key. Then we came straight here." He coughed. "Chief, Rachel doesn't seem to the type to get hysterical."

"She's not. Rachel's a veritable yogi."

And I ignored her instincts this morning.

"Right, so when she asked me to come with her to check out the house, I figured something might really be wrong."

Caleb's chest tightened. "Did she see anything?"

Jack looked down at his feet. "Afraid so, Chief. I tried to convince her to stay outside, but she absolutely insisted on coming into the house. She refused to go. Once she saw the body, she ran out."

"Okay. Take me to Mary Jane."

I can't use the word body.

From the evidence kit Caleb pulled a pair of neoprene gloves and a mask before entering the house, but the sickly-sweet stench of death penetrated through and assaulted his nostrils. It had been a long time, but the odor of a dead human body was not something he could ever forget. It was absolutely the worst part of police work.

He climbed the stairs and entered the bedroom ahead of Jack. A hint of cigarette smoke hung in the air. Neither Mary Jane nor Elliot were smokers. He drew a pen and small spiral notebook from a pocket and jotted a note.

Did Mary Jane have a visitor who smoked?

Drop sheets lay along the far wall. A paint can, roller tray, roller, and several brushes sat in the corner. The queen-size bed had been pushed to the center of the room, its headboard concealing its occupant. He stepped around it.

"Oh, God."

What he saw socked him in the gut, causing his breath to catch. The room tilted and his head felt light.

Splayed out on the bed was Mary Jane Bennett, the fabric of her nightgown twisted around her body. A red and black scarf was tied around her neck and attached to the headboard. Her face was blue over a pale, waxy body. The odor was lessened only slightly by an electric fan pushing air out through two open windows.

Focus, Caleb. Pull yourself together. You can mourn later.

"Was this fan on when you came in?"

"No, but the smell was so bad I had to turn it on."

"Hell, Jack, you disturbed a crime scene?"

Jack flushed and stuttered. "Between the stench and the heat, it was really bad. Even with the windows open."

"At least tell me that you wore gloves when you touched this stuff."

"Of course, I did."

"We're gonna have to have a long talk when we get back to the station. But now, we need to focus on what happened here."

He moved in closer and hesitated, steeling himself to examine Mary Jane's body. No rigor mortis.

"Mary Jane was with us Friday night. Today is Monday. She could have died at any time over the weekend."

He opened his cell phone and dialed the station. "Sandy? Get the state police over to 246 Pine Mountain Road. We have a dead body. And use the phone, I don't want this getting out."

"Will do, Chief. Did you say 246? Isn't that Mary Jane and Elliot's place?"

"Yeah, it is. Please make the call, Sandy."

Caleb turned. "Jack, get the crime scene tape and secure the site. Make sure nobody comes near this house until I say so."

"Chief, it's pretty obvious she killed herself."

Caleb took a deep breath. "Jack, you went to the academy, you've read Geberth's *Practical Homicide Investigation*, haven't you? What is the first officer's duty on arrival?" he asked.

"I determined that the victim was dead and took necessary action. I called you."

31

"And?" Caleb prodded him.

"Safeguard the scene and detain any witnesses or suspects. But there were no witnesses and no perpetrator present. She killed herself."

At least he had it memorized, Caleb thought. Too bad he didn't know enough to follow the instructions. He took a moment before answering.

"Jack, we don't know what this is."

"But there's no evidence of a break-in."

"And how long were you looking things over before you called me?"

"I got here, found Mary Jane, and called you."

"So, all of, what, ten minutes?" He shook his head. "Tell me what you've found so far."

"While I was waiting, I looked at all the doors and windows on the first floor and in the cellar. They're all locked. And the screens on the second-floor bedroom window are intact. Nobody could've gotten in."

"You mean nobody could've gotten in without a key. Or nobody could have gotten in without being invited." He stopped and gazed at Jack's slovenly uniform. "Or maybe somebody who knows how to pick a lock could have gotten in."

The officer's face flushed crimson. He swabbed his head again.

"Listen, we're a tiny police department with neither the tools nor the personnel to handle this. Other than the car accident that killed Katie Wakefield, I don't know when the last unnatural death happened in Queensbridge. We're gonna need help from the state police."

"Yes, chief," Jack mumbled and wiped his face.

"So, neither of you touched anything?"

"No. I put gloves on right away, and Rachel was only here for a minute."

"Okay, let me talk to her. Then take her home and come right back. I'll wait for the state crime scene people to get here." He paused, the gears whirring in his head. "I want you and Scott to canvass the neighbors to see if they saw or heard anything. Anything at all. We don't need the state cops to do that. When he's done, I want all of you to go over all the neighbors' statements to see if you can find anything that might give us a clue as to what happened. Maybe from several sets of eyes we'll get something."

He realized as he gave the order that it might be pointless. Houses on the mountain were so spread out that neighbors couldn't see from one to the other.

"Also, I want you to tag along with the CSI guys. Make sure they don't miss anything, like the trash in every room, and the trash cans in the garage."

"Yes, sir."

"And Jack, tuck your shirt in."

Caleb started to leave the room, but an idea struck him. The girls had been painting. Mary Jane was pregnant and wouldn't want to breathe any paint fumes, even with VOC-free paint. Of course, she would have slept with the windows open. He went over to the windows to see if either screen had been tampered with. As Jack had said, they were both intact.

What the hell happened here? Suicide? Mary Jane?

"Where's Rachel now?"

"I think she ran into the woods to be sick . . ."

Caleb walked out onto the porch and scanned the area. He saw Rachel sitting on the ground near the edge of the woods, her back against a white birch tree. He remembered the first time he had ever laid eyes on her. It was his senior year at Hamilton, and he was playing Frisbee on the main quad with his friends. He spied a pretty fresher leaning against the trunk of a massive oak, reading a book. He deliberately threw the disk across the lawn in her direction. The disk landed with a thud on her backpack. She looked up and calmly threw it back. As he looked over at her, he saw the glint in her eyes, two sparkling, almond-shaped emeralds. He tumbled into love and never climbed back out.

Now, he walked over to where his wife sat, staring blankly into the distance. A ray of sunlight that had managed to penetrate the tree branches caught the red highlights in her hair. He sat down and wrapped his arms around her. He could detect a faint aroma of spearmint gum and vomit.

Rachel looked up. "We walk together every morning. I waited and waited, but she didn't come. And now this. I can't believe it. I don't believe it. Why would she ever have killed herself? She seemed so happy."

"I agree. Something's not right, but let's not jump to conclusions. I'll do my job. That's what I'm here for. Now, Jack's gonna take you home. I want you to pour yourself a brandy and try to relax. Sandy will come up and stay with you. We'll talk later after I've had a chance to look at things here."

Rachel moaned and burrowed into her husband's shoulder. "I never thought we'd have to mourn another friend."

He, too, had been thinking of his best friend and partner in the NYPD, Manny Hernandez, gone almost eight years now.

Caleb stood and extended his arms to help Rachel up. As she rose, he pulled her to him, and she rested her head on his chest. They remained that way for a few minutes until Jack appeared, a few respectful feet away. Caleb pressed his lips to the top of her head, then walked her to the cruiser and opened the passenger side door. As she fastened her seat belt and looked up at him through the open window, Caleb's chest tightened. As close as they already were, they would now both know the pain of having lost their best friends.

— • • • —

After Jack left with Rachel, Caleb settled into one of the green Adirondack chairs on the front porch and waited for the state's crime scene investigator from the Lee barracks. He took deep swallows of cool, pine-scented air and listened to the kanock-kanock-kanock of a distant woodpecker that seemed to mirror the drumbeat of his heart. He closed his eyes, remembering how he and Elliot had painted the chairs one Sunday afternoon, taking one swig of 413 Farmhouse Ale for every few strokes of the brush. Mary Jane had wanted to stencil the chairs with a kissing lovebird design, but Elliot had nixed that as "too cutesy."

Caleb ran his hand back and forth over the smooth surface of the wood, following the grain of the chair's arm. The motion calmed his nerves just as it had when he was a young boy hiding from his father's wrath. How many times had he burrowed behind winter coats and woolen blankets in the cedar closet, running his hands over the smooth planks and inhaling the spice of the wood? To this day, the smell of cedar triggered memories of his parents' fights.

CAROL GOODMAN KAUFMAN

As chief of police, Caleb knew that he had to stay cool and in control. But as a friend of the dead woman lying on the bed inside, well, that was another matter. He kept stroking the wood.

The crunch of tires on gravel and the slam of a car door broke his reverie. Caleb opened his eyes and stood up to greet the CSI team. Instead, he was surprised to see Elliot Freund coming toward the house.

"Hey, Caleb. Is this a welcome home party?" he asked as he approached the front porch stairs.

Caleb held up a hand to stop him. "Elliot, I have to ask you to stay outside. I'm sorry."

Elliot frowned "What're you talking about? This is my house."

Caleb stepped down from the porch, effectively blocking Elliot's entry. He reached out and placed a hand on his friend's shoulder.

"Elliot, I don't know how to tell you this anyway but straight out. Mary Jane is dead."

Elliot's knees buckled. Caleb barely managed to catch him before he hit the ground. He put his arm around his waist and lowered him to the porch steps, pushing his head down between his knees. He then went to his cruiser to retrieve a bottle of water. When he turned back, Elliot was gone. He heard footsteps pounding inside the house and ran to catch up. He managed to grab his friend by the arm just as he reached the bedroom he had shared with Mary Jane.

Thank God the bed is facing away from the doorway.

"Believe me, you don't want to go in there, Ell. You don't want to see her like this."

"What happened?" he wailed.

36

"We don't know yet, but you can be sure we'll get to the bottom of it."

"She died, just like that?" Elliot said snapping his fingers. "How could that be? She's such a health nut."

"We know nothing yet. It was very sudden."

"But how did she die? Was she all alone?"

"Like I said, Ell, we don't know anything yet. All I can tell you is that it appears she strangled on her scarf."

Elliot gasped. "Strangled? How could that be? Did she get caught on something?"

Caleb didn't respond.

"What about the baby?"

Caleb felt himself getting lightheaded. "The baby's gone, too."

"Oh, no! She was so happy and I . . ." Elliot buried his head in his hands and groaned.

Caleb led him to a chair and stood by with a hand on his best friend's shoulder while sobs racked his body. After several long minutes, Elliot sat up, wiped his eyes, and blew his nose. Caleb led him back to the front porch, settled him in an Adirondack chair, and handed him the water bottle he still carried.

Elliot moaned. "My beautiful Mary Jane."

I can only imagine the pain he's in. What would I do without Rachel?

"I'll call an officer to take you down to my house. Rachel is there with Sandy, so neither of you will be alone."

Elliot looked disoriented. "Huh? Why's Sandy there?" he asked.

Caleb took a deep breath, wondering how much to explain. "Rachel raised the alarm when Mary Jane didn't show up for their regular morning walk. She saw the —" He caught himself. "She's in pretty rough shape herself right now, so I sent Sandy to stay with her for a while. I'm waiting for the state police to come now."

"State police? You can't handle a death?"

"Ell, it's an unattended death, and my department isn't really equipped for a full investigation. You know I have to call it in." Caleb decided to keep his feelings and knowledge close to the vest, so he just repeated himself. "I'll call Scott Cruz to drive you down to my house."

Within minutes, a black-and-white pulled into the driveway.

Caleb held out a hand and said, "You okay to stand up now?"

With one hand Elliot grasped Caleb's, and with the other pushed on his knee to hike himself up. Caleb saw that his good friend appeared to have aged ten years in the span of ten minutes. As difficult as it would be, he would still have to question him, and soon. That interview would be the test of a lifetime, and he didn't look forward to it.

CHAPTER SIX

Caleb corrected himself. Having to notify a family that a loved one had died was even worse than finding a corpse. Although he had no idea what had led to it, death had found one of his closest friends, and now he had to tell her father. He drove into the village and parked in front of the low-rise brick building that housed Earl Bennett's liquor store. Now, his mouth dry and his palms sweating, he prepared himself to inform Earl that his only child was dead.

He straightened his shoulders, took a deep breath, and entered. Through a partially open door behind the counter, he could see Earl sitting at his desk. The clerk was in the back of the store, so he went straight in, knocking lightly as he did.

Earl looked up and scowled. "What do you want?"

That kind of attitude must bring in lots of business, Earl.

"I'm afraid I have some bad news."

Earl's eyebrows raised in curiosity. "Spill it, Crane. I don't have all day. I have a business to run, in case you didn't notice."

Deep breath. "Mary Jane was found dead this morning."

Earl's face drained of all color, and he slumped in his chair. Caleb jumped to the other side of the desk to catch him.

No sooner had he gotten to Earl's side than the man righted himself. His face was a bizarre mask of shock and fury.

"What did that bastard do to her?" he shouted.

"Who are you talking about?"

"You know exactly who I'm talking about! Freund! That SOB murdered my baby!"

I can understand shock and grief, but accusing Elliot of killing Mary Jane? Where is that coming from?

"At this point it's not even clear how Mary Jane died. The medical examiner will have to do an autopsy."

Earl leaned forward and put his elbows on the desktop, his head in his hands. "God, no. No autopsy." His voice was a whisper. "People will find out."

"Find out what?"

"None of your goddamn business."

"It's no secret Mary Jane was pregnant, Earl."

"That bastard."

"I know this has to be hard, Earl, and I'm so sorry. Mary Jane was a close friend. Can I call someone to be with you?"

"I don't need anybody. Get out, Crane. I've got things to do. You know where the door is." He went back to his computer and began to type.

"Earl, I'm going to need to ask you some questions, but we'll talk more when you've had a chance to process."

He looked at the man behind the desk for a moment before letting himself out. As he exited the store through aisles stocked with hundreds of wine and liquor bottles, he realized that Earl had never asked how Mary Jane had died, or where she was found.

— • • • —

That evening, Caleb, Rachel, and Elliot sat on the Cranes' porch, stunned and lost in their own thoughts. The quiet of the sultry evening air was broken with the staccato flit-flit of moth wings flailing against the screens, and the creak-creak of the rocking chair.

"They're desperate to get to the light on the porch ceiling," Caleb said.

"Go away," Rachel said, waving a rolled-up newspaper at them. "You don't belong here."

"Earl would have a field day with that observation," Elliot said, and snorted. He didn't look up, but sat hunched on the wicker sofa, staring at his clasped hands. Caleb and Rachel talked quietly, not trying to engage him in conversation but letting him know he was not alone.

After a while, the warm, gentle breeze began to blow harder, and the night air took on a sudden chill, forcing the friends indoors. Rachel went straight to the stove to make tea and stood with her hands hovering over the wheezing kettle, hoping for warmth. Caleb reached into a large ceramic apple on the sideboard and pulled out a handful of oatmeal raisin cookies. He put them on a colorful majolica plate and placed them on the kitchen table.

"Eat," he said to Elliot.

"I'm not hungry."

"Eat one anyway."

A loud knock at the door startled them. Caleb went to open it and found Zoe and Dennis on the porch. They entered the house and went straight to the table, seated themselves on either side of Elliot, and wrapped their arms around him.

"Elliot, I'm so sorry," Dennis said and hugged him again.

"We're here for you, Elliot," Zoe said.

"Is your family on the way?" Dennis asked.

"Sure. My dad and brother are coming in. They'll be here tomorrow. There's nobody else."

"What about cousins?" Dennis asked.

"They all live in California and Arizona. They wouldn't come out for this."

"Are you sure? Have you called them?"

"My brother Josh said he'd take care of it. I don't have the energy to deal with all that."

"Where will they be staying?" Rachel asked.

Elliot looked up, puzzled. "With me, I guess. I've got the room."

Even though the CSIs had already done their thing, Caleb didn't want Elliot back in his house just yet.

"Why don't you stay here with us? You shouldn't be alone," Caleb said.

"But what about my dad and Josh?"

"I'm afraid we won't have the room since Tenley will be staying with us," Rachel said.

"They can stay with me. I've got lots of space," Dennis offered.

"I'll need to get my stuff," Elliot said.

"Sure. I'll drive up to the house in the morning," Caleb said. "In the meantime, we have toiletries and pajamas you can use."

"What about funeral arrangements?" Dennis asked.

Elliot grunted. "Earl's in charge. Since Mary Jane and I weren't married, I'm not next of kin and he won't let me in on anything. He's always hated me, and now he's sure I'm responsible for her death. He even called to accuse me of murdering her." He hiked himself off the sofa. "Listen, I'm really wiped. I need to go to bed. Rachel, where do you want me?"

"I'll get you all set up. Follow me."

"I'll be up in a minute to help," Caleb said.

Elliot nodded to everybody and left the room.

Zoe and Dennis remained at the table, sipping their tea quietly and picking at the cookies.

"I doubt Elliot will get any sleep tonight," Dennis said, pouring more hot water into his mug. "He looks awful."

"I'm worried about him. His face is positively gray," Zoe said.

Dennis sighed. "There must be something we can do."

"We can just be there for him," Caleb said. "He'll need his friends now more than ever."

"Caleb, why didn't you let Elliot go home? Do you think the house is a crime scene?" Dennis asked.

Caleb steadied his nerves. "Elliot's had a terrible shock. He shouldn't be alone. He needs our support."

"Do you think Mary Jane was murdered?" Dennis asked.

"Dennis, we're just getting started. I have no idea if there's been a crime 'cause I haven't heard back from the medical examiner yet."

"Medical examiner? Why do you need him?" Zoe asked.

Caleb explained. "Mary Jane's was an unattended death. That just means that she died alone without any witnesses available to report on the manner of death. Because Mary Jane was a healthy young woman and not under the care of a physician for a known medical condition, the medical examiner has to do an autopsy."

"But she did have a known medical condition," Zoe said. "She was pregnant. Oh, it must have had something to do with that. Maybe a blood clot?"

Caleb kept his thoughts to himself. There was no need to divulge the manner of Mary Jane's death at this point. And there was no way he believed it was suicide. He exited the kitchen and joined Elliot in the spare bedroom.

Rachel came in with an armful of sheets and towels. She and Caleb set about making the bed while Elliot sat on a wingback chair, a dazed expression on his face.

Once the room was all set and Rachel had left, Caleb hung back, leaning against the doorjamb.

"Can I get you anything, Ell?" he asked.

"Yeah, you can get Mary Jane back. You think you can handle that?" Elliot's eyes were puffy and red-rimmed. His face sported a heavy five o'clock shadow.

"I wish I could, buddy. I really wish I could."

Caleb looked at his friend, wondering about the things that go on in people's private lives, behind closed doors. He decided to tread lightly.

"At this point, I don't know what to think, Ell, but we will get to the bottom of this, I promise you. I'm going to look at every possible angle. I just want to ask you one question. Can you tell me the last time you spoke with Mary Jane?"

Elliot pressed his lips together. "I called her from the hotel on Friday afternoon to tell her I'd arrived. And then she called me that night, after she got home from your house."

"So about what time was that?"

"I remember exactly what time it was because she mentioned how tired she was even though it was only ten

44

o'clock. We laughed about how she was turning into an old lady."

I'd better stop now. He's in such bad shape, there's no need to aggravate him.

"Okay, why don't you try to get some rest? The next few days are going to be busy and stressful."

"I doubt I'll get any sleep . . . but thanks for putting me up. It means a lot."

— • • • —

Later that night, Caleb sat on an upholstered chair in the corner of the bedroom he shared with Rachel, quietly mulling over myriad thoughts about the day's events. A loud sob brought him to attention. Rachel was perched on the edge of the bed, crying as she clutched a wad of tissues in one hand. He got up and crossed the room to be with her.

"The last time I saw Mary Jane was when she was here for dinner. I should have noticed if something was off."

"Rachel, how could you possibly have known?"

"She was my oldest and closest friend. We talked just about every day. I should have realized something was up when she didn't return my phone calls over the weekend. I just figured she was enjoying a nice summer day. I can't help thinking she might be alive today if I'd gone over there to check." She covered her face with her hands.

Caleb saw her shoulders trembling and reached for her. "It would've been too late, Rachel."

She blew her nose again. "But why would she strangle herself? It doesn't make sense."

"We have to wait for the ME's report. And please don't tell anybody what you saw, especially Elliot. I want this investigation to be clean."

Rachel leaned back onto the pillows piled against the headboard, her face drained of all color. "But you think something isn't right, don't you?"

He didn't respond, but picked up a glass of water from the end table and gave it to her. She took a few sips, then set the glass down again.

He leaned forward and said, "Are you okay to answer some questions?"

Rachel nodded.

"Mary Jane and Zoe were here for dinner Friday night, and then you all worked on the book sale. What time did they leave?"

"They both left about a little before ten. Mary Jane said she was really tired."

"Did the two drive together?"

"No. They had their own cars."

"What about Zoe? Did she have any plans?"

"Let me think. It was late, Caleb. I'm pretty sure she was heading home, too. Do you want me to ask her?"

"No," he snapped.

Rachel's eyes widened.

"I'm sorry," he said, taking her hands in his. "Leave the questioning to me. I don't want you involved with this at all."

Rachel squeezed back.

"Did Mary Jane ever say anything to you that might have indicated she was depressed?"

Her brow furrowed as she considered the question. "She was really hurt and angry with Earl. He was being horrible to her. So, yes, maybe a little depressed."

"Was she afraid of anybody?"

"God, no, Caleb. I would have told you immediately if anybody had ever threatened her." She looked up. "Do you think she was murdered?"

"Rachel, I don't know what happened, but some things just don't add up for me."

"You're right. There's no way Mary Jane would risk her own life. Or her baby's."

"What about at school? Anybody in competition with her for a plum position?"

"She was an elementary school teacher. She wasn't applying for the principal's job or anything else, not that there were any job openings. She loved what she was doing and didn't want to move into administration."

"Did she ever complain about anybody? Have any quarrels or fights with anybody?"

"Mary Jane didn't get into fights. She always tried to bend over backwards to understand the other person's point of view." She hiccupped. "Oh God, Caleb. I can't imagine what she must have gone through."

Rachel stopped talking to take another sip of water and collect her thoughts.

"I don't think anybody hated Mary Jane. I mean, she could be a little sarcastic at times, but that wouldn't be enough to get her killed, would it?"

"Depends on whose nose got out of joint. But again, Rachel, we don't know that she was murdered. We only know that she's dead."

Rachel pulled another tissue from the box on her nightstand and blew her nose. "Caleb, when I saw Mary Jane lying there, her nightgown was all twisted, like she was struggling. Do you think she changed her mind?"

Or she tried to fight off an aggressor.

"I noticed the same thing, but I'm gonna wait until the ME's report comes back. Then we'll know more."

"What did Earl say when you told him?"

Caleb shrugged. "It was weird. He didn't even ask how she died. Or where."

"He must be in shock." Then she bolted upright. "Caleb, plenty of people heard Earl say that he could wring her neck. He was absolutely livid about her pregnancy. Do you think he could kill his own daughter?"

"Earl can be a real piece of work but . . ." He slapped his thighs and stood. "Let's try to get some sleep. Things will seem clearer in the morning, I hope."

CHAPTER SEVEN

Early Wednesday morning, Tenley Crane, all five-foot-ten inches of her, swung deeply tanned legs toned by years of tennis out of Caleb's SUV. She ran towards Rachel with arms out. Bringing her sister-in-law into her embrace, she held her for a long moment.

"Thank God you're here, Tenley," Rachel said. "I didn't think I needed help, but now that you're here, I can see that you are the perfect medicine."

"Rachel, of course I'm here for you. You're not just my sister-in-law. You're my sister-in-fact."

Caleb began to unload the luggage to bring it into the house. "By the look of these bags, I think she's planning to move here permanently. You must've taken up all the plane's cargo space."

"Now don't start criticizing me right away, Caleb. I've brought all kinds of comfort goodies from the city. I'll be here as long as you need me. Or want me."

At that moment, Elliot and Zoe came out through the front door. Tenley crossed the yard and threw her arms around him, then gave Zoe a hug and a peck on the cheek.

"You must have gotten up at the crack of dawn to catch such an early flight to Albany. And you just got back from Europe. You must be exhausted," Zoe said.

"Mary Jane was my friend, too, Zoe. Of course, I'd come."

Caleb interrupted. "I have to do my rounds now. I'll see you all later." He pulled Tenley aside and whispered in her ear. "Keep a close eye on Rachel. She's pretty shaky."

He left the group of friends on the front porch and hopped into his cruiser. As he drove up the village's main roads and down hidden lanes, he saw that the houses and the stores, flowers, and trees all looked the same despite the cataclysmic news that had shattered village life just forty-eight hours before. Things should somehow be different. They should look sad, shocked, angry. Something other than the way they appeared last week. What was going on beneath the surface?

Picture postcard village my ass, Zoe.

He drove over the bridge that gave the town its name, then turned onto Main Street, where he saw shopkeepers preparing for the day, unfurling awnings, washing windows, and sweeping sidewalks. Business as usual. Then again, maybe not. The merchants worked with shoulders hunched, backs rigid. Suspicious. As if somebody had released a toxin into the air that affected their posture. As he drove past, they looked up and signaled with short, stiff waves. Were they relieved to see his cruiser, a symbol of safety? He felt like a fraud. A beloved member of their community had died suddenly.

Caleb's gut told him that there was more to the story of Mary Jane's death. He headed back to the station to start an investigation in earnest.

For what he considered the town's first suspicious death, Caleb Crane didn't want anybody who came into the police station to have access to information on their progress in the investigation, so he decided to take over a small conference room in the back as a command center. He cut brown packing paper from a large roll and taped it over the glass pane in the door. He closed the window blinds, then he called his staff together.

Jack, Sandy, and Scott gathered around a wooden table scored and stained from years of use. Caleb turned to his team.

"Okay, let's hear what you've got. Scott, you first."

"I went door-to-door and interviewed half the neighborhood. Nobody saw or heard anything."

"The neighbors are so far apart I'm not surprised," Sandy said.

"And Mary Jane did die in the middle of the night," Scott said.

"It was worth a shot. Some people don't sleep well and are up at night," Caleb said. "Jack?"

"Same here. I did the other half. Nobody saw or heard anything."

"Who knew Mary Jane? Scott and Jack, go interview all the teachers and staff at the school and any other place she spent time. Try the craft center and the library."

"Consider it done," Scott said.

"What are you gonna do, Chief?" Jack asked.

It's time to pull on your big-boy pants, Caleb.

"I'm gonna talk to Elliot."

— • • —

Elliot led Caleb up to the bedroom, the first time back in his own home since the discovery of Mary Jane's body. Every surface was still covered with black fingerprint powder. A slight odor of paint hung in the air.

"What's going on here?" Elliot asked, looking at the drop cloths and paint cans.

"Rachel and Zoe were helping Mary Jane redecorate the bedroom and prepare a nursery. It was supposed to be a surprise for you."

"Oh, hell." Elliot's hands flew to his head, his fingers grabbing the curls of his hair.

Were those gray hairs there before all this?

"Ell, I know this is difficult, but I want you to take a really good look around. Does anything look out of place?"

"Aside from the fact that everything in the room is moved?"

Caleb couldn't blame Elliot for the sarcasm. The bedroom was in total disarray.

Elliot walked over to the dresser. On top sat a silver picture frame that held a photograph of himself and Mary Jane. He picked it up, brought it to his chest, and closed his eyes.

"She loves this picture. We took it last year up on Mount Greylock."

He rummaged through the dresser drawers one by one. Then he crossed the room to the closet and pressed on a panel concealing the built-ins he had constructed. He stood still, staring at its contents. After a moment he said, "I can't really tell. She has a lot of stuff. Jewelry, clothing, scarves."

Again, Elliot was talking about Mary Jane in the present tense. Caleb's heart went out to his friend.

Elliot turned. "I don't know why I'm even checking this closet. A burglar wouldn't have known about it with the doors closed."

"Unless the doors weren't closed."

"True. But they are now."

"Ell, did Mary Jane ever mention feeling uncomfortable about anybody?"

"No. I mean, aside from Earl, who wins worst-father-of-the-year award."

"So, no arguments? Disagreements? Fights?"

"Nope. She gets along with people. Better than gets along. She's a gem."

"When you spoke with Mary Jane that night, was anything bothering her? Did she seem at all depressed?"

"No. She was really happy that they had gotten a lot of work done on the book sale. And she said she had a surprise for me."

"So, no indication that something was wrong?"

Elliot frowned. "No, she actually sounded a little bit mischievous. I thought it had something to do with the surprise she was planning."

"Ell, I promise you I'll figure this out."

— • • • —

Next morning, Caleb was getting into his cruiser when his phone pinged to reveal a text message from the ME's office. It was time for a drive to Holyoke.

Dr. Bertrand Butler closed the refrigerated morgue drawer with a click. Pushing half-moon glasses up onto his head, he greeted Caleb with an extended hand.

"Chief, I'm sorry this is the way we have to meet for the first time. I heard that Ms. Bennett was a friend."

"Thank you. And thanks so much for getting the autopsy done so quickly."

Caleb knew the state suffered from an underfunded ME's office and that backlogs could be horrendous, so he was grateful for his attention. But he also knew that it would take several more weeks to get the full toxicology results. And those could be helpful to his investigation.

"We haven't had a single unexplained death since I got to Queensbridge seven years ago," he said, "and the state police weren't interested in hearing my theory that this was a suspicious death."

"Chief, this isn't a murder. I think you'll see why when I take you through my process. It confirms their theory that she died at her own hand—although accidentally." Butler turned toward the notes on his desk. "I'll take you step-by-step through the autopsy and my logic."

Caleb released a deep breath. "Please do."

Butler walked over to the autopsy table and pulled back the sheet. "My conclusion is that Mary Jane Bennett died of strangulation."

"That much I had figured out."

Caleb stood with his hands clasped behind his back, his forehead creased in concentration.

"Hear me out. Strangulation is a form of external pressure on the neck that causes a lack of oxygen due to closure of the blood vessels and/or air passages of the neck. There are three forms of strangulation: hanging, ligature, and manual. What we're looking at here is ligature strangulation. This happens with a rope, or a telephone cord, or —"

"Or a scarf?" Caleb asked, his jaw beginning to tighten.

"Exactly. Now, you need to know the anatomy of a neck if you want to understand the clinical features of a strangulation victim." He turned Mary Jane's head to the side. "Deep inside the neck are the carotid arteries. There's a pair of them located on each side. They're the major vessels that transport oxygen-rich blood from the heart and lungs to the brain. Jugular veins, on the other hand, transport deoxygenated blood from the brain back to the heart."

Caleb interrupted. "Doc, slow down. I never took anatomy."

"Okay. Bottom line: the victim can lose consciousness when the carotid arteries are blocked, depriving the brain of oxygen, or when the jugular veins are blocked, preventing deoxygenated blood from exiting the brain."

"So, is that what happened here?"

"Bear with me. Loss of consciousness could also happen a third way: by cutting off the airway, causing the victim to be unable to breathe. See this small horseshoe-shaped bone? It's called the hyoid bone, and it helps support the tongue. The larynx—the voice box—is made up of cartilage, not bone, that consists of two parts: the thyroid cartilage and the tracheal rings."

Caleb asked, "How much pressure are we talking here?"

"To close off the trachea, thirty-three pounds of pressure is required, but to cause a victim to lose consciousness, a person need only put eleven pounds of pressure on both carotid arteries for a total of about ten seconds."

Caleb was rigid as he listened to the pathologist, trying not to remember that the "victim" was Mary Jane. His jaw was beginning to ache.

"Now, what is interesting here is that there are no scratches or abrasions of any kind on the body, and no defensive wounds or skin cells under her nails, which we would expect if the victim had been attacked. And see these tiny red spots around the eyes and on the neck? They're called petechiae, and they're due to ruptured capillaries."

"Capillaries are the smallest blood vessels, right?" Caleb asked.

"Exactly. Now, if we had seen sub-conjunctival hemorrhages—deep blood red where the white sclera of the eyes normally is—that would suggest a particularly vigorous struggle between the victim and assailant. But we don't see that here.

"Also, if the victim has been strangled from behind, the impression from the ligature—in this case, the scarf—generally will be horizontal at the same level of the neck. Compare this with the mark left from a hanging. In a hanging, the ligature mark tends to be vertical and teardrop shaped. Also, with strangling from behind, the mark on the neck would be below the thyroid cartilage—the 'Adam's apple'—while in hanging, it is usually above. Finally, in strangulation by ligature, the hyoid bone and/or thyroid cartilage are often fractured. In hanging, these are usually intact. Here, the victim's hyoid bone and thyroid cartilage are both intact."

Caleb closed his eyes, trying to picture the scenario. A wave of nausea swept over him.

"So, between the lack of both sub-conjunctival hemorrhages and abrasions, plus the vertical ligature marks, I believe that she died accidentally as a result of experimenting with autoerotic asphyxia, having tied herself to the headboard. And the CSI report did say that the headboard the scarf was tied to was fairly high, so it was in the right position for strangulation."

Caleb tried to picture the antique bed frame. Before yesterday, he had been in that room only once, when he had helped Elliot carry the bed into the house and up the stairs. Mary Jane had found it at the Brimfield flea market and fallen in love with its twisted columns and detailed chased medallions. Expensive, but a real work of craftsmanship.

Butler paused here and laid his hand on Caleb's shoulder. "I'm sorry, Chief. As much as a homicide would make what happened to her, in an odd sort of way, somewhat more palatable, we never like to think of our loved ones as, um . . ." His voice trailed off.

"Were there any drugs in her system?"

"Like a roofie, you mean?"

"Anything."

"I wouldn't know that without a tox screen. But do you really want to delay the funeral? Chief, I'm absolutely certain of the cause of death. If she had been drinking or doing drugs, would that have made a difference?"

Caleb sighed, but it sounded more like a moan. "Mary Jane had dinner with us Friday night. She didn't drink. And she certainly wouldn't have been taking recreational drugs. She was pregnant."

"Yes, I know. I'll release the body tomorrow so her family can plan the funeral." Butler hesitated before speaking again. "Chief, you never know what goes on behind closed doors."

There's that phrase again. "Behind closed doors."

"The state police did find a pornographic DVD in the bedroom that supports my theory."

Jack said nothing about finding a DVD. Did he screw up again?

Caleb's stomach churned. The ME's ruling meant that the state police wouldn't investigate further. He took a deep breath, then thanked Butler and left the morgue. He got into the SUV, pushed the ignition button. He sat still and stared out the windshield, trying to absorb all he had been told.

He put the car in gear and headed back to Queensbridge. As he reached the Turnpike exit, he decided to stop by Elliot's place before going home.

This is gonna be awkward.

On seeing Caleb pull into the driveway, Elliot rose from his seat on the front porch.

"Hey. What's up?"

Caleb climbed the stairs. He wavered between sitting and leaning against a porch post, finally deciding to sit.

"Ell, I know this may be uncomfortable, but I'm going to have to ask you at some point."

"Go ahead, if it'll help you figure out what happened."

He took a deep breath. "Okay. Was Mary Jane into anything kinky?"

"Kinky? You mean sexually? Not at all. I mean, she has a healthy appetite, very healthy, but nothing weird. Why?"

Still using the present tense.

"Just asking."

"Just asking? You want to know what she does in bed? You don't think she committed suicide, do you? That's why you're asking?"

"I can't talk about this yet, Ell. I just need to ask questions."

"You asked me before if Mary Jane was at all depressed. I've been thinking about that. She was feeling bad, almost guilty, about getting pregnant while Rachel was having so much trouble." He gulped. "You don't think she harmed herself, do you?"

Caleb shrugged. "I don't know anything yet."

"Or do you think she was murdered? And you think I had something to do with it? Is that why you're asking all these questions? Am I a person of interest?"

Nobody's off the suspect list yet.

"Elliot, you knew Mary Jane better than anybody. You can give me background that I can't get from anybody else. Consider yourself a witness."

"I'll give you anything you want. You need to figure this out because I'm going crazy here, wondering how she could have strangled. And no, Mary Jane wasn't into anything unusual."

"Thanks, buddy. You can trust me to find answers."

"I'm not sure I can trust anybody now. Somebody killed Mary Jane, and we both know it."

CHAPTER EIGHT

The day after his visit with the ME, Caleb headed back to the station and called his team into the conference room. He stood at one end of the table.

"Since the ME ruled that Mary Jane's death wasn't a homicide, the state guys aren't going to give us any more support. So, we're on our own."

"On our own for what?" Jack asked.

"I'm convinced Mary Jane's death was not an accident and I don't think she committed suicide. I want us to pursue this as a possible murder, full bore."

"What makes you say that?" asked Scott.

"Just call it my gut instinct."

"You sure that's not acid reflux, boss?" Jack said.

Caleb looked at Jack over the rim of his coffee cup. "I can't see her ever risk hurting her baby, Jack. And by the way, when were you planning to tell me about the DVD?"

"I'm sorry, Chief. I guess it's been so busy I forgot. I'll get it from the state guys."

Caleb's jaw clenched.

Sandy broke in. "Your gut has been pretty accurate before, Chief. What do you want?"

"I want Mary Jane's phone logs and credit card bills. And I want you to check where she bought the DVD. If she bought it. And any unusual telephone calls. Elliot's too."

"You seem skeptical, Chief. You don't think she bought the video herself?" Sandy asked.

"I'm having a hard time accepting that Mary Jane was into either porn or paraphilia. And I don't need to tell you that this is all just among us. I don't want anybody in town knowing what we're doing yet."

"Our questions will raise some suspicion," Jack said.

True enough. Unconsciously, he ran his left hand over the edge of the table, back and forth, feeling the silky smoothness of the wood worn down by generations of villagers.

Drumming her pencil on the tabletop and biting her lower lip, Sandy watched her chief in what she called his "process mode." Then she looked up and said, "Chief? If I were going to buy porn, I wouldn't want any record of my having purchased anything like that. I'd have paid cash. An Internet purchase would probably be out of the question."

"Good point. Get Mary Jane's computer. Look at her internet search history to see if you can find anything. She may have browsed for titles without purchasing anything."

"Yes, sir."

"That leaves us with video rental stores. Jack, make a list of stores in Berkshire County and see if any of them sell this particular DVD, and if anybody happens to remember who bought it."

"That's going to be a lot of legwork, Chief."

"Then you'd better get started. And, Jack, see if any of those stores have video surveillance. We'll want everything they have."

He turned to his right.

"Sandy, I want you to check out Elliot Freund's alibi that he was in Chicago giving a seminar at the time of the murder."

"I've actually already done that. Chief, I know how hard Mary Jane's death has been on you, so I thought it would be best to check Elliot out right away. As her partner, he has to be at the top of the list of suspects. If she was, in fact, murdered."

"So, what did you find?"

"I was able to get an electronic copy of the program book from the organization that sponsored the conference. Elliot was on the agenda Saturday morning. Plus, the *Chicago Tribune* featured an article about the conference and quoted him in it."

Caleb mulled over this information. "Did the reporter interview Elliot in person, or by phone?"

"Good question. I'll try to track her down."

"And check the conference schedule against the airlines to make sure he couldn't have flown here and back."

"Will do, Chief. You're really covering all your bases here. I'll even check to make sure Elliot actually did speak at the time he was scheduled."

"I want to be absolutely sure. And, frankly, this part is easy. Nobody has to know we're investigating yet."

Caleb went to the white board hanging on the north wall of the conference room and wrote a list of tasks to be done, along with the names of the officers assigned to them.

He turned to Scott. "What have you found?"

"Jack and I interviewed all the staff at the Sunnybrook School. At least, all of them we could actually talk to. More than half were away on vacation when Mary Jane died."

Jack interrupted. "Yeah, what do they need so many teachers for? There're teams of at least four teachers in each class. You've got the specialists, and the interventionists, and the special ed people, and on top of that you've got the office staff. Holy crap, that's a lot of people to talk to."

"That's your tax dollar at work, Jack, and a future educated society. But I would really like to stay on task here," Caleb said.

"Right. Sorry."

"So?"

"So what?"

"So, what did you learn?" Caleb was tempted to roll his eyes but elected to take a deep cleansing breath instead and run his hand along the edge of the chair in front of him. Sandy looked as if she just might get up out of her wheelchair and shake him.

Scott jumped in and summarized their findings. "Every teacher and staff member had a solid alibi for Friday night. Everybody loved Mary Jane, from kids to faculty and staff. We found the same thing at both the library and the craft center. But there was something," he said. "Apparently, one of the teachers and her boyfriend are into kinky sex. She talks about it in the teachers' lounge."

Caleb leaned forward. "And?"

"Well, given how Mary Jane died, I was kinda wondering if maybe she got herself involved with this couple."

"How tight was their alibi?" Caleb asked.

"They said they were together. At a key party."

The knot in Caleb's stomach tightened. "You're thinking they could just be alibiing each other?"

"Yeah."

Jack sat up. "I'll check out the key parties," he said.

Sandy grimaced.

"I'll check it out, Jack," said Caleb. "Rachel teaches at the same school. And she knows Mary Jane. She'll know what's going on there. Now Sandy, what else have you got?"

"I decided to check our files to see if anybody's requested a vendor's permit in town, thinking that maybe an itinerant salesman might be our guy. Nothing there. So, I checked with the local Boy Scout troops to see if they had anybody in the area selling candy and might have seen something hinky during the day."

Jack sat up in his chair. "What, no cookie salesgirls? Aren't we being just a little bit biased?"

"Cookies go on sale in the winter, Jack," Sandy said. "And you can wipe the smirk off your face."

"Play nice, children," Caleb said.

"What about you, Chief?" Scott asked. "How about the days leading up to the murder? Did Elliot say what Mary Jane had been up to?"

"Do you think she told Elliot every single thing she did during the day?" Jack asked.

"Rachel tells me everything, including her conversations with the produce manager at the Price Chopper. And no, Elliot said there was nothing out of the ordinary."

"I'll bet partners keep secrets from each other," Jack said.

"You're just jealous, Jack," Sandy said.

Or we really didn't know Mary Jane well at all.

Caleb turned and left the room, went back to his desk and, sighing, picked up his notebook and a pencil. At the top left corner of the page, he wrote Suspects. Bile rose in his throat. It was only a word, but what a loaded one. Everybody on the list would be a neighbor, a friend, or God help us all, family.

Across the top of the page, he scrawled Motive, Means, and Opportunity.

He began to fill in the column under Suspects with the names of Mary Jane's family, friends, co-workers. As he wrote, his jaw began to tighten. He knew that 80% of murder victims are killed by people they know. Friends or family.

The first name on the list was Elliot Freund. After all, he lived with Mary Jane and had the greatest access to her. And Caleb knew that Elliot wasn't at all happy with Mary Jane's pregnancy. In fact, he had suspected that she'd gotten pregnant on purpose. But Elliot was his best friend. He knew this man like a brother and couldn't believe that he would, or could, kill someone. He chided himself for his emotional reaction but wanted to give Elliot the benefit of the doubt.

The phone rang, interrupting his thoughts. Caleb held the phone away from his ear, trying to preserve his hearing during a particularly angry harangue from a resident about a neighbor's bothersome roosters. He figured the fowl couldn't possibly be as loud as the caller. After promising to speak to the offending neighbor, he hung up the handset. As he swiveled his chair to face the window looking out onto Main Street, he spotted Rachel's auburn head bobbing through the shoppers at the weekly farmers market on the village green.

Perfect timing!

He jumped up out of his chair and headed out to meet her. The scent of fresh fruits and vegetables permeated the air, and Caleb inhaled several times to fill his mind with the wholesomeness he so sorely needed. The temperature was such that he couldn't tell the difference between his skin and the air until a soft breeze ruffled the hairs on his forearms.

He found Rachel sorting through a bin of peaches, scrutinizing each one before depositing it into a paper bag. The sight of her made his heart ping. He placed a hand on her back. She turned and smiled, but joy didn't reach her eyes, under which were dark smudges.

"Is guarding the produce part of your job now, or do you have news?" she asked.

"Nothing yet."

Rachel's face fell, making the dark circles even more prominent.

"Got a minute?"

She frowned. "For you? Of course." She paid for the peaches, then took him by the hand to a bench in a far corner of the green.

Caleb got right to the point. "Have you ever heard anything in the teachers' lounge about Mary Jane and kinky sex parties?"

"You don't think Mary Jane had anything to do with that?"

"This isn't for public consumption, but the CSIs found a pornographic video in Mary Jane's DVD player."

"Oh, my God."

"And it was pretty hardcore. So, have you heard something?"

"Well, one of the very young teachers, Bari Watson, likes to talk about the escapades she and her boyfriend get into. I tend to think a lot of her talk is for show. But, then again, you never know."

"Was Mary Jane friendly with her?" Caleb asked as he leaned forward.

Rachel seemed to be considering her choice of words. "Mary Jane was friendly with everybody on staff, but certainly not to the point of friendship with Bari."

"Thanks. That helps." He noted the pain in Rachel's eyes.

"Caleb," she said, "I really can't see Mary Jane into that kind of stuff. I've known her all my life. It just wasn't like her."

CHAPTER NINE

Friday, the sky was a robin's egg blue with a scattering of cottony white clouds the afternoon Mary Jane Bennett was buried, the medical examiner having finally released her body. Birdsong filled the air, and a slight breeze relieved the late August heat, ruffling villagers' hair. Caleb thought it was obscene that a funeral could take place on such a perfect day.

What a way to spend the day, he mused. He positioned himself off to the side under a large sugar maple. He watched friends, family members, students, and their parents, all pale-faced and somber, make their way up the steps and into the white clapboard church. Rachel and Tenley stood together next to the brick path leading to the church, greeting people with hugs and tears. Caleb joined them.

"Have you spoken to Elliot's father and brother?" he asked.

"Yes," Rachel said. "They seem a little shell-shocked. Mary Jane was very close to them."

"I think Earl may also have something to do with their discomfort."

Rachel's eyes widened. "Oh, no. What did he do this time?"

"He was pretty much himself. When Elliot's dad went over to express his condolences, Earl turned his back on him.

Elliot's pissed, but I convinced him to breathe. How about I go over and serve as a buffer?"

"There's something wrong with that man, Caleb. Who acts like this?"

"I'd just stay out of his way. Earl's toxic."

As he walked away, Caleb turned his attention back to the crowd. He wasn't exactly sure what he was looking for there. But he knew that, despite the popular perception encouraged by television, a perpetrator doesn't usually return to the scene of a crime. Unless, of course, he was an arsonist. Or a serial killer. And that was a possibility he didn't even want to contemplate.

He was looking for something that might give him a clue. But what that clue was he didn't know. All he did know was that his gut was telling him that his good friend did not die accidentally. And definitely not on purpose by her own hand.

Somebody who didn't seem sad. Somebody who seemed too sad. Somebody who didn't belong here, who didn't know Mary Jane or Elliot. The autopsy report was clear that the death was caused by accidental strangulation, but Caleb's gut wasn't accepting the ME's conclusions. He realized that his negative reaction to the report might simply be the result of his being Mary Jane's friend. But his instinct had always served him well in the past. Could it be telling him something here, too?

You're not a homicide detective. Wouldn't Father be gloating now? You should've stuck with the legal career. Look where you'd be now. Yes, Father, I'd be a miserable SOB like you.

A commotion to the left caught his attention. When he turned his head, he saw Zoe struggling up the slight rise toward the church. Rachel raced to her side. The two friends hugged and kept their embrace for a long minute.

"Oh, my God, Zoe," Rachel said. "I should've called you! I should've picked you up."

"No need. Dennis dropped me off and then parked. He'll be here any minute. But I really can't stand too long with these crutches. How about if I see you inside? I'll save seats."

"I'll help you up the stairs."

The two friends headed toward the church, arm in arm. Caleb turned his attention back to the crowd, although he still had no idea what he might see.

When Rachel returned, she said, "Thank goodness Zoe has Dennis."

Caleb nodded in agreement. "He's been a tremendous support to her."

She sighed deeply. "Between Mary Jane's death, Zoe's foot, and the car accident on Route 41, Friday night was not a good one for this village. I guess it's true that bad things come in threes."

If only.

After the ceremony, Caleb switched on his cruiser's light bar and led the funeral cortege over hills and along the Housatonic River to the cemetery, slowing at some of Mary Jane's favorite spots in her beloved Berkshires before reaching her final resting place.

CHAPTER TEN

The next morning, Caleb pushed his chair away from the breakfast table and stood up. He tucked the *Berkshire Eagle* under one arm and picked up his coffee mug with the other, then made his way to the screen porch. The old wicker creaked as he sank into the soft, yielding cushions of his favorite chair. The furniture had sat in the sunroom of Rachel's parents' summer home and migrated here when they had redecorated. Rachel insisted on calling the faded floral upholstery "shabby chic," preferring good memories to new fabric.

He set the newspaper aside and gazed out at the serene summer morning, listening to a symphony of chirping birds and lowing cows. The perfume of freshly mown hay drifted in on a soft breeze and a massive cloud of pure white cotton candy fog filled the valley, obscuring the rising sun. Caleb knew it would burn off as the day progressed, so he leaned back to take it all in.

The banging of a screen door roused him out of his reverie. Rachel was standing next to him, dressed in her workout clothes.

"Going somewhere?" he asked. "It's early. The sun just came up."

"I couldn't sleep again last night. Horrible thoughts keep bouncing around in my head. I can't stop thinking about how Mary Jane died. How she looked. But what about you? Aren't you going to work?"

"You're always after me to smell the roses, aren't you? Well, I decided to stop and smell them. Except I'm smelling grass."

Rachel's tipped her head to one side, her brow furrowed. She touched his arm. "Are you okay?"

"I'm fine. Really. Now that I'm doing what you want, you're worried? Isn't this why you wanted to move to the country, so we could breathe fresh air?"

Caleb knew even as he said it that he was lying. He couldn't move out of the city fast enough after that terrible night in the Meatpacking District. He and his partner, Manny, had just finished up a long day surveilling a suspected meth house and decided to stop for a beer before going home. They figured they'd get to their favorite hangout just in time for last call. It turned out to be Manny's last call. As the two walked toward Herlihy's, a stray bullet from a fight in an apartment across the street caught Manny right in the chest. He had died in his best friend's arms, his blood seeping out to mingle with the grit embedded in the concrete sidewalk.

Despite attending department-mandated counseling, Caleb had roller-coasted between anger and guilt and back to rage for months afterwards. Rachel had lobbied hard for the move, hoping that the tranquility of the country would help him find some peace of mind. Ultimately, he agreed, and they relocated to Queensbridge. Little did he know that another one of his best friends would die violently in this little corner of Eden.

He smiled at Rachel and patted her on the backside. "Go. Take your walk. The fresh air and exercise will do you good."

She frowned. "Okay then. I guess I'll be off."

"Why don't you go over to Zoe's and have coffee with her? You both could use the company."

"Not today. I need to be alone."

The screen door banged again as she exited. Caleb picked up the newspaper, scanned the headlines, and drained his coffee cup. He gathered up everything from the table and brought it into the kitchen, placing the cup into the dishwasher. Then, he grabbed his jacket off the peg in the back hall and zipped it up, smiling at the memory of Rachel scouring flea markets and yard sales in search of the antique brass doorknobs that she had turned into coat hooks. He checked himself in the wall mirror and noticed that his hair was beginning to curl over his collar.

Time for a haircut.

He headed out for his regular morning tour of the village. He drove slowly down Main Street, taking in the shopkeepers' pre-opening rituals, his senses attuned to catching anything out of place, but somewhat surprised—even offended—that everything seemed normal. He almost preferred their hunched shoulders and suspicious eyes. Flora Swenson swept the sidewalk in front of the Three Sisters bookshop, sand puffing into clouds around her feet. The morning sun shone through her silver hair, forming a halo around her head. George Roberts cranked open the green and red awning in front of his market. The walkway in front had already been swept and hosed down, and water still dripped off the curb into the gutter. Harriet Jablow was talking with him, her hands waving as she pulled something green and vegetable-looking out of her shoulder bag.

He noticed that Hallie Cartwright was already at work, probably getting ready for a delivery of fresh flowers. The trellis in the alley next to the shop was covered with magnificent cerise roses that highlighted the pink and white-striped awnings over the front windows, making the place look delicious—more like a French patisserie or a confectionery than a flower shop.

Caleb, a firm believer in the broken windows theory, admired the care that the shopkeepers took with their properties. Keeping control of littering, graffiti and other mischief could prevent an escalation into more serious crime. Of course, Queensbridge was no urban setting, but he also knew that, despite Zoe's vision of the picture postcard, no place was Eden. People were people, and at any moment something could happen to shatter the peace. Something *had* happened. Now it was his job, his responsibility, to solve it.

He finished his rounds and headed back to the station. His phone rang as he walked into his office.

Zoe's voice was frantic. "Caleb, somebody's been in my house."

"Get out now. I'm on my way."

Caleb grabbed his service weapon and his keys and ran to the cruiser. Within minutes he found Zoe standing at the bottom of her driveway, leaning against her car, her crutches by her side. He motioned to her to get in.

"Are you okay?"

"I'm terrified. Thank God you're here. What's going on? Mary Jane is dead. My house is broken into . . ." She clutched his arm so tightly that he knew there would be a nice black-and-blue mark on it later.

He released himself from her grip and said, "Let me check out the house first. You stay in the car."

He drove up the steep driveway and parked, then went inside. He went through the first floor of the house room by room, opening every closet door. Entertainment center, computer, and printer were all in place. He then proceeded up the stairs to the second floor. The hallway was empty save for a console table that held a bowl of ostrich eggs. He checked out the bedrooms and bathrooms. Nothing was tipped over, nothing ripped or broken.

He then descended into the basement, one step at a time, his ear tuned for the sound of breathing, his nose sniffing for the smell of a human presence. Then, halfway down the stairs, he spotted a man in front of him. Heart thumping, he drew his service revolver from its holster and aimed for center mass.

From an oval cheval mirror standing at the bottom of the stairs, Caleb saw his own image reflecting back at him. He let out a breath, shook his head and laughed, but kept his weapon drawn while he checked out the rest of the basement. Gradually his heart rate returned to normal.

I've only drawn my weapon once in my career and just now I almost shot a mirror.

He went back upstairs to the front door and signaled for Zoe to join him. "Nobody's in the house now."

"I'm sure somebody's been here. I can feel it," she said.

"You're sure you didn't inadvertently leave the door unlocked when you went out?"

"It was wide open!"

"Okay. We'll go through the house together. Take your time. There's no rush. Tell me if you see anything missing or out of place."

Slowly and carefully, they moved through the great room, the kitchen, and her office.

"Everything seems to be here," she said. "I don't understand."

"You may discover something missing later when you go to look for it. Let's check the bedroom."

"My jewelry!" She hobbled up the stairs to the second floor, dragging her crutches behind.

In the bedroom, Zoe headed for her dresser. She pulled open the wide top drawer to reveal three sections containing loads of bracelets, necklaces, and earrings.

"Damn, Zoe! How much jewelry do you have?"

"Remember, Caleb, I deal in image. I have jewelry for every type of potential client. Bohemian, Upper East Side . . ."

"Can you even tell if any pieces are missing?"

"Give me a minute. I'll check."

Zoe pulled out a file folder from a drawer. It held a large, folded sheet of paper on which was printed a spreadsheet listing all her jewelry.

Caleb laughed. "Wow. Zoe, you said you liked things organized, but this is amazing. You even have photos of every piece."

"I did tell you that, didn't I? Let me check the list to see if anything is missing." She scanned the spreadsheet. "Oh, no! There are a few pieces gone."

"Why these pieces in particular? Is any of this stuff expensive and worth pawning?"

"It's very nice stuff, but not precious gems. Except, of course, my diamond engagement ring."

"Is that here?"

She reached into the back of the drawer and fished out a tiny blue box. Holding her breath, she opened it and let out a deep sigh.

"It's here. Thank God. Evan gave me this." She held the box close to her chest. "Caleb, just the thought of somebody being in my home, my sacred space, gives me the creeps," she said, "Do you think the Turners will let me install a system before we close on the house?"

"I'm sure they'd be okay with that, and I think it's a good idea, especially since you live alone."

"I'll call today."

"Zoe, send me photos of the missing pieces. I'm not optimistic we'll be able to recover your stuff, but I can share the images with area departments." He looked around the bedroom one last time. "Maybe you should stay with us until you get that alarm system installed. Elliot's back in his own house, so we have room."

"That's really sweet, Caleb, but you've had enough company for a while. I'll just have Dennis come over."

"If you change your mind, Rachel would love the company. You could each use the other's support."

"The last two musketeers." She lifted her head and smiled through tear-filled eyes.

— • • • —

Caleb stopped by the Queen Bee and picked up a tuna wrap before heading back to the station. He sat down at his desk to sort through his notes before joining his team, taking bites of his sandwich while reading. Within minutes, his cell phone rang. He swallowed before picking up. It was Rachel.

77

"Zoe just called to tell me about the break-in," she said. "She said you invited her to stay with us. That was the right thing to do."

"She declined the invitation."

"Do you think she'll be all right?"

"She's not that brave. Dennis is coming over to stay with her."

"Caleb, do you have any idea who did it?"

"Not yet. But I've been thinking about it. Why would somebody break in and only take a few little pieces of costume jewelry and not the expensive electronic gear?"

"Maybe he figured that jewelry is easy to hide in a couple of large pockets or a backpack."

"True, and if it was a kid, he wouldn't know the good stuff from sparkly costume jewelry."

"I'm sure you'll figure this out. You always do."

"Hmm," Caleb mumbled.

"Be careful what you wish for." He had wanted challenge, but certainly not at the expense of a good friend.

And now I have to go talk to Earl. I hope he's calmed down a little since his performance at the funeral.

CHAPTER ELEVEN

Earl Bennett lived in a tidy white cape house with black shutters. The front lawn and hedges were trimmed with a razor sharpness that made Caleb think of the aisles of shelves in the man's liquor store. He lined up the bottles with the same precision. Green was the only color in the yard, although there were a dozen shades of it. No wonder Mary Jane had loved her flower garden, with its profusion of hues from every point on the color wheel.

He paused to gather his thoughts before opening the car door, trying to imagine a father killing his own child. He couldn't help the feeling that something squirrely was going on.

He swung his legs out of the cruiser, walked up the straight brick path, mounted the freshly swept front steps, and pressed the doorbell. He heard what sounded like a drawer slamming shut followed by shuffling.

Earl opened the door and glared. "What do you want?"

"Can I come in, Earl? I want to ask you some questions if you're up to it."

"Do I have a choice?" he asked.

"I'm trying to find out what happened to your daughter, Earl."

Caleb's words seemed to throw Earl off balance. "You know Freund did it."

"No, I don't know that Elliot did anything."

"Well, then come in but be careful where you walk. I've been working here."

As he followed Earl through the living room and into the kitchen, Caleb looked around. The furniture was dated, but the house was neat and dust free. At least he hadn't let the house go to hell.

Earl got down on his knees and resumed pulling up the kitchen floor.

"Sylvie was after me for years to replace the linoleum with wood. I hope she can see from where she is that I'm finally getting to it."

When Caleb didn't respond immediately, Earl said, "You mourn in your way, I'll mourn in mine."

"When did your wife die?"

"Sylvie passed eighteen years ago."

"How long were you married?"

Earl glared at him. "Fifteen years."

Caleb did some quick math in his head. "So, Mary Jane was conceived out of wedlock?"

Earl braced himself on a kitchen chair to ease himself up from the floor. His face was red, whether from exertion or anger, Caleb couldn't tell. Until he clenched his fists.

"Sylvie got pregnant. That's why I married her," he said. "She was a nice woman and a good mother, but not the love of my life. I did my duty, and I was faithful, but I always felt trapped. I didn't want the same thing to happen to Mary Jane."

"It had to have been hard, raising a teenage girl by yourself. And you were still a young man."

"We managed. I loved her. She was my only child." Earl's breath was coming out as a shallow wheeze.

"You had a hell of a way of showing it."

"What's that supposed to mean?"

"You said some very nasty things to her, Earl. You called her a slut. You—"

"What do you know? You don't have children."

Caleb felt a sting in his throat but continued.

"You never even asked how Mary Jane died. Or where. Why are you so convinced she was murdered?"

"Because I know my daughter. There's no way she hanged herself." He paused. "And I hear things. This is a small town, Chief." He said the last word with a sneer.

"So, Earl, where were you the night Mary Jane died?" Immediately, he was ashamed of himself for his need for payback.

"I won't dignify that question with an answer."

"Would you prefer to come to the station with me?"

Earl huffed and paced the room, his hands balled into tight fists.

"Earl, answer the question."

"People will talk about how my little girl got herself pregnant." He dropped into a chair.

"People are already talking, Earl. They're talking about what a shit you were to Mary Jane and Elliot." He paused, trying to control his own anger at the man. "Maybe people might think she killed herself because of the way you treated her."

Earl's eyes bulged. "Chief, leave my house now. If you want to arrest me, then do it. But I have nothing else to say to you. You're wasting your time here."

Instead, Caleb persisted in his questioning. "Earl, you say you loved your daughter, but you certainly haven't demonstrated it. We're wasting precious time dancing around when we could be focusing our attention elsewhere. Help me out here so I can do my job. Mary Jane strangled to death. I need to find out how and why."

Earl glared at him for a moment. Then, his head fell forward, and he began to sob, his shoulders shaking. Caleb stared at him in wonder. Why was he so unwilling to help him understand how his own flesh-and-blood had died?

He pulled a pristine white handkerchief from his pocket and wiped his tears. "Do you really think I could murder my own daughter? Everybody loved Mary Jane. She was a child of this village. Why aren't you checking out Freund?"

Caleb's stomach cramped. "What would make you think she was murdered?"

"Mary Jane would never kill herself. She was a good girl."

"A good girl or a slut, Earl? Which is it?"

Earl glared at him.

"So, again, where were you that Friday night?"

"For Chrissake, I was watching a movie on TV. Did you think I'd be out clubbing?"

"Did you talk to anybody that night?"

Earl was silent.

Caleb repeated the question. "Did you talk to anybody that night?"

"Who would I talk to?"

"Earl, you might've seen something, even if it didn't register at the time. This is the way we investigate. I'm asking everybody."

"No. I saw nothing. I wasn't there at the house. You happy?"

He's hiding something.

Before he could pursue his line of questioning, Earl shouted, "Why don't you check your good buddy? His plane was two hours late taking off. Why don't you ask him about that?"

"How do you know that?"

"Mary Jane told me."

Caleb's radar went up. "You talked to Mary Jane the day she died?"

"Yeah. I talked with her in the evening."

"Then why didn't you say so before? What time was that?"

Earl looked out into space as he thought. "About 6:30. Yeah. I'd just closed the store and was on my way to the gym."

That was just before she came to dinner at our house.

"I'm telling you, Chief, you have to check him out."

This is a desperate man.

He brought the focus back to Earl.

"Do you have any enemies?"

"Enemies?"

"Yeah, enemies. It's no secret that you're not the easiest person to get along with. In fact, you can be a real pain in the ass. Is there anybody you've ticked off so much that they might want to get back at you by hurting Mary Jane?"

"So, you do think it's murder?"

"I'm exploring every possible avenue to understand what happened."

Earl blew out a puff of air and ran his hands through his hair. "I know I'm not everybody's favorite person, but I've always been honest in my business, and I always did my best with Mary Jane. Especially after Sylvie died."

"Well, if you think of something, anything, give me a call," Caleb said and turned to go. "Don't get up. I'll let myself out."

As he made his way back to the SUV, he mulled over their conversation. Earl had been adamant about Elliot's flight being delayed. Did he actually believe that Elliot would murder Mary Jane? Or was he trying to divert attention from himself or somebody else?

CHAPTER TWELVE

Sunday night, a nightmare jolted Caleb awake. His heart pounded as he checked the numbers on the digital clock glowing red in the dark: 4:24 a.m. He tried to slow his ragged breathing by counting: in four, hold seven, out eight. Breathe, he commanded himself. In and out. He shuddered at the memory of his dream. In it, a very pregnant Rachel was standing over Mary Jane, the red scarf wrapped around her hands, an evil grin spread across her face. His father, a martini glass in hand, stood to the side, his lip curled in derision.

But Rachel was sleeping soundly at his side, her soft breath lifting the sheet with every exhalation. He closed his eyes and worked at regulating his own breathing. What was that dream all about?

He wondered if he was up to the job of investigating his friend's death.

Snap out of it, Caleb. You're a professional, for crying out loud. It's only because this death struck so close to home that you're having nightmares. Right?

His heart still pounding, he knew he wouldn't fall back asleep. So, noting that the sun would be up in another hour, he got out of bed, dressed, and did his morning rounds before going to the station.

The station was eerily quiet when he let himself in at six o'clock. He turned on the coffee maker. Five minutes later when he heard it beep, he poured the scalding liquid into an oversized mug that had been a gift from Rachel. It was so old that the original Red Sox insignia had long worn off. He took it to his desk and, as he drank, he turned to look at the photo of himself and Rachel that sat on the low file cabinet below the windows. Caleb contemplated it now with new eyes.

Rachel had been deeply shocked by the news of Mary Jane's death. The two did everything together. Everything except get pregnant. Could the love of his life, that gentle, caring woman, have been so jealous of Mary Jane's pregnancy that she had had something to do with the woman's death? And, in such a perverted way? In his heart he couldn't believe that, yet he was a cop. He needed to rule out the possibility methodically.

Where was Rachel when Mary Jane died? Could she have killed her at some point over the weekend? He sat quietly, his eyes closed in thought. What did the ME's report say was the time of death?

Caleb opened his eyes and reached for the manila folder that contained the ME's preliminary results. Time of death: about one a.m. Saturday, give or take. At one a.m. Rachel had been in bed with him. He was a light sleeper, so there was no way Rachel could have gotten out of bed, driven to Mary Jane's, and murdered her without waking him up.

But just as the tension in his neck and his gut began to recede, a memory jolted him. On that fateful Friday, he hadn't been in bed all night. At around midnight he had been called out for that car accident on Route 41. And Rachel had even mentioned it at the funeral.

He hauled himself out of his chair and headed over to the Queen Bee. He needed breakfast. And better coffee.

— • • • —

Sally pushed through the swinging door from the kitchen, the sounds and aroma of bacon sizzling on the grill following her.

"Hey Chief, I've been meaning to tell you. I'm seeing so many hummingbirds this summer. Thanks so much for getting me set up with the feeder. They are just the most amazing creatures."

Sally's really trying hard to pretend that all's normal in the village.

"Indeed, they are, Sally. They'll be here every day of summer and then find their way back to the very same place every year."

"Just like our second homeowners," Earl Bennett piped in. "We can't get rid of 'em."

"If it weren't for those second homeowners, half this town wouldn't have a decent income," Sally said.

Earl jumped off his stool and turned toward Sally, his arms akimbo. Veins bulged from his muscular arms, something Caleb always found inconsistent with the man's sedentary job.

"I could wring her neck," he had said. *With hands strong enough to strangle a woman?*

"We could get by just fine with tourists coming through and going home. We don't need those people."

Caleb knew that Earl had to be hurting, but sometimes he just really wanted him to shut up. He tried to change the subject before Earl launched into one of his usual rants but was interrupted by a group of tourists coming in together for breakfast. Mercifully, Earl fell silent, allowing Caleb to enjoy his scrambled eggs and hash browns in peace.

Just as Caleb sipped the last of his coffee, he heard Earl gearing up again with another diatribe against New Yorkers. Fearing the worst, he slid out of the booth, grabbed the man by the arm, and led him outside.

"Earl, you are certainly entitled to your opinions, but if you do anything to hurt Sally's business with your incessant crap, or attack one more person in this village, I will have you in cuffs. Do you understand me?"

Earl's eyes bulged. "Are you threatening me?"

"I'm telling you what will happen if you continue on the path you've chosen. I will not tolerate your aggression."

He released the man from his grip, then crossed the street to the police station. He went back to reviewing the ME's autopsy report, his officers' reports, and the notes he himself had taken at the scene, stopping every few minutes to take a phone call. Frustrated, he got up from his desk and went over to Sandy's desk.

"What'd you find?" he asked.

"Nothing unusual at all in her phone or credit card statements," Sandy reported.

"Anything in Elliot's?"

"Not unless you count lots of money spent on woodworking tools."

"Okay, thanks."

"But there was one other thing, Chief. Earl told you there was a delay in Elliot's departure, but that would've been totally irrelevant. His flight took off at two on Friday. He landed at five o'clock, our time, and met with the reporter at seven for about half an hour. There's no way Elliot could have boarded a flight to come back here, kill Mary Jane, and then be back in time for his presentation at 9 a.m. Even presuming he could find a flight in the middle of the night, which he couldn't. If he had turned around at O'Hare and come right back in the afternoon, he wouldn't have been able to talk with the reporter. And I checked to see if he had made a return flight. Nada."

"Good work, Sandy. Now I've got another job for you," he said.

"Sure, Chief. What is it?"

"I want you to find out everything you can about autoerotic asphyxia."

Sandy's mouth formed an O. "Why's that?"

"It's how the ME thinks Mary Jane was strangled. I want to understand exactly what's involved to see if it makes sense."

"Okay. I'll get right on it. Sorry I haven't had a chance to read the report yet." Sandy spun her wheelchair around to face her computer.

"You've had a lot on your plate, Sandy."

He headed back toward the coffee pot. He dumped used grounds that smelled vaguely like stale cigarettes into the trash. He opened the refrigerator, took out the pitcher of chilled water, and started a fresh pot. While the coffee was dripping, he paced the halls, going over the evidence in his mind.

Suddenly, he stopped. The smell of stale cigarettes! He headed back to his office, the tick-tick-tick of Sandy's keyboard in his ears. He rifled through his notes until he came upon one he had jotted down the day Jack discovered Mary Jane's body.

Smell of smoke in the room. Damn! How could I have forgotten that?

He jumped up and made a beeline toward the front of the station.

"Sandy, round up every officer you can find, part-timers too, and send them up to Elliot's house. And Scott, I want you to lead a team there."

"What're we looking for?"

"See if you can find a cigarette butt anywhere inside or outside the house. And make a large circle."

"Cigarette? What're you thinking?"

"Not sure yet, but I distinctly recall smelling smoke in Mary Jane's bedroom. She wasn't a smoker. I made a note at the time, but then got sidetracked."

"You got it, Chief."

Caleb looked at his watch. "There's still plenty of daylight left to get the job done."

— • • • —

By two o'clock Caleb had drunk enough coffee to keep him sailing through the rest of the week. The sounds of people talking and phones ringing made for background noise to his musings. He had been sitting at his desk for over an hour, trying to make sense of the witness statements, the ME's report, and the scant evidence collected so far, but not making much progress.

Sandy's voice broke through his reverie. "Chief, Luisa Burke is on the line."

He picked up the phone on his desk.

"Chief, I need to talk to you. Can you meet me at Stevens Glen?"

"Can't you come to the station, Luisa?"

"No, I need to talk to you in private."

"I'm kinda busy. How about if I send Scott Cruz?"

"No, I don't want anybody else to hear what I have to say."

"Well, you've got my interest, Luisa." He could feel a surge of adrenaline. Could this be something important?

"Thanks, Chief. I'll see you at the head of the trail in ten minutes."

Nine minutes later, Caleb pulled over to the shoulder and jumped out of the car. About fifty yards down the hill he spied the ramrod-straight Luisa pacing back and forth. On hearing Caleb's footsteps on the gravel, she looked up and gave him a tight smile.

"Nature is really something, Chief. Did you know that Queen Anne's lace and poison hemlock look alike?"

"Uh, no. I didn't."

"That something so beautiful can look like something so innocent. Yet be deadly."

There we go with that Purim theme again.

"Luisa, is that why you called me?"

"Of course not. I need to talk to you about Mary Jane Bennett."

Caleb tensed. "What about Mary Jane?"

"Well, it's actually about Earl. He told me that you came by to question him."

"Yeah, I came by to see if he could give me any information that might help us figure out his daughter's death. I asked him where he was the night Mary Jane died. He was quite evasive."

"He was with me. We had dinner and then watched a movie. There is no way he could have—or would have—killed her. And yes, I think she was murdered."

"He was with you?" While ashamed to admit it, Caleb had never thought of Luisa as having a personal relationship. Just shy of 40, she dressed like a lumberjack and had a manner as smooth as P12 sandpaper. He hoped his surprise at her revelation hadn't been too obvious, so he continued talking to smooth over his gaffe. "I didn't say he was a suspect. He's a potential witness."

"Earl's a wonderful guy. We've been seeing each other for about a year now."

"Then why didn't Earl tell me this? It could've saved him a lot of grief, and this investigation a lot of time."

"Earl's a gentleman. He doesn't kiss and tell."

Caleb felt acid rise in his throat as Earl's words came back to him. "People will talk."

What a hypocrite. He was willing to be with Luisa, but only on the sly, and then deny his daughter's right to be with the man she loved.

"I know what this looks like. I'm so much younger than Earl. But we really love each other."

"So much so that you have to keep it secret, Luisa?"

Luisa's face flushed.

"You wouldn't understand, Chief."

"You're right, Luisa. I wouldn't understand. But I do appreciate your telling me. Is there anything else I should know?"

"What do you mean?" She looked puzzled.

"I mean if you have any other information relevant to this investigation, I need to know. Now. The further we get from Mary Jane's death, the harder it will be to solve."

"I've got nothing else." She hesitated a moment, then said, "Listen, Chief, I liked Mary Jane. Didn't everybody? She was a child of this village. I'd like nothing more than to catch the monster who killed her."

"A child of the village." I guess Luisa is spending lots of time with Earl. That's the second time I've heard that expression.

— • • • —

Caleb returned to the station and added a note about Luisa and Earl to the whiteboard. As he stood pondering, he heard a cough and turned toward the sound. Sandy was sitting at the conference room door.

"Chief? Got a minute?"

"Sure, Sandy. What's up?"

"First of all, you have a bunch of calls." She handed him a pile of pink message slips. "But I've been thinking." She stopped and bit her lower lip.

"Go on. What's bothering you?"

"I'm looking at the notes you're writing and wondering about Earl and Luisa. Did Mary Jane know about their affair? Do you think Luisa might have killed Mary Jane? I mean, there's a huge age difference between the two lovers. Mary Jane might have given them a hard time."

"Interesting thought. I'm pretty sure she didn't know about the affair or Rachel would have mentioned it, but I'll ask her. In fact, let me call her right now."

A few minutes later, Caleb had his answer. "Rachel said that Mary Jane was actually hoping Earl could find somebody. She figured that would take the pressure off her and Elliot. Too bad Earl felt the need to be so secretive."

"Well, how about we take another tack. Earl must have a will, right? If Mary Jane is dead, who inherits his estate? Do you think Luisa might be a beneficiary of the will?"

"Sandy, that's an excellent point. We should check that out today."

"Should I send Jack?"

Caleb puffed up his cheeks and blew out air. "No, Jack has all the subtlety of dynamite. I'll do it. I might as well go now. I'm not getting anything accomplished around here."

Earl's history of loud and very public disdain of Elliot was well known, as was his generally cantankerous, if not outright obnoxious, behavior. He had been livid at Mary Jane's living with Elliot, and downright verbally abusive on learning of her pregnancy, hurling hateful names at her. But murder his own daughter?

Grieving father or vengeful killer?

Caleb shook his head. "I need to get back to Earl and find out what's going on in that warped little mind."

He picked up his phone and dialed the liquor store. The clerk answered the phone and informed him that Earl hadn't come into work.

Ten minutes later, Caleb was back at the white clapboard house. When Earl opened the door, he was shocked to see how much the man's appearance had deteriorated in the short time since his previous visit. His skin was sallow, and his eyes were red.

"You again? What do you want?" Earl hissed.

"Earl, are you feeling all right? You look like hell."

"Of course, I look like hell. You woke me up," he said, a scowl crossing his face. "Do you have any news for me?"

"Not yet, Earl, but can I come in? I have a few more questions."

"Might as well." He turned, leaving the front door open. Caleb followed him into the house. Every shade and curtain had been drawn shut, and a sour smell of old socks filled the place. He tried not to gag but was sorely tempted to throw open every window in the house. How could the house have changed so fast?

Earl plopped down onto his easy chair while Caleb took a seat on the sofa. He sank so deeply into the old cushions that his knees were pushed above waist level.

"Earl, did Mary Jane know about you and Luisa?"

Earl's head shot up, now fully awake. "How do you know about me and Luisa?"

"She told me. She knew that you wouldn't tell anybody, and she also realized that you needed an alibi. So, tell me. Did Mary Jane know?"

"I never told her." Earl squared his shoulders. "If she knew, she never told me."

"So, she never said anything negative about the relationship to you?"

"I just said, I don't think she knew."

"What about Luisa? Do you know if she ever approached Luisa?"

"No."

"No, you don't know? Or no, she didn't approach her?"

Earl looked confused for a moment, then said, "No, I don't know. But Luisa would've told me if she had."

Caleb wondered if that was true. After all, Luisa had divulged the relationship in order to provide him with an alibi. Would she have kept a confrontation with Mary Jane quiet to protect him?

"All I can say is that you should ask Luisa. Now that she's spilled the beans," Earl said.

Caleb started to rise but sat down again. "Earl, do you have a will?"

"Of course. I know what happens when people die intestate."

"Who are the beneficiaries?"

Earl frowned. "Mary Jane's the only one. She was an only child. Sylvie's gone and I don't care for my brothers and sisters." He stroked his chin and seemed surprised to find stubble on his normally clean-shaven chin. "I guess I should call my lawyer to change it. I'm not getting any younger."

Was Sandy on the right track?

"Who will you name as beneficiary, Earl? Luisa?"

"Jesus, Chief. Do you really think this was about money?" He shook his head. "No, I'll give it to charity. Maybe a little to Luisa."

Then another thought occurred to Caleb. An alibi for Earl was also an alibi for Luisa.

"So, what did you and Luisa do that night?"

"The night my daughter was murdered?" Earl coughed and cleared his throat. "We went to a steakhouse in Springfield, then came home. We watched a movie and then went to bed."

Springfield. So, nobody would see them? His gut was tightening, but instead of saying something he might regret, Caleb decided to keep the conversation friendly. "We like Bernie's in Chicopee. You ever go there?"

"Yeah. But they only do take-out now. Listen, I'm not proud of my behavior, but I'm all alone here. I'm lonely. You wouldn't know about that, would you?"

Caleb chose to ignore the barb. "Do you have a receipt from the restaurant?"

"Of course. I do run a business, y'know." He put his hands on the chair arms and pushed himself up, then went to a side room he used as a home office. In less than a minute he returned with the receipt. On it were listed two house salads, two regular cut prime ribs, a lemon meringue pie, a rice pudding, and two coffees.

That Luisa sure has a good appetite.

"So, then you came back here?" Caleb asked.

"No, we went to Luisa's." Caleb remembered that Luisa's house was deep in the woods. Again, a place where nobody would see them.

"What movie did you watch?"

Earl narrowed his eyes at him. "Casablanca."

"Did you watch it on TV or DVD?"

"It was on cable."

Caleb checked the notes of his previous conversation with Earl. He had said he watched a movie on TV. He didn't say where he'd watched it. Or with whom. He made a note to check the TV listings for the night of the murder, then thanked Earl and headed back to the station.

CHAPTER THIRTEEN

Caleb and Rachel sat side by side in the old wicker rocking chairs on the screen porch, having their after-dinner coffee. The musical plash of rushing water from the backyard stream provided a soothing background. Raindrops from an afternoon sun shower had caught in the screening, rendering the view of the hilly landscape into a sparkling Impressionist painting.

"Well, look at us, two old folks rockin' away our evening," Rachel said.

"Yup. Where's my knife? I should be whittlin'."

She set her coffee cup down on the small table and held out her hand. Caleb took it in his and the two rocked in comfortable silence for a while, the creaking of the chairs in rhythm with each other.

Caleb decided to break the quiet. "So, how about you? Are you okay?"

"What do you mean?"

"Rachel, your best friend is dead. She was pregnant, and you want to be."

"Yes, I want to be, but you're still ambivalent. I'm not sure I'd feel comfortable having a baby until you're ready."

"I know this is hard for you, but you know why I feel the way I do. I don't want a repeat of my childhood if I can control it. My father is a cold, manipulative son of a bitch. My sister went through some very, very wild times in rebellion. And my mother . . ." Caleb choked up and had to wait a moment before he could continue. "My mother lived a life of privileged misery with him. I sometimes wonder if she was happy to die."

Rachel stopped rocking. She took a deep breath and turned to face him. "Caleb, I know why you feel this way. I do. But I also think you're not thinking straight. You can control it."

Caleb raised his head and looked into Rachel's eyes, a deep ocean green in the light of the setting sun. What was she thinking, this love of his life?

"Caleb, you seem to think that a baby of ours would somehow inherit an abuse gene. But we won't be the same parents as yours. We won't provide the same environment. You are not your father. You are a kind, gentle man, despite your father, and I am a strong woman. We both have so much love to give a child." She paused, waiting for a response, but Caleb continued rocking. Then she whispered, "What about adoption?"

"I don't think so."

"Why not?"

Caleb's blue eyes were dark and brooding, like a summer storm on the horizon.

"I don't know if I could do it. I'd worry about the parents' habits—drugs, alcohol, who knows? And what about any genetic traits the mother doesn't tell us about?"

"Traits like what? Honey, there are no guarantees out there. You know that. And, you just said that you didn't want your father's genes. You can't have it both ways."

Caleb's chest ached as he remembered his own childhood. His father's rages, his mother's clenched jaw and wet eyes. Rages and silence. On the one hand, he loved Rachel, and Rachel really wanted a baby. On the other hand, he was terrified of being like his father. He sighed.

"You know, you do have a point there. How did I marry such a smart woman?"

Rachel smiled. "You got lucky, sir. You married me for my looks but got brains in the bargain."

Caleb reached out again for Rachel's hand and they rocked, alone in their own thoughts. They didn't notice the flaming red ball settling into the Taconic mountain range.

When Caleb's cell phone rang, interrupting their reflections, he picked it up. Sandy True was on the line.

"Chief, I know it's late and hope it's okay to call you at home. I have that information you asked for on autoerotic asphyxia."

"That's great, Sandy. Let me just go inside where it's quieter."

No need to let Rachel hear this conversation.

He stood and walked with the phone into his study and closed the door, thinking how lucky he was to have Sandy. Although Sandy was a civilian and confined to a wheelchair, no less, Caleb thought she was a better cop than some of her able-bodied colleagues on the force.

"I got this information from an article by a forensic psychiatrist named Stephen Hucker. He's at the University of Toronto. The guy's legitimate."

"I don't doubt you, Sandy." Too keyed up to sit, he paced while she talked.

"Okay, here we go," Sandy said. "Autoerotic asphyxia is a form of self-strangulation to bring on hypoxia, or oxygen deprivation. It is thought to heighten sexual response. Hucker says that the number of deaths attributed to autoerotic asphyxia is probably under-reported."

"How is that?"

"Family members may tamper with the death scene before the police arrive."

"Because?"

"Because they may be embarrassed by the way the body is found, so exposed. Also, sex toys and pornography are often found with the body, and that, too, can be a big source of discomfort to loved ones."

"Anything else?"

"An interesting fact: the vast majority of people who participate in autoerotic asphyxia are male and under the age of forty. Not surprisingly, they also usually do it alone. This is a solitary amusement. And Hucker says that if done at home, it takes place at a time when nobody else is around. Both of these descriptions fit our scene."

"But not the male part," Caleb said.

"Right, not the male part. But even though it is unusual, it's not unheard of for females to participate."

But Mary Jane just doesn't—didn't—seem like the kind of person to do this kind of stuff, Caleb thought for the umpteenth time that week. Why was he so resistant? Was he allowing his judgment to be colored by loyalty to his friend?

"Hucker says that people who do this are often in healthy relationships. You can't always tell, and there are no easy ways to identify somebody who practices this paraphilia, or atypical sexual practice."

Caleb nodded. "She and Elliot had an excellent relationship."

Sandy continued without acknowledging Caleb's comment. "Another interesting point is that people who die from autoerotic asphyxia are often in a good mood and looking forward to the future. Wasn't Mary Jane expecting a baby?"

"Yes, she was. And very excited about it," he said. "She was also really into healthy living. Why would she jeopardize her baby's safety? Or her own?"

"Was there anything at the scene that would indicate that Mary Jane had a fail-safe mechanism in place?" Sandy asked.

"Fail safe?"

"Autoerotic asphyxia is a risky practice. If not done right, the person could lose consciousness. Or die. Because of that, the person usually has some kind of safety mechanism at hand. Something to get them out of trouble. If they do it with a trusted partner, they set up a safe word to signal when to let go. When doing it alone, they should make sure to have a fail-safe, maybe like a pair of scissors or a sharp knife. If they use a rope or belt—or scarf—they won't tie it too tight. I read of one case where a man rigged his chains in such a way that he would have needed a bolt cutter to release them."

"Making Mary Jane's experience unusual in two ways," Caleb said. "A woman with no fail safe."

"Yes," Sandy said. "And another thing. I'd have thought that if Mary Jane made a practice of this, she would have had marks on her neck."

"Unless this was her first time." Caleb felt his stomach turn to stone.

Or if it wasn't her first time, he thought, perhaps all those scarves in Mary Jane's closet were there for a reason. To hide the marks.

"Wouldn't Elliot have noticed marks on her neck?" he asked. "They did live together."

"Good point, Chief. Or . . ." Sandy hesitated before continuing, "Maybe Elliot did know about her, uh, proclivities, but doesn't want us to know. Or maybe they did it together."

"Elliot says that Mary Jane wasn't into kinky sex," Caleb said.

"Sure, but he might just have been embarrassed to admit it. I know I would be."

"But he was out of town when she died. So, unless she had another partner—and we have no evidence that somebody was in the house with her—Mary Jane was alone when she died."

Caleb tried to organize this thoughts. No forced entry and all the signs pointing to a sex game gone bad. Mary Jane's death may actually have been a really bad accident.

Or it was set up to look like one.

But then there was that cigarette smoke.

Caleb ended the conversation only to hear the phone ring again. The caller ID displayed Scott Cruz's name.

Scott launched right in. "You were right, Chief. We found a cigarette butt. Gauloises."

"I want that cigarette tested for DNA. Scott, this killer is either careless or cavalier."

"And pretentious."

CHAPTER FOURTEEN

On Tuesday morning, Caleb was at his desk in the police station, leaning back in his chair and staring at the ceiling, going over everything he had learned so far. The lamp on his desk provided the only illumination in the office, casting a whitish circle on the blotter where his coffee was getting cold. The only sound was the tap-tap-tap of his pencil against the arm of his chair. Again, he had been unable to sleep, so he had come to the office to try to sort through the very weird situation that was Mary Jane Bennett's death.

"I just can't believe this," he said aloud and shook his head. Despite the ME's opinion, he couldn't see Mary Jane being into an activity that entailed such great risk, especially while pregnant. He had to admit that you could never tell what goes on in people's private lives, and his job was to think logically, but when he told Elliot the ME's conclusions, his friend collapsed, seemingly unable to absorb the news that his life partner had put herself in such danger.

After an hour of stewing, Caleb slapped the desktop. It wouldn't do any good just to sit there. He got into the SUV and drove toward Monument Mountain. A strenuous hike might just clear his head. He focused on the scenery along the road in the gathering light, giving himself over to the thickly forested hills that looked like mounds of tightly packed broccoli.

Fifteen minutes later he locked the car and set off, pushing himself hard to work out the tension that had tied knots in his neck and shoulders. The sweet tang of spruce tickled his nose as he trod on the pine needles carpeting the ground. That fragrance never failed to bring back memories of summer camp. He thought about those carefree days of walking through the trees with his bunkmates, excited about the next baseball game or canoe race.

But then he heard his father's voice coming to him from a long-ago trek up Mount Monadnock. "Push, dammit, push! Caleb, if you want to accomplish anything in life you have to push."

But what—or whom—should he be pushing to figure out what happened to Mary Jane?

After a good forty-five minutes of stepping over tree roots and rocks, Caleb reached Peeskawso Peak and sat down on a large flat rock to catch his breath. He pulled a bandana from his back pocket and wiped the sweat from his forehead and neck. From his perch he looked out over the valley, a bucolic scene of houses and farms tucked into green hills. The view had never failed to relax him and help him think. This time it barely made a dent in his stress level. He closed his eyes, turned his face to the now-full sun, and soaked up the warmth as the vibrant red illuminated his eyelids.

He decided to request the state police files on the case. Formally. But first he had to run home, shower, and change. His shirt was soaked through with perspiration.

Once back in the house, he poured himself a tall glass of water before heading upstairs. When he entered the bedroom, he found Rachel sitting on the striped wing-backed chair by the window.

"Hey," he said.

Rachel looked up, her eyes red from crying. Next to her on the bed was a crocheted blanket she had made before the first miscarriage. His chest tightened.

"What's happened?" he said as he rushed over to her side.

"I got my period. Again." She hiccupped and dabbed her eyes with the tissue. "I'm never going to get pregnant."

Caleb pulled her toward him and held her close. He could feel Rachel's tears soaking the shoulder of his uniform shirt where it wasn't already damp from sweat.

"It's not fair. Mary Jane got pregnant so easily." She barked out a sudden, cynical laugh.

Caleb rubbed his wife's back and stroked her hair, running his fingers through her auburn waves. The memory of his nightmare came charging back.

No. Get that thought out of your mind. Rachel may have been envious, but she's not a killer. She cannot be a killer.

"It's okay. It'll happen," Caleb whispered. He rocked her gently, his chin resting on her head.

But do I want it to happen? Will I ever be ready for kids? What kind of SOB am I that I'm relieved when Rachel gets her period?

"I wanted lots of babies, close together. I hated being an only child. It was so lonely."

Caleb continued to hold her close as she wept silently.

"You know, you're always talking about mind-body connections. Maybe we're both just too tense. A little relaxation is what we need," he said, making sure to use the plural pronoun. "How about if we take a long weekend away? We could go to the Cape or to Vermont. What do you think?"

Rachel sniffled, and then reached for the tissue box. "That sounds good. But you have to finish this case first. You have to figure out what happened to Mary Jane." Then, wrinkling her nose, she said, "Oh my God, you smell. And you're wet."

"That's the thanks I get for comforting you?"

Rachel began to sputter until tears ran down her cheeks.

"Until then, maybe we can do something here to relax," Caleb said. "How about Tanglewood?"

"No. Too many memories there. How about a nice hike and a picnic? Just the two of us."

— • • • —

The air conditioner blowing frigid air provided a shock as Caleb entered the station. Tall plastic take-out cups filled with iced coffee had replaced the regular ceramic mugs on the desks, their condensation dripping onto the wood grain plastic laminate. Jack's uniform shirt was sweat-stained from the simple act of crossing the street to buy the coffee at the Queen Bee and bringing it back to the office.

"I know this is summer, and it's supposed to be hot, but I'm sapped," Jack said. "I sure hope no bozo decides to get into trouble today."

"Yeah, let's hope every would-be criminal is at least as miserable as we are and decides to stay home in the AC," Sandy said.

"Okay, guys, stop complaining," said Caleb. "We have work to do. Let's go to the conference room."

107

Sandy, Scott, and Jack all stood staring at the whiteboard, trying to sort through witnesses already interviewed, potential witnesses, and physical evidence. Caleb and his team were used to posting bits of evidence on it when working through a crime, whether it was a souvenir store theft or vandalism at the town cemetery.

"Okay folks. What do we have? Is there any evidence at all that what we're looking at is anything other than an accidental death?"

Jack cleared his throat and pulled at his collar.

"Jack, you look like a kid outside the principal's office. What's up?" Caleb said.

His face reddening, Jack cleared his throat again before speaking. "Chief, did anybody interview Rachel? I was busy securing the area, and then you asked me to bring her home." He cleared his throat again and wiped his forehead with a handkerchief.

Sandy's eyebrows shot up. "Rachel Crane? I was with her at the house, but I'm not authorized to interrogate her."

Caleb froze. The nightmare of Rachel with a scarf in her hand was still haunting him. Was Jack thinking of Rachel as a suspect, or as a witness, or a source of information?

"I talked with her," Caleb said. "Since they were such good friends, Rachel was an excellent source of background, but she couldn't tell me anything that would help us."

"So, where was she Friday night?" Jack asked.

"In bed with me," Caleb said.

"But weren't you at the car accident on 41?"

So now Jack chooses to act like a real cop.

"Sure, Jack, but how would she have known there would be an accident?" Sandy asked. "Would she just jump out of bed and decide to go kill her best friend?"

Jack smirked. "Yeah, a best friend who had something she wanted. A baby."

How did Jack know that? This really is a small town.

Caleb's gut churned. "Let's hear him out, Sandy. We need everybody's input."

"Okay, humor me," Sandy said, lifting her chin. "Chief, what time was the accident?"

"Around midnight. At least, that's when I got the call. You can check the phone logs."

"How long were you at the scene?"

"Maybe two hours, until the ambulances left and the area was cleared."

"So," Sandy continued, "would Rachel have been able to get over to Mary Jane's house, strangle her, and then get back into bed in two hours?"

"Yes," said Jack.

"Is it at all reasonable that she would have had a murder plan in her pocket, just waiting for the Chief to leave in the middle of the night?" Sandy asked.

"Okay, okay. I get it. Rachel's off the hook," Jack said. Then, with a smarmy smile, he said, "But the Chief isn't."

Sandy sighed and rolled her eyes.

Caleb realized that his nightmare had really rattled him, but he still had a nagging feeling that he should explore his fears. He took a cleansing breath and changed the subject.

"What about Dennis Hendrikson and Zoe Bouvier?" Caleb asked. "Has anybody interviewed them yet?"

"Both were on my list," Scott said. "The night Mary Jane died—Friday—Zoe was at your house for dinner until about ten. That was also the night she sprained her ankle. Dennis took her to the emergency room."

"So, I guess they both have pretty good alibis," Jack said.

"Again, Jack, I was thinking of them as potential witnesses," Caleb said, "Not suspects. We still don't know for sure that this was a crime."

"What time did they arrive at the emergency room?" Jack asked.

Caleb realized that all his closest friends were now under the microscope. He had to remind himself that Jack was doing his job.

Maybe he can be trained, after all.

"Jack, check out the hospital, will you?"

"Sure, Chief." He left the room and returned a few minutes later, a piece of notepaper in his right hand. "Dennis Hendrikson brought Zoe Bouvier to the BMC emergency room at about 2 a.m. That would have been Saturday already. So, it looks as if they're both in the clear. He was with her, and Zoe couldn't possibly have killed somebody with a sprained ankle."

"Unless they murdered Mary Jane at one o'clock and then went to the hospital," Sandy said quietly.

Jack snorted. "They could've been in it together."

"They wouldn't need a key if Mary Jane knew they were coming," Sandy said.

Caleb considered this. "Yes, they were good friends. Mary Jane would have opened the door to friends. But both Mary Jane and Zoe were at my house Friday night 'til about ten. Mary Jane told them she was tired and was going straight home to bed. How likely is it that Dennis and Zoe would just show up at her house that late at night?"

Scott shrugged their shoulders. "I don't know. Her good friends knew that Elliot was out of town, and she was home alone. Maybe they wanted to cheer her up?"

Sandy interjected. "But what kind of good friend would wake up a pregnant woman?"

"Let's keep digging, folks," Caleb ordered, then headed for the door. "I'll be right back with more cold drinks for all of us."

— • • • —

At about four o'clock, Jack charged into the Chief's office and dropped a plastic bag onto his desk. Caleb and Sandy looked up.

"Here it is, Chief."

"About time. What took you so long?" Caleb asked.

"Sorry, Chief. I kept forgetting. Anyway, there was only one DVD in the room, and it was still in the player. The CSI dusted both the jewel case and the disk. There was no cellophane wrapper, so maybe it wasn't the first time she'd used it. But . . ." He paused to catch his breath.

Caleb felt a shiver go up his spine. "But?"

"There were no fingerprints on the disk itself or the jewel case. Nada. Zip. Zero. Zilch."

Caleb's eyebrows went up.

"And . . ." Jack paused again.

"Are you waiting for a drum roll?" Sandy asked.

"Remember what the CSIs said about the other prints on the furniture that didn't match either Mary Jane's or Elliot's?"

Sandy interrupted. "It's in the case file, Jack. Rachel and Zoe were helping Mary Jane move furniture and paint the bedroom on the Friday she died. I fingerprinted them both here. There were no other unidentified prints in the room."

Jack nodded and started to leave the Chief's office, but then stopped and turned. "Chief, why wouldn't Mary Jane just get her porn from the Internet? Everybody under the age of fifty knows that you can get it online, some of it even free."

"Everybody, Jack?"

He turned toward Sandy. "Did you find anything at all in her browsing history?"

"No, nothing."

"Well, that answers that question, doesn't it?"

Caleb closed his eyes and leaned back in his chair to process what Jack had said. Why, indeed, wouldn't Mary Jane view whatever she wanted online? Had she deleted her search history? And with the DVD, why would she bother to wipe her fingerprints off a disk in her own home?

He opened his eyes and sat up. "Or did somebody else wipe them off? And, if so, who didn't want his prints found?"

"Jack, I want you to find out who bought that DVD and where they bought it."

"Yes, Chief." He went straight to his desk, picked up the phone, and began dialing.

Twenty minutes later, Jack slammed the receiver down in the phone cradle and grumbled.

Sandy looked up from her computer screen. "What's wrong, Jack?"

Waving the DVD in his right hand, he said, "Not one freakin' video store in this county sells that damn DVD. And Sandy said her credit card statements show that she didn't get it online. So, where did it come from? The sky?" He hoisted himself out of his chair with a grunt and strode toward the refrigerator in the corner.

Hearing Jack's outburst, Caleb came out of his office and watched as he poured cola into a Texas-size mug. Its inside was stained brown from hundreds, if not thousands, of refills of caffeinated beverages. When was the last time he had washed it? Was not cleaning it some sort of superstitious ritual, like that of Little Leaguers afraid to jinx a winning streak by changing shirts? He shivered at the thought of what his living quarters must look like. That mug was his special security blanket, he thought. He had an exclusive on it; nobody else touched it. But then again, who would want to?

Sandy straightened in her chair. "Jack."

"Yeah. You want something to drink?"

"No, I just thought of something. Why not call the people who actually made the DVD? They would know where they were distributed. It might be that only a few stores carry it."

"That's a great idea, Sandy. I only wish you had thought of it earlier."

"It's not like you wore out any shoe leather on this. On top of that, there just aren't that many video stores around anymore, what with on-demand video."

Jack mumbled something under his breath.

Sandy rolled her eyes and moved toward his desk. Taking the jewel case from him, she examined its label. Multiple O Productions.

"Clever name. I'll call the company."

"You're a gem, Sandy."

"And you're one lazy son of a bitch."

CHAPTER FIFTEEN

The heat finally broke late that afternoon with a booming, yet mercifully brief, rainstorm that crashed through town. Once it was over, Rachel went from room to room, opening windows to let in some refreshing air.

"I'm going to make some nice strawberry soup and pasta with pesto and we're going to eat supper on the porch tonight," she announced. "It's been so hot I can't wait to enjoy a nice breeze."

"That'll be nice. I'm getting tired of air conditioning. Is the garden producing a lot? I haven't been out there in a while."

Tenley laughed. "Brother, it's almost fall. We've had a bumper crop of everything. Haven't you noticed that you've been eating a lot of veggies this summer?"

Caleb realized that he had been so totally absorbed in the investigation that he had not, indeed, noticed what he had been eating much of the time.

"I'll be right back," Caleb said, heading out the door.

Twenty minutes later, he burst through the kitchen door, Elliot in tow. "Look who I brought for supper."

Rachel looked up from her perch over a large pot and said, "Excellent. We'll need help eating this feast."

"What needs doing?" Caleb asked.

She gestured with her cooking spoon. "We need a salad, and the table needs to be set. Tenley, will you go out to the garden and pick a bunch of basil for the pesto?"

"Sure thing."

Elliot stood stock still in the middle of the kitchen floor, eyes closed, forehead creased.

"You okay, Ell?" Tenley asked.

"I'm fine. I was just remembering how much I loved cooking with Mary Jane. Our house always smelled delicious. It made me feel that I was coming home. Especially in winter when she would make all those soups and stews."

"I loved it when she put up her famous raspberry jam," Caleb said.

"Remember the look on her face when little Jacob Ellis got into the jars cooling on the counter?" Rachel said, her eyes filling with tears.

The memory made Elliot smile. "Do I ever," he said. "He was covered from head to toe in sticky red goo. I thought I would crack a rib I was laughing so hard."

"Mary Jane stripped him, washed his clothes, and had him looking good as new just as Tricia came in the door to pick him up," Caleb said. "Super efficient."

"You mean super scared that Tricia would find out and never ask her to babysit again," Rachel said.

"And Rachel manned the lookout post in the front window, shouting Tricia's progress up the driveway," Caleb said.

The friends laughed at the memory.

"I wish I had seen that," Tenley said.

Elliot suddenly sobered. "She was so worried that she wouldn't know how to take care of our baby. That she would drop him into a pot of jam or something."

Tenley and Rachel went to their friend and hugged him. The soft sounds of Django Reinhardt playing acoustic guitar wafted from speakers placed on shelves among cookbooks and vintage cookie jars. After a minute, Rachel cleared her throat and wiped her eyes. She said, "Okay, get to work, you slackers. I'm hungry."

Caleb noted that Elliot had said "our baby."

"Ell, it sounds as if you were starting to get on board with the whole baby thing," he said.

"Yeah. Mary Jane was so damn happy about it that I guess I caught the fever, too."

"She was happy," Rachel said. "She was glowing."

"Oh, God," Elliot moaned, then sank into a chair. "I'm not sure how much more of this I can take. I need to go home."

"Ell, stay for supper. You need to eat."

"Sorry, guys. I just need to be alone."

I have to solve this case. Soon. Mary Jane's death is tearing him apart.

— • • • —

After dinner, dishes washed and leftovers put away, Caleb, Rachel, and Tenley gathered on the porch. Tenley had picked up a quart of raspberries from her favorite farmstand in Richmond and placed a bowl of them on the table to share.

"This is so cozy. I could really learn to love this place," Tenley said.

"You say that every time you're with us. Why not get a place here, Ten?" Rachel said. "It would be so nice to have you close by when you're not globetrotting."

"I'll bet some of your New York friends are here, so you wouldn't be entirely cut off from civilization," Caleb said with a glint in his eye.

Tenley popped out of her chair. "I'll be right back. I forgot the ice cream!"

Rachel lowered her voice. "Caleb, did you ever find out where the DVD came from?"

"No," he answered in a whisper that he hoped wouldn't carry. "We struck out locally. Jack called every video store in the county and came up empty."

"What DVD?" asked Tenley as she walked back onto the porch.

"Oh God, I'm sorry, Caleb. I thought she couldn't hear," Rachel said.

"Wow, you do have good hearing," he said nodding at his sister. "This is not for public consumption, but we found some porn in Mary Jane's bedroom."

Tenley raised an eyebrow. "Still waters, huh?"

Rachel hesitated for a moment. "What if it wasn't purchased locally?"

"It probably wasn't. Sandy had the same idea, so she called the company that made it. It's an older video, from the late '90s. They gave her a list of all the places that had ordered it, and she called them all. I guess it wasn't very popular because the only stores that still had it in inventory were New York, Chicago, Los Angeles, and Miami."

"That doesn't really narrow it down very much, does it?" Tenley said.

"Not by a long stretch, Ten. If we're going to find out who bought that DVD, we'll have to go to those stores and see if they have records on who bought it. And pray that they can even remember the person. If they have video surveillance, that would be a miracle. But I just don't have the staff to go knocking on doors around the country. I'm afraid we're up a creek."

"How about if I help out?" Tenley asked.

Caleb looked up from the bowl of raspberries and caught Rachel's eye.

Ladies-who-lunch Tenley?

"What did you have in mind, Ten?"

"Well, for starters, you said that you came up empty when you looked for porn sellers in the county, right?"

"Right."

"Well, porn is available everywhere, not just here. If I were going to buy the stuff, I would never use the internet and have the charges show up on my credit card statement. I would pay cash."

"That's what Sandy said."

"But I also would go shopping where nobody knew me. Far away."

Caleb raised an eyebrow. "Like where?"

"Like a big city. Anonymity. Cash purchase. Lots of people doing the same thing."

"Lots of people, Ten. How would a vendor remember one person?"

"We won't know if we don't try. I can leave for the city in the morning."

"I'll go with you," Rachel said.

"Hold the phone," Caleb said. "I don't think so. This could be dangerous and neither of you are trained cops." The two women's faces fell.

"What about your old friends on the force? Would they help?" Rachel asked.

"I do keep in touch with some of the people I worked with, but I could only ask them for a small favor, not something so labor intensive. And we don't even know where the porn was bought. Also, if this was a murder—and I really believe it was—it didn't take place in their jurisdiction. Why would they spend time on my crime when they have enough of their own?"

"For a fellow man in blue?" Tenley asked.

Caleb grimaced.

"Actually," Rachel said, "What's keeping you here in the village? Doesn't solving this murder take precedence over the usual crimes that we have here in Queensbridge? Can't Jack and Scott and the part-timers take care of the speeding and the leaf burning?"

Caleb looked at Rachel and raised his right eyebrow. "You know what, you're right," he said. "I'll ask Sandy to compile a list of every vendor in the Northeast who sells this particular video. I'll start in New York."

"Why New York in particular?" asked Rachel.

"It's as good a place as any to start. I know the city cold, and it seems that half the cars in Berkshire County have New York plates on them, as Earl loves to go on about. Who knows? We just might get lucky. I'll have Sandy print out a list of all the adult video stores in the five boroughs that sell this particular DVD."

"There probably aren't that many video stores of any kind anymore, Caleb," said Tenley.

"You're right. That's the good news, but there are still plenty of them around."

"Caleb, you can use my apartment. It's empty and it's at your disposal," Tenley said. "And, while you're there, Rachel and I can do some serious retail therapy at the Sheffield antique shops."

"Now, that's the sister I know and love."

CHAPTER SIXTEEN

The roar of trucks and crash of garbage cans outside Tenley's East Side apartment woke Caleb early. He had mapped out all the video stores that carried the DVD Jack had found in Mary Jane's bedroom and planned his day by their hours of business. Some of these places were open twenty-four hours, seven days a week. In the middle of the night, a guy could get a craving for pizza and porn and would have no trouble finding either in this city. Amazing, Caleb thought, how quickly and completely he had gotten used to the quiet of country life.

Twenty minutes after coffee and instant oatmeal, he was out the door and walking toward his first destination. It was a gorgeous day, but despite a full sun, only slivers of clear blue sky were visible between the buildings towering on both sides of the street. The weather had changed dramatically, bringing a chilly snap to the air. Caleb zipped his jacket and prayed that the forecast for clear skies would hold. Then he searched for a sunny patch of sidewalk.

On his way downtown, he passed stores decked out for Halloween. Already? They start pushing holidays earlier and earlier every year, he noted. He stopped in front of one display window where a bittersweet memory of trick-or-treating with Tenley flooded his mind. He was dressed as

C3PO, she as Princess Leia. He smiled when he remembered their mother standing far back on the curb, keeping a watchful eye on her charges.

He shook his head, "And now, to visit porn shops," he muttered.

The first two stores he visited were dark and musty, even in the bright of day, and made Caleb want to pull out a bottle of hand sanitizer. While both vendors had the DVD in inventory, they hadn't sold one in several years. Discouraged, but determined to get through the lower Manhattan stores before lunch, he continued on his quest. He arrived at the last store on his list, "eXXtra XXX," and entered, triggering a buzzer.

He had expected it to be as rank as the others, but the interior of this shop was clean and bright. Rows of shelves and glass cases extended front to back and lined the perimeter of the small store, displaying the inventory of videos and sex toys. A ponytailed man who appeared to be in his late twenties, with a nametag that said Mike, was behind the counter in the front corner.

Pulling out his badge, Caleb introduced himself and put the disk on the counter.

"I know I don't have jurisdiction here, but I'm hoping you can help me. We've had a murder in my town and I'm trying to trace down who might have bought this DVD. Do you happen to carry it?"

Mike picked up the DVD case and looked it over. "Yeah, we did," he replied.

"Did? You don't carry it anymore?"

"Nah, it wasn't so popular, so we haven't reordered."

Caleb chewed on this for a minute. "Popular videos?"

The clerk looked at Caleb as if he were a naïf. "Of course. They're reviewed just like regular feature films."

Caleb tried to imagine who the Vincent Canby of skin flicks might be. "Can you tell me when it was last sold?"

"Sure, just give me a minute."

Caleb watched as the clerk pulled up records from the computer. *High tech comes to porn.*

The clerk looked up and said, "Somebody bought the last one from the clearance bin last April."

"I guess everybody loves a bargain," Caleb said, encouraging him. "What about the others?"

"There was only the one. Like I said, it wasn't popular."

"How did he pay for it?"

"Cash. Most of our customers pay cash. Y'know, they don't want their wives finding out."

"Do you have a name on the slip?" Caleb asked, praying for a miracle.

Mike snorted. "Nah. If we took names, we wouldn't be in business."

Caleb gave a short laugh, then paused to consider his next steps.

"This is a pretty sophisticated shop you run here. Do you have video surveillance cameras?"

"Yeah, we do."

His heart leapt. "Can I see the video from that date?"

"Nah, we don't keep the record more than a couple weeks."

Caleb felt his heart drop into his gut. *Damn. Another dead end.*

Disheartened and beginning to tire, he decided he needed something to eat, but as he turned to head uptown, his cellphone rang. He reached into his pocket and saw Rachel's name on the Caller ID.

"Hey. What's up?"

"I wanted to let you know there's a forecast of heavy rain, maybe even ice up here, for this evening. You should probably head back now."

Ice this early in the year? Caleb looked up through the concrete forest for what he realized was the first time since the morning and saw that the sky had indeed filled with dark, heavy, rain clouds. At home in Queensbridge, he mused, he could see the sky wherever he was, even from his office window. Here in Manhattan, he had to make an effort to see it.

"I've got a few more places I want to check out before I leave."

"Please don't take any chances. Stay overnight if you're going to be too long. You've got Tenley's apartment so there's no need to drive back tonight."

"I'll start before there's a problem."

Caleb could hear Rachel sigh on the other end of the line. "I've heard that line before."

CHAPTER SEVENTEEN

After driving all night through torrential rains and high winds, Caleb slept in, so he didn't arrive at the station until ten o'clock, carrying an extra-large take-out cup filled with Sally's strongest brew. He settled into his office chair and checked his messages, hoping for revelation. The sounds of phones ringing and the rumble of voices emanated from the front of the station. A couple of minutes later, Sandy appeared in his doorway.

"Jonas Summers just called, reporting a suspicious person at the cemetery. He said it looks like the guy is painting a headstone. I sent Jack over to check it out."

"Thanks, Sandy. Let me know if anything turns up."

Then, stiff from the previous day's drive, Caleb got up to stretch his legs and work out the kinks in his back and neck. As he returned to his seat, the radio crackled. It was Jack. "Nobody at the cemetery."

"Did you get out of your cruiser to check it out?" Sandy asked.

The line was silent for a few seconds. Had she insulted Jack? Or caught him in yet another lazy-man's way out?

"Yeah, I got out. There was nobody in the cemetery."

"Okay but keep an eye on the place." After she hung up, Sandy turned in her chair to face Caleb through his open office door. "Do you think Jonas actually saw something up there?"

Caleb shrugged. "Who knows?"

— • • • —

After supper that night the friends gathered around the kitchen table.

"Here, tell me what you think of these," Rachel said as she placed a pineapple upside down cake among a half-dozen other dishes in the middle of the farm table.

"What's the occasion?" Caleb asked. "It's not a holiday."

"I'm researching more foods for my Purim project. It's really amazing the diversity of dishes you see in the different Diaspora communities around the world."

"Like what?"

"Well, for example, here in the United States all we ever hear about is hamantaschen."

"I love hamantaschen," Tenley said.

"Of course, you do. They're delicious, but they're not the only special food for the holiday. In Morocco they make a dairy couscous with dried fruit. And in the Caucasus Mountains, they make a semolina-based halvah. They call it Hadassah, after the Queen."

"I thought her name was Esther," Tenley said.

"Hadassah is her Hebrew name. Anyway, I thought I might add some new recipes that really illustrate the message of the holiday."

"So, we're basically your lab rats?"

"Basically. Normally, I'd have had Mary Jane rate these, but . . ." Rachel took in a quick breath and pressed her lips together.

Zoe jumped into the awkward silence. "What's the significance of pineapple upside down cake?"

Rachel sighed and gave her friend a look that said "thank-you." "It stems from the line in the Scroll of Esther that says that on the very day of the king's edict to execute all the Jews in the Persian Empire, 'it was turned to the contrary.' The Jews were not only saved but ruled over their former enemies. So, you see, things are upside down."

"So, pineapple upside down cake is a traditional food for Purim?" Dennis asked.

"Oh, no! There were no pineapples in ancient Persia. I just made it up because it's upside down."

"Very clever," Zoe said. "And it looks delicious."

"You're going to a lot of trouble for Sunday School," Dennis said.

"This is my first year at the school. I want to do a good job."

Zoe offered her opinion. "You'll definitely make an impression with these desserts. They're all beautiful. And appearances are so important."

"Do you really believe that?" Caleb asked.

"Caleb, my income depends on it. If it didn't, I'd be wearing jeans and a tee shirt all the time," Zoe said. "But people hire me to fulfill their dreams of domestic perfection. I have to look the part. I never know who I'm going to run into, so I've always got to be prepared to meet a new client."

"Have you ever seen Zoe's jewelry drawer?" Rachel asked. "She's actually got jewelry for every kind of client."

"I have. It's amazing," Caleb said.

Zoe laughed. "I'll let you in on a secret. My upstairs is a holy mess. It's where I relax, in sweats or pajamas."

"I'd never suspect that!" Tenley said with a deep-throated laugh.

"Don't get me wrong. My job is great. I love nothing more than turning a sow's ear into a silk purse."

"Well, Elliot would be a real project for you," Caleb said.

"Hmm," Zoe said with an exaggerated frown. "I could try to tackle that, but it would take some time. And time is money."

"He likes being comfortable," Caleb said. His eyes turned misty.

"You did help him pick out a nice suit," Rachel reminded her.

Caleb intervened. "Hell! Enough talk. Let's eat."

Everybody dug in, taking a sample of every dish on the table.

"Rachel, what do these other foods have to do with your holiday?" Tenley asked.

"One of the lessons of Purim is that things aren't always as they seem. Quiet, demure Esther was a heroine while the exalted Haman was a villain. Nothing is really as it appears to be. We wear disguises to celebrate the holiday."

"And the little lava cakes?" Zoe asked.

"There's something hiding beneath the surface. Just as Queen Esther had to hide her Jewish identity in the king's palace."

Zoe was quiet. After a moment she looked up and said, "Haman had a secret."

"Agreed," said Caleb. "Every evildoer has a secret. That's how he gets past his victim's defenses."

The group mulled that idea as they munched on their treats, each one wondering what secrets their little village was keeping.

Later that evening, as Caleb was wrapping up the leftovers, Rachel turned to him.

"I wanted to talk about what I did with the kids at the after-school program today."

"Why? What happened?"

"We were playing Clue. You know, Colonel Mustard in the dining room with the candlestick? Professor Plum in the kitchen with the rope?"

Caleb laughed.

Rachel opened her eyes wide in a look Caleb knew only too well. He'd better listen.

"I know you're going to say I read too many mystery novels, but it occurred to me that you could go to different hardware stores and find out where the rope that strangled Mary Jane came from. They could tell you if they sell that particular brand, and then maybe who bought it."

Caleb tensed. "Why do you think it was a rope that strangled her?"

Rachel looked puzzled. "Why? What else could it have been?"

Caleb was silent. Rachel had been in Mary Jane's bedroom and had seen her. Had she been in such shock that she didn't actually see the scarf? Or, if his nightmare was based on reality, was she simply pretending?

"Rachel, it wasn't a rope that strangled Mary Jane." He paused, watching her reaction. "It was one of her scarves."

"Oh, God." Rachel's face drained of all color before she hurtled toward the bathroom. The sounds of retching filled the air.

Unless my wife is a really good actress, she can't be involved with Mary Jane's murder. Thank God.

CHAPTER EIGHTEEN

Caleb stared at the blank expanse of a second whiteboard he'd had brought into the conference room. Picking up a black marker from the narrow tray running along the bottom of the board, he began to write the facts he and his team had gathered during the investigation.

1) No fail-safe mechanism near the body
2) No evidence of a break-in
3) No suicide note
4) No record of Mary Jane having bought the DVD
5) The odor of cigarette smoke in Mary Jane's bedroom
6) Cigarette found in yard
7) No unaccounted-for fingerprints in the bedroom
   And, weirdest of all, he thought:
8) No fingerprints at all on the DVD jewel case or disk.

Caleb still couldn't bring himself to write the names of potential murder suspects on the whiteboard. Even with the windows covered, he didn't want to risk posting them there for a nosy neighbor to see. The list would be an admission that the verdant, peaceful village in which he had settled was, in fact, a façade. And it could start some vicious gossip. Just as Rachel had said, things weren't always as they seemed. He shook his head and tried to focus on the case.

Back in his office, he lowered himself into his chair. How many talks had he and Manny had in the precinct squad room in New York, working out the facts of a case? Manny with his feet up on his desk, Caleb with his own feet propped up on his desk drawer, his back leaning into the worn fabric cushion of the standard issue office chair. He really could use Manny's help right now.

He closed his eyes and went through the facts yet again. First, there was no fail-safe mechanism in place, so maybe Mary Jane did attempt suicide. But there was no suicide note. Then again, there was that pornographic DVD that would point to autoerotic asphyxia. The twisted nightgown could be an indication that she changed her mind about suicide. Or that she had forgotten to have the fail-safe. Or that she struggled against an assailant. But there were no skin cells under her fingernails. Unless, of course, she was strangled by a killer wearing gloves and long sleeves. Was there anything at all under her fingernails?

He reached across his desk to retrieve the file containing the ME's report. Scanning through it, he found an interesting item he hadn't noticed before. All the skin from her elbows to her fingertips had been cleansed with hand sanitizer.

And what about that cigarette? An artifact or a clue?

He picked up the phone and dialed the medical examiner's office.

"Chief Crane, what can I do for you?"

"Is there a reason that Mary Jane Bennett's arms and hands would have been sanitized? Did you do it?"

"No reason for that and no, I didn't do it. I did note it, however, but assumed the woman had done it herself. Given the nature of how she died, perhaps it was part of her ritual. She may have felt a need to cleanse herself."

Or somebody sanitized her to wipe out any possible trace.

"Thanks, Doc."

— • • • —

Later that afternoon, the sun was streaming through the blinds when Sandy knocked on Caleb's open door. She propelled her wheelchair into the office, making sure it shut behind her.

"It took me a while to reach her, but the reporter confirmed that she did speak with Elliot face-to-face on Friday afternoon. She said he gave a very good interview, and she even commented on his un-lawyerly ponytail, pointing out how it didn't seem to go with the really nice suit he was wearing."

Caleb exhaled. "I'm sure he gave a great interview, being his usual voluble self. And the suit was Zoe and Mary Jane's doing."

"Just to be sure, I decided to check on the off chance that Elliot took a private charter back from Chicago."

"That would've been really expensive, Sandy. Like thousands of dollars."

"I know. I just wanted to be thorough. Anyway, there's no record of him hiring a private plane from anywhere in Chicago to any airport in this area. He just couldn't have been here in Queensbridge."

"Good job, Sandy."

For the first time in days, Caleb felt his stomach begin to relax. He got up to stretch his stiff muscles. As he was working out the kink in his neck, he heard his vertebrae pop, and something Elliot said suddenly jogged Caleb's memory. "One of these days he's gonna offend the wrong person and that person's gonna pop him." Caleb wondered if that "somebody" could hate Earl enough to murder his only child. Mary Jane was the apple of Earl's eye. What better way to wreak revenge than to get him where he would really hurt? Elliot's words haunted him. ". . . and that person's gonna pop him."

What am I missing here?

CHAPTER NINETEEN

Caleb began his morning rounds with a drive on Pine Mountain Road. As he neared Elliot's house, he spied his friend walking out onto his front porch with a mug in his hand. He pulled into the driveway, parked, and got out.

"Hey. What're you doing up so early on a Saturday?" he called out. "It's only 6:30."

"Couldn't sleep. I haven't slept well since, you know . . ." His voice trailed off.

"How about some of that coffee? I could use a cup."

"Sure. I'll make a fresh pot." He turned and went into the house

Fresh pot? What's he been drinking? Caleb leaned over and sniffed Elliot's mug. It smelled of whiskey.

Elliot returned a few minutes later and set the coffee mug on the table next to his own before sitting down.

"How're you doing, Ell?"

"I don't know, Caleb. Everything has changed. The house just feels different."

"Different how?"

"When Mary Jane was alive, the house was always sparkling with energy, even if it was just the two of us. I'm not sure how I can go on living here without her."

"You need time, Ell. But you also need to lay off the booze first thing in the morning."

"Don't tell me how to handle my grief. Have you found anything at all that will figure out who killed her? I know she didn't die at her own hand."

"I'm inclined to believe you. Can I look over the house again?"

"Why? D'ya think you might have missed something?"

"I don't know. I just want to make sure that Jack and the state guys did a thorough job."

Elliot took a noisy sip from his mug. "You know, you inherited Jack from Larry Ledbetter. You didn't have to keep him."

"I know. I've been trying to shape him up but, frankly, we don't have much serious crime here in Queensbridge." He caught himself. "As a rule."

"As a rule."

Caleb changed the subject. "Ell, who has a key to your house?"

"Let me think. You and Rachel have one, of course. And Zoe. Earl has one, although I'm surprised he didn't throw it in our faces when he found out Mary Jane was pregnant."

"Anybody else?"

Elliot's brow wrinkled as he thought.

"Oh, of course. Ned Reese has one."

"Ned does more than plow?"

"Uh-huh. When we go away, he checks on the heat and the water."

Caleb nodded. He finished his coffee and brought the mug into the kitchen and placed it in the dishwasher. He then began to move through the house methodically, checking out the main room first. African masks and Middle Eastern tribal rugs, as well as artifacts from Europe and the Far East, covered walls and the wide-planked wood floor, testifying to the couple's love of travel. Bookshelves lining two walls were organized by interest. History, philosophy, and psychology volumes shared space with literature and crafts.

Caleb went upstairs and moved slowly through every room on the second floor, checking windows for signs of entry, but found nothing. Eyes sharp, he descended the stairs, running his hand over the hand-carved newel posts and the railing. As he reached the landing, he spied a book lying open on the window seat. Edith Wharton's *The Age of Innocence*. He groaned inwardly.

Irony. Gotta love it.

As he turned to continue down the stairs, something bright caught his eye. Nestled where the cushion of the window seat met the wall was a string of garnet beads. Using his pen, he lifted the bracelet and examined it. The clasp was in perfect condition. It couldn't have fallen off Mary Jane's wrist. Why would she have taken it off? He removed an evidence bag from his pocket and placed the bracelet into it.

He repeated his rounds on the first floor and was about to start on the basement when Elliot joined him.

"Elliot, help me move this stuff outside so I can get a better look down here," he said.

"Sure. It's pretty crowded down here. Mary Jane couldn't bear to part with things from her mother. And you know how she loved a good yard sale."

"And flea markets, and estate sales, and auctions," Caleb said.

"She and Rachel have done—did—some serious damage," Elliot said.

Caleb saw Elliot flinch and his face go dark.

The two men carried a bed frame, a large table, and an antique mirror out to the backyard. Back indoors, Caleb picked up a pile of folded striped canvas from a shelf.

"What's the hammock doing in here?"

Elliot's eyes misted up. "I had to bring that inside. That hammock was Mary Jane's favorite place to be in the summer. She loved lying out in the yard with a glass of iced tea, a good book, and the view. As much as she loved teaching, she really loved her down time." He coughed and wiped his eyes. "Let me get us something cold to drink."

While Elliot was gone, Caleb looked around the basement. Nothing unusual here, either. No dropped matchbook, no scrap of torn clothing, no blood stains. Nothing. He had assumed that at some point something would turn up, but the trail was going to go cold soon.

Standing in the open doorway, he looked out to the mountains on the other side of the valley. Out of the corner of his eye he saw something. Suspended from the handle of a watering can tucked under the stairs was a single, gray work glove. He turned to call Elliot but found him coming down the stairs with two bottles.

Caleb took the water bottle, twisted the top off and drained it, then dropped it into the blue recycling bin under the staircase. He then turned to Elliot, who was holding a dark brown bottle.

"It's only a beer, Caleb, not the hard stuff. And we've been working our asses off."

If I hadn't seen the whiskey in the coffee cup, the beer wouldn't have made much of an impression. How much is he drinking?

He held up the glove. "Is this your glove?"

"That's not the kind I use. I have no idea where it came from."

"I'm gonna take it, okay?"

"Sure. Whatever you need."

"Ell, do you check your doors before you go to bed?"

"Of course, I do. You know what they say, 'You can take the boy out of New York, but you can't take the New York out of the boy.'"

"Do you lock all doors? Like the cellar door?"

"I wouldn't even think to check unless we had actually used that door, and then I would lock it when we came in. Why?"

"Have you had any work done at the house lately?"

Elliot gazed into space, thinking. "No, not since last winter, when we had problems with the boiler. Caleb, you don't believe Mary Jane's death was an accident either, do you?"

Caleb didn't answer but continued with his questions. "Ell, did Mary Jane ever talk about somebody bothering her?"

Elliot looked surprised. "No, never."

"Had she had a fight with anybody?"

"No. Mary Jane was well-liked. You know she was a sweetheart."

Caleb mulled over the facts in hand and came to two tentative conclusions. One: somebody with a key, or with access to somebody with a key, got into the house. Or, two:

Mary Jane had let somebody she knew and trusted into the house.

He needed to talk with a key holder.

— • • • —

A car, a pickup truck, and a disconnected snowplow blade were jammed into the driveway at Ned Reese's house. Caleb pulled up onto the front lawn so as not to get clipped by a passing car on Swift Road, then picked his way along a flagstone path that wound through a lavish display of flowers and tastefully placed statuary. He mounted the three steps to the front porch, where a cat seated on a bench looked up briefly, then continued grooming itself.

Caleb knocked on the front door and a dog started barking inside.

After a minute, Ned came to the door, drying his hands on a rag. "Chief," he said by way of greeting.

"Hey, Ned. You have some time to talk?"

"Sure, come on in." Ned held the door for Caleb to come through and led him into the kitchen. "I was just puttin' in a garbage disposal. Now that we've got a sewer line, we don't havta worry about the septic tank gettin' clogged up."

"That's great. I know Rachel wishes that the line would go as far as our house."

A little tow-headed boy wandered into the room, followed by Ned's wife, Rose. When he saw the uniform, he saluted Caleb, who reached into his pocket and pulled out a police officer action figure. "Is it okay to give him this, Rose?"

"From the Police Chief? Of course. What do you say, Eddie?" Rose said.

Eddie stopped moving, his eyes laser-focused on the figure. "Thank you," he said.

"You're welcome, Eddie. Now, your Daddy and I have some work to do, so can you put the officer to work in the other room?"

"Yes!" Eddie took the doll and clutched it to his chest. He ran from the room.

Rose laughed and, with a slight wave of the hand, left the kitchen.

"Coffee?" Ned asked.

"Sure, thanks." He took a seat at the kitchen table covered in a red-and-white checked oilcloth. Old, but clean and neat. The house was well maintained.

Ned reached for the coffee pot, poured the brew into two big mugs, and set them down on the table before taking a seat himself. He slurped some of the steaming hot liquid, then let out a contented sigh.

"So, what's up, Chief?"

"Ned, Elliot Freund told me that you take care of the house when he and Mary Jane aren't around." Caleb blanched when he realized that he had referred to Mary Jane in the present.

"Yeah. That's not very often 'cause they don't go away that much. But I do clear their driveway 'cause they don't have a plow."

"Did you happen to be by the house around the time Mary Jane died?"

Ned looked over Caleb's head, squinting at an imaginary calendar. "Nah, I don't think so. No, definitely not. It was late August when Mary Jane died. There was nothing for me to do then."

"Elliot was away on a business trip."

"Oh yeah? Well, Mary Jane would still be there, right? She'd only call me if something like a tree went down in the driveway."

"Did she ever say anything to you about somebody bothering her? About anything strange happening at the house?"

"Bothering her? No way. Everybody loved Mary Jane. People were always at her house."

"Did you know her growing up?"

"Sure. I knew her from kindergarten on through high school."

"You're the same age?" Caleb realized as he said it that he sounded incredulous.

Ned laughed so hard that coffee sprayed from his mouth.

"Hard outdoor work," he said by way of explanation as he wiped his face with a napkin.

Caleb looked more carefully at Ned. Under the deep crevices in his skin made leathery from years of outdoor work, he could see that Ned Reese must have been handsome once. He had a thought.

"You said that Mary Jane had lots of people at her house."

"Yeah. They were always doing some kind of craft. Needlework. Painting. You know . . ."

"How did you know that?"

Ned looked at him as if he were an alien newly landed on Earth. "Chief, this is Queensbridge. It's a small town. I ride by there all the time, goin' from house to house on my rounds. I see the girls out there on the porch or in the backyard."

"Did Rose ever go there?"

"Nah. Rose isn't much of a joiner. She's more into gardening. You should see what she's done with the yard. C'mon. I'll show you."

Caleb stood and followed Ned out to the backyard, where indeed there was a magnificent flower garden, a riot of reds, purples, yellows, and pinks set among meandering bluestone pavers and strategically placed benches and trellises.

"This is really something, Ned. You must have half an acre here, and it's all beautiful."

"Yeah. I'm real proud of Rose. She's taking classes to become a landscape architect for when the boys are both in school full time." Ned's chest seemed to puff up a bit as he spoke about his wife.

Caleb was quiet for a minute, counting on Ned to talk. When nothing came, he plunged in. "Ned, did you ever go out with Mary Jane?"

Ned threw his head back and laughed. "Me? Hah! She was way out of my league."

"Did you have a crush on her?"

Ned laughed again. "Of course. Every guy did."

This guy was open, Caleb thought. No guile here. Unless he was a true psychopath.

The two returned to the house.

"Ned, do you take care of other houses around here?" he asked, switching direction.

"Sure. I do the plowing in winter, mowing in summer," he said, unfazed by the change of topic. "And I check on the houses when people are away. There are so many second homeowners here in the village now, we see lots more license plates. Y'know, Rose and I collect 'em."

"Collect them?"

144

"Yeah, we write them down in a notebook when we're in the car. We've had up to 25 different states in just one Sunday drive to Williamstown and back."

Caleb thought of Earl ranting against New Yorkers. Why is Earl so obsessed with that particular state? It couldn't just be that Elliot came from there. Could it?

"So, you have a key to all these houses?"

"Sure." Ned extended his arm to point at a pegboard with a couple of dozen keys hanging from hooks. "Those are all the houses I look after."

Caleb wondered who besides Rose had access to those keys. He moved closer to the pegboard to look at the keys and lifted one off its hook. "Ned, these tags don't have names on them."

"Right. I use codes so if I lose a key, there's no chance anybody can figure it out."

Smart guy. "What's the code?"

"It's something my friends and I worked out in middle school so the teachers couldn't understand notes we wrote to each other."

"Any of those friends still in town?"

"Nah. They all left after high school."

Caleb looked at Ned with curiosity. He pulled a work glove out of his pocket. "Is this yours?"

Ned leaned forward to take the glove, and Caleb detected the smell of cigarette smoke on his clothes.

His eyes lit up and his smile widened. "Yeah, it is. I've been looking all over for it. Where'd you find it?"

"In the cellar at Elliot's house."

Ned's brow furrowed and he was quiet. Again, he looked over Caleb's shoulder as if an answer were written on a billboard hanging there. After a long moment he let out a puff of air.

"Of course! I was doing some work on the boiler. I must've dropped it then."

"When was that?"

"Oh, Jeez, around February." He stopped and looked into the air again. "Yeah, it was 'cause we talked about the weather, how weirdly warm it was. If it would be nice enough outside to grill."

Caleb looked closely at the caretaker and wondered if Ned had just thought up that excuse, or if he had kept it in store for just this occasion. He did seem genuinely surprised to see the glove. In any case, Caleb could—and would—check out his story with Elliot.

"Chief, if you're done with me, I promised Michael I'd go to his T-ball game today, but I've got some work to finish up first. If I'm late, Rose'll kill me."

"You don't want that, for sure," Caleb said. "Just a few more questions. Do you remember where you were the night Mary Jane died?"

"It was a Friday night, right? I would've been at the VFW for a couple of beers, and then I'd be home. Rose and I always put the kids to bed and then we watch TV. *Blue Bloods* was on. It's Rose's favorite." He paused, then smiled. "I think she's got a crush on Will Estes."

Time for another switch.

"Ned, what brand of cigarette do you smoke?"

"Gauloises. Why?"

"That's a pretty fancy brand to smoke."

Ned guffawed. "Yeah! My whole gang smoked 'em. It was a thing for us. We thought it made us look sophisticated. Stupid kids. Now I'm addicted. And Rose can't stand the smell."

Caleb mulled over what Ned had said. He watches the house. That could be why there was a cigarette butt at the scene. Or maybe not.

"Any of your gang still in Queensbridge?"

"No. Tim Genest is in California, and Hollis True is all over the world with the Merchant Marine. And Justin, of course, is dead."

But Hollis True is here. "The whole gang smoked 'em."

"Thanks," Caleb said, and extended his hand to shake. "And Ned, if you think of anything that might help, please give me a call. It might seem trivial to you but let me decide." Caleb reached for his wallet and took out a business card. He placed it on the table.

As soon as he was settled back in the SUV, he picked up his cell phone.

"Freund." The deep, gravelly voice came over the line.

"Hi, Ell."

"Calling me at the office? You have news?"

"Not yet. I just want to clear up something. You had trouble with your boiler last winter?"

"Huh? My boiler? There's a question out of the blue."

"Just confirm, okay?"

"I already told you this."

"Who fixed it?"

"Ned Reese came over. Why?"

"Was he wearing gloves?"

Elliot was silent. Caleb could practically hear the gears working in his brain. "I think he was. Why?"

"Thanks, bud," Caleb said.

"That's it? You're not gonna tell me what this is about?"

Caleb didn't respond.

"Come on, Caleb. This is Mary Jane we're talking about. Give me something. Are you investigating Ned Reese?"

"I was just following up on the glove we found. You gave me the reason it was there. That's it."

"If he had anything to do with this—"

"Ell, at this point there's nothing to report. I promise you I will let you know when I know something."

He disconnected the call and dialed again. Jack picked up.

"Chief?"

"Jack, I want you to follow up on Ned Reese's alibi that he was at the VFW the night that Mary Jane died. When did he get there and when did he leave?"

Ned Reese had a key to the house, and he admitted to having had a crush on Mary Jane. Was a teenage crush likely to have ramifications decades later?

As he turned the key in the ignition, a thought popped into his head. Had Rose known about Ned's affection for Mary Jane? Could she have been jealous enough to do harm? Caleb groaned as he realized that everybody he came in contact with had a potential motive to kill Mary Jane, however small and seemingly insignificant. I'll have to pay her a visit soon, he thought, before she has a chance to work on her story.

And when Eddie isn't around to see me interrogate his mother.

CHAPTER TWENTY

Caleb was just finishing the morning paper when Zoe walked into the Queen Bee. He waved to her, and as she settled into the booth across the table from him, a waitress came over with the coffee pot.

After ordering, Zoe said, "I love this place. Sally's done a wonderful job fixing it up."

"Yep. The Queen Bee is Village Central. Everything that happens in town starts here."

Zoe forked a piece of Caleb's blueberry pancake and popped it into her mouth. "Yum. The best pancakes ever."

"They are. Elliot's brother Josh likes them so much that when he visits, he eats breakfast here every day."

"You two guys couldn't be more different from each other if you tried," Zoe said, pouring milk into her cup from a black and white porcelain cow. "But you're the best of friends."

Caleb chuckled and wiped his face with a napkin. "Why do you think we're different?"

"Elliot's what we call in the design business a 'fixer-upper.' He looks more like Grizzly Adams than a lawyer."

Caleb started to laugh but choked on his coffee and coughed. Zoe jumped up and slapped him on the back a few times. "Elliot does seem a bit un-put together," he admitted.

He realized that this was the first time he had laughed in weeks.

"Maybe capable of being rehabbed," Zoe said. "Even if he's a Yalie."

Caleb laughed again. "And he is a top-notch lawyer."

"I could never figure out why he chose to do Legal Aid."

"He believes that everybody deserves the best legal representation possible. Elliot could never do the corporate law thing."

The waitress brought Zoe's order to the table and topped off their coffee. Zoe split her bran muffin in half and watched the steam rise before buttering it. She took a small bite and closed her eyes with pleasure.

"But you're so very Boston Brahmin. And always dressed impeccably, if casually. You even wear your uniform well. Yet you left the law to be a cop."

"So maybe we aren't so different after all."

They were quiet for a moment, Caleb pushing a forkful of blueberry pancake through a puddle of deep amber maple syrup, Zoe buttering the second half of her muffin.

She looked up, the muffin still on the plate. "You know, now that I'm really going to be here full time, I should get involved with something in town. I think it will help me settle in, especially being alone."

"Like what?"

"Well, there's the annual Pumpkin Festival in the fall. With Mary Jane gone, Rachel will need help with that . . ." Zoe stopped to wipe a tear from her eye and blow her nose. "Or I could get more involved with the Friends of the Library. They have their annual book sale every summer and need all kinds of help. Or I could do both."

Caleb smiled. "That's a great idea, Zoe. You really should get involved if you're going to make a life here. And helping Rachel would mean a lot to her."

"That's what best friends are for, no? We could do this in Mary Jane's memory and make it really special."

"Right. Listen, Zoe, I'm gonna need to talk with you soon. Away from prying eyes and ears."

"Of course. I want to help in any way I can."

"I'll be calling you."

— • • • —

At precisely one o'clock, Caleb followed the limestone path from the driveway to Zoe's kitchen door, which opened the instant his right foot landed on the steps.

"Caleb, come on in. I've just made lunch. I've got caprese salad and ciabatta."

"All right, you've convinced me."

He pulled out a chair from under a round table set into a deep windowed bay, making a scraping noise on the clay tile floor. The sun-filled niche housed a variety of tropical plants, and a light breeze wafting through the window screens lifted an earthy jungle scent from them. Zoe poured coffee and passed the cream and sugar. He poured a generous amount into his cup, then took a big bite of the sandwich.

He chewed slowly, savoring the taste.

"This is delicious, Zoe. Thanks for making time to see me today."

"Mary Jane was one of my closest friends in the world. I want to help you in any way I can." She took a sip of coffee, and her head dropped.

"I know. You and Rachel were like sisters to her."

"I just can't believe she's gone," she said, resting her elbows on the table. "You know, I was with her the day she died."

Caleb noted Zoe's avoidance of the word "murdered" or "killed." He wished he could do the same, but he had a job to do.

"To help paint?"

"Uh huh. Rachel and I were both there, helping her set up the bedroom for redecorating. We moved the bed into the middle of the room 'cause Rachel and I didn't want Mary Jane doing it, being pregnant and all."

"What time was that?"

"From about eleven 'til about four thirty. Mary Jane made lunch for us and even baked those fabulous ginger cookies of hers. We all scarfed down way too many of them with iced tea."

Caleb remembered the chewy gems, packed with chunks of crystallized ginger. He wondered if he could ever eat one again.

"Oh, I almost forgot. I was also there later in the day."

"Why?"

"To return a scarf I'd borrowed. I'd forgotten to bring it earlier."

Caleb felt a catch in his throat. He coughed. "Which scarf was that?"

"A gorgeous, long red and black shibori design in a magnificent silk."

Caleb held perfectly still. The same scarf that was wrapped around Mary Jane's neck.

"She said it would go perfectly with my black dress," Zoe added. "I had a dinner with a potential client and wanted to make a good impression. That was Mary Jane. Generous to a fault."

Zoe's eyes filled with tears. She reached to get a tissue from a box on the counter behind her. After she dabbed at her eyes and blew her nose, a wistful smile came to her lips.

"It smelled of jasmine. I remember she took it and pretended to be a belly dancer. She said she was going to surprise Elliot when he got home with her routine. Mary Jane could be pretty raunchy when she wanted to be."

This was news. Had Elliot lied about Mary Jane's proclivities? Then again, a little strip tease wasn't particularly kinky, at least in his book.

"After the belly dance, where did she put it?"

Zoe thought for a moment, her eyes scrunched. "I think she just left it folded up on the back hall table. She was in a bit of a hurry. We were going to your house for dinner, remember?"

Suddenly she gasped and sat up straight. "Did that scarf have something to do with her death?"

Caleb didn't answer the question but proceeded with his own. "Did anything happen while you were there that day that stands out in your mind?"

"Like what?"

"Did anybody come to the door? Did she get any phone calls?"

Again, Zoe closed her eyes to think. "Elliot called to say his plane was about to take off. She said it had been delayed. And then Earl called just as I was leaving."

"Did Mary Jane tell Earl about the plane delay?"

"I don't remember. She was mostly talking about a doctor's appointment he had coming up. From her end of the conversation, it sounded like she was arranging to pick him up to drive him."

Caleb switched directions. "Did Mary Jane ever mention that somebody was bothering her?"

Zoe shook her head. "No. Who would bother Mary Jane? She was wonderful."

"Maybe somebody who might have had an unrequited crush on her?"

Zoe snorted. "A crush? Like in high school? No, I don't think so."

Caleb finished the last of his lunch and pushed himself up from his chair. "Thanks, Zoe. If you think of anything that might help, you know where to find me."

Zoe also stood and put a hand on Caleb's arm. "I keep thinking I should've driven her that night. I should've come in and checked the house. I probably should've stayed with her. She was alone all weekend."

Caleb was silent.

She sighed. "And if I'd been there with her, maybe I wouldn't have sprained my ankle."

"Magical thinking, anyone?"

Zoe sniffed again and wiped her eyes. "I guess you're right."

As he turned toward the door to leave, his hand on the doorknob, Caleb stopped.

"Zoe, Rachel needs your support. She's hurting as much as you are."

"If not more. You don't even have to ask."

CHAPTER TWENTY-ONE

In his office, Caleb picked up the phone on the first ring. "Crane," he said.

Sandy's voice was low, almost a whisper. "Chief, Mr. Gorham is here. He's on his way down the hall."

The Town Manager is here at the station? What could he possibly want?

"Thanks, Sandy."

Tom Gorham appeared at his door, wearing casual Friday khakis and a pale blue polo shirt that highlighted his azure eyes. Caleb liked the town manager. He was a sharp administrator with vision, and a real asset to the village. He often wondered why Gorham had chosen to work in such a small town when he was sure he could have gone to a much higher paying job in a big city. Then again, he thought, he was here as the chief of police. Was Gorham also running from bad memories?

"Chief, got a minute?"

"Sure. What's up?"

"I wanted to give you a heads-up."

"Heads-up? About what?"

"Word has gotten out that you're going around town asking questions about Mary Jane Bennett's death. They're worried that you're bringing undue attention to the village, that tourists might stop coming if they think there's a killer loose in town."

"Tom, this is just between us, but I believe there is a killer loose in this town, and I mean to find him."

"They all think you're on a wild goose chase, and that Mary Jane died in a horrible way by her own hand."

"Do you think I'm on a fool's errand?"

"It doesn't matter what I think. I'm just the hired gun. The elected officials get to tell you what to do."

"In other words, they think I'm wasting their money. Since when are graffiti and shoplifting more important than murder?" Caleb said, his voice lowering with tension. "Never mind, I know. They don't think it's a murder. Of course, if it was their kid . . ."

"I will tell you that Earl has been trying to bend every ear he can get to."

"Ah, well that may be the problem. Earl can tick people off to the point they don't want to help."

"Bingo," Gorham said.

"Thanks for the warning."

"And don't forget that half of the Select Board members are new to the commission. They were second homeowners before making Queensbridge permanent. They may be more interested in their property values than justice."

Caleb grunted.

"You'll want to tread softly," Gorham said.

"I'm not stopping."

"If it makes you feel any better, I'll back you up on this, but don't expect a miracle."

"What would make me feel better is if I could figure this damn thing out. Soon."

— • • —

That afternoon, the police station was filled with a group of third-graders rambunctious enough to challenge Harriet Jablow's prodigious crowd management skills. Caleb had just delivered his annual safety presentation and was in the process of fingerprinting the kids when Zoe Bouvier strode into the police station and approached the counter. Under her bloodshot eyes were dark smudges. Stray hairs sprang randomly out of her normally well-behaved coif, and her salmon blouse was only partially tucked in.

Sandy True rolled over to a section of the counter that was lower than the rest. She smiled and said, "Hi, Zoe. How can I help you?"

"I want a gun permit," Zoe said.

"You want a license to carry? For what purpose?"

"Purpose?"

"Yes. Do you plan to hunt?"

"Hunt? No, no. I want a gun for protection."

Sandy frowned. "Has somebody threatened you?"

"Yes. I got a letter. A really frightening letter."

"Come around the counter and have a seat while I get the Chief. I keep a nice chamomile tea in my desk for occasions like this. Can I get you a cup?"

Zoe sighed, wringing her hands. "Um, okay. Thanks."

Sandy turned in her chair and made her way over to the hot water dispenser, where she prepared the tea and signaled to Caleb. She then placed the mug in the cup holder on the side of the chair and rolled back.

"Oh, Sandy, I'm sorry. I should have done that."

"I'm perfectly capable, Zoe."

"Oh, I didn't mean —"

"Enough of that. Now, take a deep breath and a sip. He'll be here any minute."

Caleb left the kids to Jack and escorted Zoe to his office, where he hoped it would be a bit quieter.

"Zoe, what's going on?"

"I'm scared to death, Caleb. I just got a letter. Somebody is threatening me."

"Do you have it with you?"

She rifled through her purse and pulled out an envelope. She waited as Caleb pulled on a pair of neoprene gloves before giving it to him, her hand trembling. Caleb removed a single sheet of paper from the envelope and spread it out on his desk.

"You're next," the message read.

"Turn it over," she said.

The hairs on the back of Caleb's neck stood up. There was a full-color photograph of Mary Jane's scarf. He checked the postmark. It had been stamped in Springfield two days prior.

"This was done on a computer. It could have come from any desktop printer in the world, Zoe."

"You'll dust for fingerprints, though, won't you?"

"I will but, frankly, I'm not sure what we'd find. Dozens of hands have probably touched the envelope already. And if the person who wrote this is clever, he would never have touched the paper himself."

Just like with the DVD. Who is this guy?

"Oh, God. First Mary Jane, then the break-in, and now this." Zoe ran her hands through her hair, mussing it up further. She sighed, her breath ragged.

"This may just be a prank," Caleb said. "A sick one to be sure."

But Caleb knew that this was no prank. It was sent by somebody who knew about the scarf. And had access to it.

"I'm scared and I don't like not knowing who's out there."

"Sandy also told me that you want a permit to carry. Are you sure you want a gun in the house?"

"Yes. I'm sure."

"Then let's go back out front."

Sandy handed her some forms over the counter. "Read this. It's all the information you'll need to help you make a decision," she said. "You'll first need to take a gun safety class. And the course has to be certified by the Mass State Police."

"Where can I find a class?"

"The Queensbridge Sportsman's Club offers classes once a month on Saturdays."

"Then what?"

"You'll have to decide what kind of license is best for you. I'd recommend a long gun rather than a handgun. It's less likely to miss the target."

Zoe sighed and ran her hands through her hair again. "Thank you." She turned and left the police station.

As Caleb watched her leave, he rued the day he had wished for some crime to shake things up. Two close friends had now been victimized, one of them fatally. Would there be more? Was Rachel safe? Elliot? What had happened to his peaceful little village?

He turned to Scott. "Dust this letter and see if you can get anything from it. Postal workers are required to be fingerprinted, so at least we can eliminate them."

"Maybe we'll get lucky."

Caleb grimaced before turning back to the third graders. Although his body was with them, his mind was elsewhere.

An hour later, the kids were gone, and the station was quiet again. Caleb went back to the conference room to add the latest piece of evidence to the mix. He was sticking the letter onto the board when his cell phone rang.

"Caleb?" Rachel's voice was raspy.

"Hi, hon. What's up?"

"Will you please come home?"

"Rachel, what's going on?"

"I just got home from school and brought in the mail. I got a letter. Actually, a picture."

Caleb tensed. "A picture of what?"

"A red scarf."

"Does it say anything?"

"Yes. It says, 'You're next.'"

He grabbed his keys and headed straight out the door and to the cruiser. He raced up the hill and pulled to a fast stop in front of the house. As he jumped out of the car, he noticed Zoe's Audi in the driveway. Rachel and Zoe were seated at the kitchen table where Zoe was pouring tea into a cup set in front of his wife. Her hand was shaking, causing the hot liquid to splash.

Rachel jumped up and ran into Caleb's arms.

"Caleb, I'm really scared. What kind of person does something like this?" She pointed to the photograph on the table. "Zoe and I both got them."

"An evil bastard, that's who," Caleb said. He pulled on a pair of gloves before looking at the sheet of glossy paper. Sure enough, it was Mary Jane's vibrant red scarf, and the wording on the back was almost exactly like that in Zoe's letter."

The killer was teasing us. Whoever took this picture had access to Mary Jane's red scarf. It couldn't have been one of my officers, could it?

He turned over the envelope.

"What are you looking for, Caleb?" Rachel asked.

"A postmark. See here, it was stamped in Springfield. So was Zoe's." He pulled a plastic evidence bag from his pocket and slid the photograph into it.

"Did you find any fingerprints on my letter?" Zoe asked.

"Nothing yet. I just gave it to Scott."

"If our stalker isn't even from the village," Rachel said, "then how would he even know us?"

Caleb pulled on his earlobe. "He could very well be from the village, but went deliberately to Springfield to mail it, to reduce the chance that somebody might see the envelope."

Groaning, Rachel sank into her chair and held her head in her hands. "I'm terrified."

"Now do you see why I want a gun?" Zoe said.

"No guns, Zoe. I'll get you both some mace to carry with you. In the meantime, you should keep doors and windows locked."

"Damn right," Zoe said. "And please catch this sicko. Soon."

Rachel shivered. "I'll never leave the house unlocked again. Even when you're home."

Caleb kissed Rachel and clapped Zoe on the shoulder. "I'm taking this with me," he said, waving the evidence bag.

He returned to the station as quickly as possible, his heart in his throat, and called his team in.

He closed the door to the conference room and stood at the head of the table.

"There's been a development in the Mary Jane Bennett case." He pushed one of the photographs with its note across the table and said, "What do you all think?"

Sandy recoiled. "This is disgusting."

"Yes, it is. But what can we say about it?"

"I can't imagine that anybody would develop a picture like this at the local CVS," Sandy said.

"You're right. Even if he came in with his own thumb drive and didn't do it online, there would always be a risk of being seen."

"Right. Somebody could walk by the monitor while he was working or see the pictures when they spit out of the developer."

Caleb lifted his pen and pointed toward Scott. "Scott, you're the photographer. What do you think?"

Scott pressed his lips together in a straight line, his brow furrowed. He got up and went to a retrieve a ruler from a canister set atop a filing cabinet. He returned to the table and measured the photo.

"This picture isn't a standard three by five, or four by six inches, like what you would get at any standard photo processor."

"So?" Jack asked.

"So, that probably means that it was printed at home. But . . ."

"But?" said Jack. "Don't drag it out. What does it mean?"

"Patience, Jack," Caleb said.

"But," Scott continued, "Look at the rich, vibrant, colors and fine details. The gradations are smooth, the blacks sharp. This picture wasn't printed on some cheap home device. This was done on a high-end, professional deal."

"Like the one you have?" Sandy asked.

"Yes. Like the one I have."

"So, did you kill Mary Jane?" asked Jack.

"Go to hell, Jack," Scott said.

"This isn't helpful, Jack. Get back on track," Caleb said. "Scott, how many of your photographer friends have printers like this?"

"Probably all of them. But plenty of businesses have them as well. Who knows how many there are in the county?"

"Or even across the border in New York State or Connecticut," Sandy said.

"So this is just a dead end," Jack said. "Unless we get a big break, we're never gonna catch this guy."

— • • • —

That night, Caleb, Rachel, and Tenley sat on the porch in a semicircle around Zoe. They watched the sun inching its way into the hills, streaking the sky with purple and coral. The detritus of dinner was scattered over the table. Tenley kept picking at a bowl of berries she held in her lap.

Rachel turned to Caleb. "Will you try to talk Zoe out of getting a gun?"

"Zoe, you're not really going to get a gun, are you?" Tenley cried.

"I'm afraid!" She blurted out. "Aren't you? First, Mary Jane is murdered in her own bed. Then my house is broken into. Who knows if the guy will come back? I'm terrified of being alone."

Tenley lurched forward in her seat. "Wait a minute! Where did you get that she was murdered? Didn't the medical examiner say that her death was an accident?"

"That's what he ruled," Caleb said. "And the state won't investigate it any further."

"But you can. Right?" Zoe said.

"Yes."

"I don't know, Caleb," Zoe said. "People are talking. Maybe I just need to feel secure."

"But a gun?" Rachel and Tenley said in chorus.

"Rachel, you have a cop in the house with you. You can afford to feel safe." She sighed. "Maybe I should rethink this whole house buying thing. At least in New York I live in a security building."

Caleb saw Rachel bristle.

"You don't mean that, honey," Rachel said. She darted across the porch to put her arm around her friend's shoulder. "Maybe you should come and stay with us for a few days. At least until this is all figured out."

"I can't do that. I have too much to do at the house. All my work is there."

"How about getting a dog? There are plenty of dogs at the shelter who need love," Caleb said.

"We can all go together to help you pick one out," Tenley said.

"A dog isn't going to protect me," Zoe said, sniffling.

"Sure, it will," Tenley said. "It will bark to high heaven if somebody were to try to break into your house. Dogs are very protective of their masters."

"But what if the killer shoots the dog?"

"A dog will give you some security," Caleb said.

Zoe clenched her hands. "If only Mary Jane had had a dog. It might've been able to alert her—and rip the throat out of any intruder. Maybe she'd still be alive."

Warning of an intruder or a fail-safe mechanism?

CHAPTER TWENTY-TWO

Back in his office the next day, Caleb sifted through his notes, hoping for an epiphany. Or at least a clue. Moments later, Earl Bennett blasted his way into the station and headed straight for the Chief's office. Without preamble, he shouted, "Chief, what are you doing about this investigation? Do you have anything to tell me yet about who killed my girl? Or are you just sitting around on your ass all day, drinking coffee?"

Caleb extended his arm, indicating the chair across from his desk. "Earl, take a seat." He couldn't help noticing that the man's normally fastidious appearance had devolved even further. His usual high-and-tight haircut was growing over his ears, and white stubble sprouted on his face. A wrinkled shirt under a steel gray cardigan hung on his skeletal frame. A seam at the shoulder had separated, but he seemed not to have noticed.

Caleb's jaw and neck muscles tightened in what was becoming too familiar a way as he tried to control his temper. And his fear. He had nothing to report yet and felt like a failure. But he couldn't fault Earl for wanting answers. He wanted them, too.

"Earl, you know I can't divulge the results of our investigation. But please be assured that my team is working very hard to get to the bottom of this," he said, recoiling at the bland, stock words he used all the time to keep people's noses out of police business.

Earl snorted.

He tried again. "Remember Earl, Mary Jane was a very close friend of ours. We are working every angle we can think of to figure this out."

That, at least, sounds genuine.

Earl deflated suddenly as if pierced by a pin. He raised his hands to his head and pulled on the desiccated straw that his hair had become. "I'll have to take your word on this, Chief. Just try a little harder, okay?"

He got up to leave. Caleb stood and offered a hand. Earl stared at it for a moment and turned away. He didn't look back.

Caleb sat back down and ran his hand over the soft, worn leather of his grandfather's blotter. Something else was niggling at his mind, but he couldn't retrieve it. He returned to sifting through his officers' reports, hoping for enlightenment, but Earl's diatribe kept intruding in on his thoughts. He stood and began to pace around his office, but soon realized that he needed some action. It was time to see Rose Reese.

— • • • —

Caleb's uniform shirt was limp with perspiration when he arrived at the Reese house a little after three o'clock. The day was hot and humid, and the air was filled with the shrill, relentless whine of cicadas. Through the screen door, he could hear music emanating from the television. *Sesame*

Street. He smiled and knocked on the doorframe. Within seconds, Rose appeared at the screen. She smiled shyly and unlatched the door. The soft flowered fabric of her maternity dress billowed in the breeze emanating from a room fan. She wore no makeup but had a glow about her that made Caleb wonder if it was true that pregnant women were radiant. A toddler wearing nothing but a diaper grasped the hem of her dress and peered out at Caleb from behind the safety of her skirt.

He smiled at the boy. "Rose, I'm sure Ned told you I'm investigating Mary Jane Bennett's death. I need to ask you some questions."

"Sure, but I really didn't know her that well since I didn't grow up here. Come on in and get out of the heat."

Caleb chose a straight-backed chair with a needlepointed seat cover. Rose sat on the sofa.

"Ned showed me your beautiful garden," said Caleb. "You're very talented. Did you always like to work with flowers?"

"Oh, yes. My mother and I used to garden together in Newport."

"When did you come to Queensbridge?"

"After Ned and I were married. It'll be ten years next week."

"Where did you two meet?"

She looked down, gazing at the flower pattern on her dress. "We met when Ned was stationed in Newport."

Caleb noted that she was blushing.

"Ned was in the Navy?"

"Yep. Anyway, I was working in my father's diner in Jamestown. He came in one day and I waited on him. He was so handsome. He said he was thinking about going into the restaurant business when he got out, so he was checking out the competition."

"The restaurant business? Was he a cook in the Navy?"

"No!" She laughed and the crinkles around her eyes deepened. "Ned was a locksmith. He just said that to get my attention."

Caleb stiffened. He had to focus on what Rose was saying.

"He kept asking for things—refills on his coffee, extra napkins—so that I would come over. A few months later, we got engaged, and he had a rose tattooed on his arm." She lifted the hem of her dress to show Caleb a tiny rose on her ankle. "I had one, too."

She was beaming, and Caleb didn't think it was the pregnancy doing it.

A horn sounded outside.

"That will be Eddie on the van from day camp," Rose said.

Caleb watched through the window as she went to the front yard to collect her son, who was wearing a backpack that featured a smiling lion's head. They went around to the backyard together, where Rose extracted a towel and a wet bathing suit that she hung on the clothesline, followed by a lunchbox and flip flops. Caleb shook his head in wonder that the little pack could hold so much, and that the five-year-old could carry it all. Rose bent over to give her son a hug and kiss, then took him by the hand. They skipped back to the house, singing. Caleb smiled.

"Eddie, can you say hello to Chief Crane?"

"Hullo," he said. "Are you here to do police work?"

"Yes, I am," Caleb said. "And your mommy is helping me."

The boy's eyes widened with excitement. "Can I help, too?"

His mother interrupted. "Sure you can, honey. But first, why don't you go into the kitchen and get your snack? It's on the table."

"Okay. But then I want to help."

"You got it. Would you like to wear my badge while you have your snack?"

A 1000-watt smile was his answer. "Yes! And I'll get the policeman you gave me." He ran off toward the kitchen.

"You're good with kids, Chief Crane," Rose said.

Am I?

"It's a skill that comes in handy to keep kids calm when there's a crisis."

"Is this a crisis?" she asked, frowning.

"No but keeping kids happy makes my work easier." He waited while Eddie went into the kitchen, then began. "Rose, do you remember the night Mary Jane died?"

"I remember hearing about it on the news. And then, of course, everybody in town was talking about it."

"She died on a Friday night."

"Oh, right."

Caleb tried to make his next question as innocent as possible. "Where were you and Ned that night? Do you think you might have seen or heard anything unusual?"

Rose closed her eyes and pressed her lips together, as if it might help her to think. "Gee, we really don't live close enough to Mary Jane and Elliot to see anything."

"And you were . . . ?"

"Oh, right. Well, if it was Friday night, then Ned would've been up in Pittsfield, at the VFW."

"Something special going on there on Friday nights?"

"Ned likes to get together with his buddies and have a few beers after work." Rose's eyes suddenly widened, and she said, "But he never gets drunk. And he always comes home before the kids go to bed so we can read them their stories."

So, Ned had been telling the truth. Or, Caleb wondered, had Rose and Ned rehearsed his alibi?

"So, he was home all night after he got home?"

"Uh huh. We watched TV after the kids went to bed."

"What time did you go to bed?"

"I was tired, so I went upstairs right after my show, at eleven."

"And Ned? What time did he come up?"

"I guess it was around one. He wanted to watch a movie."

One? Caleb felt his heart do a backflip. Could Ned have gone out and murdered Mary Jane in that time? "That must have been one great movie on TV."

Rose laughed. "No! Ned falls asleep in front of the TV every night. When his snoring wakes him up, he comes upstairs."

"Does he wake you up when he comes upstairs?"

"He always wakes me up. I'm a very light sleeper. But I don't mind. I like to see him next to me."

"Did Ned ever talk about Mary Jane?"

Rose stopped to think. She stared over his shoulder just the way Ned had, as if a teleprompter was feeding her lines of dialogue. "Sure. After she died, he talked about how he had known her in school and how all the boys had crushes on her."

"Did that make you jealous?"

Rose looked at him with surprise in her eyes. "That was a lifetime ago. I know Ned loves me." She bent over to pick up a stuffed giraffe from the floor and placed it on the coffee table. "He did talk about how she had changed after her mother died. How she became sort of a mean girl."

Mean girl? This was something new. I'll have to follow up on that.

"Rose, does anybody else have access to the keys on the board in your kitchen?"

"No."

"You don't have anybody coming in to help? A repairman maybe?"

Rose laughed. "No! Ned is all the repairman we need. He does everything."

"What about friends?"

Rose's eyes widened. "Do you think somebody took the key to Mary Jane's house?"

Caleb kept his voice even. "We don't know. We're looking at anything and everything that can help us figure out this puzzle."

He decided to wind up the interview. He wanted to get back to the station and add the new information to his timeline and follow up on it. At that moment, Eddie came in from the kitchen, cookie crumbs stuck to his chubby cheeks.

"Can I help now?" he asked.

"Sure thing. Eddie, I need a neighborhood watchman. Do you think you can do the job?"

"Oh, yes!" he said, his eyes gleaming with excitement. "I'll help you catch all the bad guys."

"Well, if you see any, you make sure to call me. Do you know about 911?"

"Yep. We learned that in school."

"Right. So, call 911 if you see anything bad. But don't you try to stop it. That's why I wear the badge."

"But I'm wearing the badge," Eddie said with an impish grin.

Smart kid.

Caleb unpinned the shield from Eddie's shirt and held it aloft. "Now, I've got it."

"Then I'm gonna be a policeman when I grow up," he said with a salute.

Back in the cruiser, Caleb tried to process what Rose had told him. Ned was a locksmith, a fact he had neglected to mention. On the other hand, where would it have come up in conversation? If he were going to murder Mary Jane— revenge for a perceived slight when they were teens?—he wouldn't have needed to pick the lock. He had a key to the house. Either way, Ned wasn't stupid. He would have to know that he would be among the first people suspected. Unless, of course, Ned counted on that rationale.

And what was that about Mary Jane being a mean girl?

— • • —

Caleb called the team back to the conference room and Jack launched right in. "Ned Reese was at the VFW for a couple of hours, but he left before seven."

Caleb calculated the timing. "It's a twenty-minute drive from Pittsfield to Queensbridge. That would get him home at about 7:15 p.m., just in time to read bedtime stories. So, that checks out."

"That might even be a little late for a five-year-old," said Scott. "In my house it's lights-out at 7:15."

"Right, but it's a Friday night. Maybe they're a little lax at chez Reese," Jack said.

"More important, what about the gap between eleven o'clock, when Rose went to bed, and the time he came upstairs?" Caleb asked.

"The ME estimated time of death to be around one o'clock, right?" Sandy said. "Ned could have driven to Mary Jane's house and back, with the house key. And Rose would have been none the wiser."

Except that Rose says she's a light sleeper.

CHAPTER TWENTY-THREE

The hours ticked by slowly on Tuesday. Caleb kept glancing at the clock on the wall, waiting until school was out for the day before he could call Harriet Jablow, but it was just noon. He played at attacking the paperwork that was piling up on his desk but couldn't keep his mind on it. What he really wanted to be working on was Mary Jane's murder, but he needed some time alone to think. He decided a break was in order, so he picked up his keys and told Sandy he would be back later. As he rounded his desk, Jack popped his head through the doorway.

"Chief, do you mind if I check out a few minutes early today? I have a job at the country club in Pittsfield tonight. Some big political party going on."

"Okay, but let's not make a habit of it. We've got enough on our hands here with this investigation into Mary Jane's death."

"Right. Thanks, Chief." Jack turned on his heel and left.

Caleb continued on his way when the word "club" stopped him in his tracks. Ned Reese's words came back to him. "Rose isn't a joiner." Perhaps, but might she have wanted to be a part of the friendship circle? He had once briefly pondered the possibility that Rose might have envied the close friendship among Mary Jane, Rachel, and Zoe, but had become distracted by the revelation of Ned's background as a locksmith. Rose certainly had access to Mary Jane's house keys. And she was a fantastic gardener. Why hadn't she gotten together with Mary Jane over their shared interest?

Or had she tried? Did Mary Jane reject her advances? If so, why would she?

And then it occurred to him. Was Mary Jane simply being protective preventing Rose's fecundity from being shoved in her best friend's face?

Was Rose Reese's alibi as solid as it seemed?

As sweet a woman as she appears, I have to explore further.

Caleb climbed into his SUV and returned to the Reese home, where he found Rose tending to the flowerpots on the front steps. Caleb pulled to a stop in the driveway. She looked up when she heard his approach.

"Hi, Chief. This is a surprise. Ned isn't here. He took our little one out for ice cream."

"I actually wanted to talk with you again about your gardening. Do you have a few minutes?"

"Of course, Chief. Come on in. Would you like some lemonade?"

"No thanks. Do you use a computer?"

Her smile was broad. "Of course. Doesn't everybody?"

"Ned told me you're studying landscape architecture. Do you happen to have an app for your gardening?"

"I do! Why?"

"I'm thinking about getting something like that for Rachel. She also loves to garden. Did you know that?" Caleb felt a twinge of guilt at his deceptive tactics but knew that he didn't want to raise any suspicion. And he liked Rose. He didn't want her to be a killer. But he had a job to do.

"Yes. I've always enjoyed the plantings when I drive past your house," Rose said with a wistful smile.

"May I see how it works?"

"I'd love to show you."

Rose led Caleb to a room that was quite obviously hers and hers alone. Along one wall were shelves filled with colorful fabrics, and racks with dozens of spools of thread. Next to these sat a sewing machine and a large table, presumably to lay out the fabric. At right angles to that was a desk with a computer set up.

"Wow. You do a lot of crafting here," he said.

"I love quilting. Just like in gardening, it requires arranging patterns of colors. Let me pull up the garden design software."

Rose pulled a chair over to the computer and began to type. While she was focused on that task, Caleb looked toward the printer sitting next to it. It was a low-end inkjet model.

A wave of relief swept over him. Rose couldn't have printed out the threatening photograph. He felt relief in one sense, frustration in another.

Caleb thanked Rose for her help and wished her luck with her studies before letting himself out. He was fastening his seat belt when she came running out of the house, waving.

"Chief Crane, please take this package of seeds to Rachel. I've had wonderful luck with these hollyhocks."

For the first time in days, Police Chief Caleb Crane felt good about Queensbridge.

He drove back to his office. No sooner had he settled into his chair than Sandy appeared in the doorway. "Chief? I just heard back from forensics."

"What did they say?"

"No fingerprints that didn't belong to postal workers, Zoe, or Rachel. So, our letter writer obviously wore gloves. But the lab was able to narrow things down a bit. The letter definitely came from a color laser printer."

Caleb frowned. "Not much help. There are probably hundreds of them in town."

"To say nothing of the county."

— • • • —

After what seemed like days, it was finally three o'clock. Caleb grabbed his keys from his desk and headed out to visit Harriet Jablow.

Her bubblegum-pink cottage would have been comfortable on the Candyland game board. The house sat on a gentle knoll that she maintained as a wildflower sanctuary, attracting butterflies and birds. According to Harriet, weeds were "merely plants growing in the wrong place."

What a contrast to Earl's yard, Caleb noted, with every blade of grass cut with military precision and only one color: green. He parked the cruiser.

Harriet appeared around the side of the house, clad in her beekeeping gear. "Come on out back, Caleb!" she called. "I've just been smoking the honeybees. It's such a beautiful day we can sit on the patio. I made a cobbler this morning from wild blueberries I picked. It'll go well with the iced tea." She removed her hat and veil.

Caleb made his way up a narrow flagstone path that wound through the flowers and walked directly into the warm embrace of Harriet's pillowy soft arms. He took a chair facing the mountains, while Harriet fussed with the pitcher and cut the cake into generous wedges.

"Here, eat. Then you can tell me why you're here."

Caleb smiled. "What? I can't just visit?"

"You haven't visited me since that bear set up shop in my orchard in April. I know this is about Mary Jane."

Caleb polished off the cake in seconds, then pulled his notebook from a breast pocket.

"Harriet, you've been a teacher in the village for a long time, right?"

"Right. And I had Mary Jane as a student. In fact, I had her twice, first in the fourth grade, and then in sixth."

Caleb marveled at Harriet's ability to get right to the point. He decided to go with the rapid flow. "What was she like? Did she have friends? Did she have enemies?"

"Mary Jane was a very bright girl and had a group of girls she hung out with, but after her mother died, she withdrew. I don't remember that she was especially close with anybody after that. It was tough for her those first few years, being a child in this tiny village."

Caleb remembered full well what that was like. He, too, had felt lost when his own mother had died during his freshman year of college. His mother was withdrawn herself, always under the shadow of her domineering husband. But then he had found Rachel and opened a new chapter in his life.

"Even as a little girl, Mary Jane was more sophisticated— no, that's not the word I'm looking for. She had more depth than the other village girls. That could just have been her sadness. But she always seemed happier when summer came. Yes, in the summer she definitely perked up," Harriet said.

Caleb nodded. "Rachel's family used to come for the whole summer. Eagle Lake Camp is where Mary Jane and Rachel met."

"And became best friends. You know that, but what you may not know is that Rachel's mom took Mary Jane under her wing. I think that really helped her out of her depression. If that's what it was."

"What about enemies? Did Mary Jane have any feuds that you knew about?"

Harriet paused to gaze at a bumblebee buzzing around a patch of red clover. She watched as it entered each flower to extract its nectar. She coughed. "I don't like to speak ill of the dead, Caleb, but Mary Jane could be pretty snarky."

"Can you give me an example?"

"Well, she didn't have much patience for the village girls who were really just normal girls with typical adolescent concerns. I remember her saying some pretty cutting things about all the glossy magazines in their lockers." She paused, thinking. "Something like, 'Theresa, has your agent called yet?' or 'Barbie, what are you wearing to the Emmy awards?'"

"Was there anybody in particular she offended?"

Harriet pondered the question. "Only one that I can remember. But she didn't make fun of that girl for being a boy-crazy fashionista. This girl wanted to go into the military, and Mary Jane was a self-styled peacenik. She gave her a really hard time."

The "peacenik" sounded like Mary Jane. "Do you remember her name?"

"Of course. It was Sandy True."

Caleb's head snapped back in surprise. "My Sandy True?"

"Yes. Sandy had always been interested in serving. She planned to enlist in the Army right after graduating from high school, but then she had the motorcycle accident the night of the senior prom."

"She rode to the senior prom on a motorcycle?" Caleb tried to picture Sandy on the back of a motorcycle.

"Yep, in full prom regalia, too. Her boyfriend, Justin Blakely, had restored an old Indian motorcycle he found lying around his grandfather's barn. That bike was a real beauty and he loved to ride it everywhere."

"What happened to the boyfriend?"

"Justin drove over the center line on a curve. A truck hit them head-on. Justin died instantly. Sandy was thrown. That's how she ended up in the wheelchair. You didn't know this?"

"She only told me it was a motorcycle accident. She never mentioned the boyfriend. Or the prom. I read everything in her personnel file when I came to town, but it didn't say anything about that."

He fell silent, trying to process this new information.

How little I know of the people I work with.

After a lull, Harriet said, "I've always believed that Sandy went to work at the police station so that she could be as close to the military life as possible, given her disability. Did you know that after she left rehab, she went to Northeastern and double-majored in criminal justice and criminology?"

"That I did know. And she's a hell of an asset to my team."

Caleb jotted down a thought in his notebook, wondering at Sandy's reticence in talking about the accident, but relieved that even if she had harbored anger at Mary Jane, there would have been no way for her to take revenge. There was nobody in town to do it for her. Her parents were elderly. There was no boyfriend.

Then again, she did have a brother. Hollis. Who just happened to be in town when Mary Jane died.

Not jealous but vengeful?

She paused, considering her words. "I think Mary Jane grew up some after she left school. She became much more open to people, both old and new."

"What about Earl? Was he as tough as he seems now?"

"Earl? Oh, how he doted on her. Mary Jane was the apple of his eye. After Sylvie died, he tried to be both parents to her." Harriet hesitated a moment. "He did go a bit overboard, I'd say. He could be overprotective. Still is."

"How about as a teacher? Did she have any problems with anybody?"

"Not at all. Mary Jane was well-liked and respected. She was generous with her time, to new teachers especially. Like I said, she grew up." She laid a hand on Caleb's arm. "I hope that makes you feel better."

"Thanks, Harriet. What I feel doesn't really matter right now. In fact, my feelings can only interfere with the investigation."

She left her hand on his arm while Caleb sat still. The only sounds on the hill were the buzzing of bees and chirping of birds.

Caleb cleared his throat. "Well, Harriet, if you think of anything else that could help me figure this out, please give me a call. It may seem like a minor detail, but let me decide, okay?"

"Of course." Harriet gave Caleb another hug. "Take care of yourself, Caleb."

"I will. I promise." He started to leave, but then turned back. "One more question, Harriet. If Mary Jane was so unhappy, why did she stay in the village? You yourself said she was very bright. She could have gone anywhere."

"Despite Earl's overbearing and overprotective side, he was also her father, and she was his only child. She loved him and probably didn't want him to be alone."

As Caleb opened the door to his cruiser, he glanced one last time at the profusion of wildflowers. So free and unencumbered, he thought. No enforced boundaries.

— • • • —

"Chief, Jonas Summers just called," Sandy announced as Caleb walked through the door to the station the next morning.

"What now?"

"He says there's somebody painting over at the schoolyard."

"Yeah, so what?" Jack asked.

"The guy is painting a picture. Of Mary Jane Bennett," Sandy said.

"Better check it out," Caleb said.

"I'll get this, Chief," Jack said.

He swallowed the last of his coffee, stood, swiped his keys off his desk, and headed out the door.

"This is getting kinda creepy. Does Jonas just stalk the village looking for crime?" Sandy asked.

"What can I say? Ever since Merna died, he's lonely. Apparently, Neighborhood Watch helps him feel useful."

"I suppose it's better than drinking."

Twenty minutes later Jack was back at the station. Caleb and Sandy looked up expectantly from their desks.

"Nope, nobody there," he reported. "However."

Caleb's ears perked up. "However?"

"There were splatters of paint on the ground over on the side of the school."

Caleb nodded his head. "This could be perfectly innocent, Jack. Painting isn't a crime."

Jack scoffed. "But painting a portrait of a dead person? Maybe that's the same guy who's been hanging out in the cemetery."

"Could be. Did you talk to Jonas and get a description?"

"Uh, no."

Hell, Jack, learn to follow up.

"Well?"

"I'll go back now and ask."

CHAPTER TWENTY-FOUR

Although the day had dawned bright and sunny, by late afternoon heavy, charcoal-gray clouds had crept in from the west, half threatening, but also half promising to cleanse the air of the oppressive humidity that had been building all week. A warm breeze caused the greenery on the property to dance in unison, swaying back and forth in time to an unheard melody.

Caleb had taken his camera into the back yard after work and settled into a chaise longue, waiting for some wildlife to appear. But instead, he stared into space, the camera forgotten on the ground next to him.

Rachel padded across the yard on bare feet and laid a gentle hand on his shoulder. "Penny for your thoughts," she said.

"I'm not sure they're worth even that."

"What's going on? Have you taken even one photo?"

Caleb snorted and sighed. "I'm thinking about Mary Jane. There's something I'm not seeing. The harder I look, the harder it gets."

"And?"

"And." Caleb sighed again and hauled himself to a sitting position. "It's also about the fact that this village isn't the Garden of Eden Zoe thinks it is."

"You're not so naïve that you'd think it would be perfect."

The wind began to pick up, blowing Rachel's hair around her face as a massive black cloud galloped across the sky.

"Of course. Death happens, I know that. But in car accidents, or drowning, or falling off a cliff while hiking. Even being struck by lightning. But I had half-convinced myself that a New York-style brutal killing would never take place here. Stupid, huh?"

"No, not stupid. Delusional, perhaps."

Caleb exhaled and gave a cynical laugh. "You're right. People are people. Human nature is the same everywhere."

"And in a tiny village like ours, life can get very close. People know everything about everybody else's business."

Rachel took Caleb's hand in hers and lowered herself onto the chaise. They sat side by side, silently. Caleb knew that Rachel was worried about him. He sat up and smiled in an attempt to reassure her. But he couldn't shake the feeling that he was failing in his chosen profession.

"Caleb, do you think the killer might be somebody who's jealous?"

"Jealous?"

"Mary Jane is dead. Zoe and I have both received horrible, anonymous mail. Everybody knows we were all very close. Could it be somebody who feels like an outsider? Somebody who may have felt snubbed by us?"

Caleb nodded. "I've been thinking along the same lines. That is a distinct possibility. In Queensbridge we know just about everybody, but who might feel like an outsider?"

A thunderclap startled them before the sky opened and released its watery contents. Caleb grabbed Rachel's hand and his camera, and together they ran across the back yard, their feet kicking up splashes from the grassy puddles. A sudden and fiercely howling wind forced the rain into almost horizontal sheets. By the time they reached the back door, they were soaked to the skin.

As they helped each other out of drenched clothes, Rachel caught sight of herself in the mirror and began to giggle at the sodden image. Her delight was infectious, and Caleb felt the tension that was his constant companion wash away. He, too, began to chuckle. They both broke into full laughter until tears filled their eyes.

— • • • —

At the crack of dawn on Thursday, Caleb jumped out of bed to a day so hot he felt he could fire ceramics without benefit of a kiln. So much for a cooling rain. He packed his gym bag and, after downing a quick glass of orange juice, headed to the town beach, hoping to get in some laps before work. Within minutes he arrived at the parking lot, having passed only two cars on the way. He did some compulsory stretches and waded in.

As he churned through the water, his strokes automatic, his mind began to wander. He felt so comfortable in this lake and in this village, but he had to admit to a bit of homesickness for the city. He missed the rush he'd get from simply crossing a bridge, hearing the tharump, tharump of automobile tires on road joints. From sunlight sparkling off the Hudson. From the exhilaration of running in Central Park. Bright lights. Throngs of people. Throbbing energy.

Caleb flipped over and began a backstroke. Beads of water fell from his arms, glimmering as the sunlight caught them. Like crystals, he thought. Or shards of glass. Suddenly a vision of the night Manny was shot flashed in his mind's eye, bringing him up short and causing him to choke on swallowed water. Treading water and coughing, he saw his partner bleeding out in his arms on a grimy city sidewalk amid cigarette stubs, broken glass, and smashed chewing gum. By the time the EMTs arrived, it had been too late to save him.

That was why they had come to Queensbridge. Rachel had begged him to leave the city. She was afraid that he, too, would be shot and killed or stabbed. Or that he would meet any number of other horrifying ends. He hadn't fought too hard to stay. He could see the terror in Rachel's eyes. But the prospect of his father's "I told you so" rang in his ears.

He resumed his workout with an energy born of grief and rage, plowing through the water without his usual enjoyment. By the time he finished circling the lake, he had burned off the anger. He trudged out of the lake, water sloughing off his body. He dried himself, running the towel over his strong and fit body, before getting back into the car and driving home.

Rachel was sitting on the porch, where the ceiling fan provided a much-needed cooling breeze. She waited for Caleb to get dressed before pouring coffee and serving the eggs, then sat quietly while he dug in. After a few minutes of silent eating, he finally looked up.

"I'm glad we moved here," he said.

"What brought that up?"

"I was thinking about all the things I miss in the city."

"And?"

"Then I remembered the night Manny died. The filth and the terror. I'm not that person anymore. The edginess of the city just isn't for me."

"But?" Rachel always had an instinct for the "but."

"But I do miss the vitality, the challenge. Sometimes I wonder if I'm wasting my life."

Rachel was silent for a moment, weighing her words. "Have you ever thought about how many people you've had an impact on since you got here?" she whispered. Her green eyes sparkled through a film of tears.

"No."

"Well, it's been a lot. Every day you make somebody's life safer. It may not be Homeland Security, but it is hometown security."

Caleb pulled her to him and buried his face in her hair.

His cellphone rang, interrupting the moment.

"Chief," Sandy said. "Jonas Summers just called. He says there's somebody throwing paint around the cemetery."

Just when I had a moment of peace.

"Can you send Jack or Scott?"

"They're both out at a traffic accident. A pickup and an SUV."

"Okay. I'm on it."

— • • —

The black wrought iron gate had been left open. The grass was still wet with morning dew, darkening the tips of his shoes.

The headstone on Mary Jane Bennett's grave was as pristine as it had been the day her name and the dates of her birth and death had been carved into the marble. No paint. What had Jonas Summers seen? Thinking another headstone might have been targeted, Caleb picked his way around the grave markers but saw nothing out of the ordinary. The cemetery was maintained well by a group of volunteers who raked up leaves, mowed the lawn, and regularly removed dead flowers from gravesites. There didn't seem to be anything out of the ordinary.

He returned to Mary Jane's grave, placed his hand on the headstone, closed his eyes, and bowed his head. He remained that way for a moment. When he opened his eyes again, he noticed some barely visible spots of color in the blades of grass. Indigo, bottle green, maroon. Was this the paint Jonas had seen? Certainly not the fluorescent colors preferred by spray can-wielding vandals. He crouched and ran his hands through the blades of grass sparkling with water droplets.

Then he noticed oil paint. The kind that artists use. Like that at the school?

Interesting. But what does it mean?

After completing his morning rounds, he returned to the station and added a note to the whiteboard. He stood staring at it for a few minutes, hoping something might jump out at him, but nothing did.

Who hated Mary Jane enough to kill her? Who was sending the threatening letters to Rachel and Zoe? It had to be the killer. Otherwise, how would he have had the scarf to photograph? But, who? And why?

He went to the door and leaned out. "Sandy, anything more come back from the lab about the cigarette yet?"

"No."

"Dammit. I feel like we're spinning our wheels."

"Chief, I think we're dealing with a very smart, very calculating person. This was no crime of passion."

"Agreed. I'm going home for an early lunch. I'll be back soon."

At home, Rachel pushed her lunch plate aside, placed her elbows on the table, and tipped her head to one side. "P.D. James," she said.

"Excuse me?"

"P.D. James always said that the motive for murder could be reduced to love, lust, lucre, and loathing."

"Are you still playing detective? Maybe you should take the police entrance exam."

Rachel shook her head. "What motive would anybody have to murder Mary Jane? We can check lucre off the list. Mary Jane didn't have any money. Or property, other than the house she co-owned with Elliot. But you're the expert. What other motives could there be?"

"There're any number of reasons. Somebody wanting to keep a secret. Revenge. Hate. Jealousy." Caleb had a flash of his nightmare of a jealous Rachel and shuddered. "A drug deal gone bad. Or an urge to protect a loved one. Then, of course, you've got radical politics and religion."

"Right."

Caleb smiled. "Most of these do fall under James's four categories. And we know that Mary Jane wasn't at all into drugs. She barely drank."

"Right. So that leaves us with lust, love, and loathing."

Caleb was quiet for a minute as the possibilities ran through his mind. There's a very fine line between love and hate, he considered. Who loved Mary Jane? Who hated her?

And could somebody have been so hurt—or rejected—by her that love would turn to hate?

CHAPTER TWENTY-FIVE

Saturday noontime found the Queen Bee crowded with locals and tourists, so Caleb took a seat at the counter.

"Hey, Chief. What can I get you today?" Sally asked.

Without even a glance at the menu, he said, "I'll take the tuna wrap."

"Extra jalapenos?"

"You know your customer," he said with a grin.

A symphony of chatter, laughter, and the clinking of cutlery on dishes filled the diner. Caleb looked around to check out the customers. He nodded at a few and greeted others by name. Then, his eyes settled on a young man seated two stools away. He had blond hair pulled back into a ponytail, exposing a small ring in one ear. His black t-shirt was emblazoned with a rock band's logo, and his forearms sported colorful tattoos. He smiled at Caleb, exposing a set of straight white teeth. *Good orthodonture or good genes?*

"Chief Crane?" The young man said.

Caleb's eyebrows went up. "Yes."

"Do you remember me? I'm Terry Jackson."

"Tim and Christie Jackson's kid?" Caleb's memory flashed to an image of a chubby boy with freckles, a cowlick, and a Boy Scout uniform.

"Yes, sir."

"Wow. I haven't seen you in a while. You must be in college now, right?"

"Yes. I'm studying art at the Rhode Island School of Design."

"Good for you. RISD is an excellent school."

Caleb's eye was drawn to the boy's arms. They were dotted with a rainbow of colors, making the blond hairs look like lollipop sticks. He realized that what he had initially thought were tattoos was actually paint. An idea struck him.

"Terry, tell me. Have you been painting in the schoolyard recently?"

"Yeah. How d'ya know that? Do you have security cameras there?"

"No, just a very curious neighbor. Why there? Isn't the schoolyard an odd place to set up your easel?"

"Not really. Ms. Bennett was my teacher. She was the only one who ever encouraged me to pursue my art." At this point, the young man choked up, and it took a minute for him to pull himself together. "I wanted to do something to honor her. I thought that if I worked near where she taught me, it might give me some inspiration."

Caleb wanted to believe this young man, but he wasn't naïve.

"Show me the painting," he said.

Terry's face lit up. "You want to see it? It's at home. I'll get it."

"Bring it to the station this afternoon."

"Yes, sir. I will."

Another thought came to him. "Were you also painting at the cemetery a while ago?"

Terry's eyes widened. "Wow. You're kinda scaring me, Chief. Like at the school, I wanted to be near Ms. Bennett."

"How did you get there? Nobody saw a car or a bike at the cemetery."

"My parents live on Stoddard Road, the street behind the cemetery. I just went through a neighbor's yard and climbed over the wall."

"How long have you been in town?" Caleb asked. "I haven't seen you around."

"I was here all summer. I had a job as an art counselor at Eagle Lake Camp."

"But you were painting at the school."

"Yeah. Camp's over for the summer and I'm back at school now. I just came home to pick up some stuff."

"Were you in town the night Ms. Bennett died?"

Terry Jackson blushed deep crimson.

"Terry?" Caleb asked again.

The kid hesitated another moment before finally spitting it out. "Yes, sir. I was with my girlfriend."

"Where?"

"Um, in her cabin."

"She worked at the camp, too?"

"Yeah. She was a waterfront counselor."

"Does this girlfriend have a name?"

"Um, Hilly Mercer."

"And will Hilly Mercer vouch for you?"

"Of course. But please don't tell the camp director. He'll never hire me again."

"For being in another counselor's cabin?"

"Yeah. He has a strict no fraternization policy."

Caleb smiled at the memory of his own violations at summer camp. Away from home with raging hormones. What a mix.

Terry paid his check and got up to leave.

Caleb thought that Terry seemed like a nice kid but knew that a call to Hilly Mercer was in order. He'd have Scott talk to her. He'd be more delicate than Jack.

Terry returned to the Chief's office with the canvas an hour after leaving the diner. Even though the painting was unfinished, Caleb could see that the kid had talent. He had captured the warmth in Mary Jane's eyes, tempered by a mischievous glint.

"Okay, Terry. Take your picture and go home. And keep in touch. I'd like to see more pictures."

"Yes, sir." He hustled out the station door.

"He couldn't get outta here fast enough, could he?" said Scott with a laugh.

"Did you reach Hilly Mercer?"

"Yeah. She was mortified but confirmed Terry's story. They were together that Friday night. She begged me not to tell her parents."

Caleb smiled. "Ah. Young love."

Later that afternoon, Caleb pulled into the parking lot at Eagle Lake. Rachel had insisted that he meet her for an early picnic supper, saying that he needed to take some time to relax. He suspected that she, too, needed some quiet time.

As he climbed out of the Explorer, he saw her across the park. Under the shade of a large maple tree, she had spread a nautical-blue-striped tablecloth over a wooden picnic table. Caleb joined her and helped set things out. From a large cooler he pulled out several cardboard deli containers holding pickles, coleslaw, and potato salad. He peeked under the wrapping around the sandwiches. Monterey Jack cheese, avocado, and alfalfa sprouts. *She's thinking about our vacation in San Francisco,* he thought with a smile. In the bottom of the cooler, he found a large thermos containing lemonade and poured some into a cup. He took a big gulp and his mouth puckered around the tart liquid. Then, with a flourish, Rachel pulled from her hobo bag a package of Caleb's favorite guilty pleasure, sour cream-and-onion potato chips.

"How's your day going?" Caleb asked, ripping the bag open. He knew that Rachel had been filling her days with activity, trying to shake off the depression she had suffered since Mary Jane's death. He hoped now that school had resumed, she would feel better.

Does time really heal all wounds?

"Nice," she said. "I walked over to Zoe's for coffee and then we went together to the Craft Center to sign up for a quilting class. Mary Jane and I had talked about doing this for a long time, so we're going to do it in her honor."

Another thing she'll have in common with Rose. Maybe they'll become friends.

She smiled, but when she turned her head, Caleb could see tears behind the dark lenses of her sunglasses.

Rachel coughed. "And how's your day been?"

"We're done interviewing anybody who had anything to do with Mary Jane. Now, I'm trying to organize my thoughts. I've got a timeline that we're filling in hour by hour, with everybody's locations. It'll take some time. We don't have a big staff." He looked at Rachel. "But we'll get the guy."

"I know you will, but I'm afraid to be alone until you catch him."

They ate their sandwiches, sharing stories of happy times spent with Mary Jane, Elliot, and Zoe. They watched as small sailboats glided along the crystal blue lake and lifted their faces to the brilliant sky. After a while, the hot sun and the big meal caught up with Caleb, and he stretched out on the bench.

"Guard those chips," he said, closing his eyes for a short nap.

Rachel laughed and grabbed a handful. "My tummy is watching them carefully. Nobody can get to them now."

Twenty minutes later, Caleb's eyes flew open. He stood up and together they loaded the back of Rachel's car with the picnic things. He watched her drive off and headed toward the cruiser.

Out of the corner of his eye he saw two women in workout gear walking on the dirt path that ran the circumference of Eagle Lake. Even from a distance Caleb could tell they were in deep conversation from the way their hands moved. As they came closer, he overheard their conversation.

"I could've killed him," said the woman in turquoise.

Her friend laughed in agreement. "Totally. Joe is in such deep trouble. If Donnie had done that, I would've had his family jewels."

Ouch. Whatever the guy had done must've been pretty bad.

He coughed in sympathy and the two women looked up.

The woman in turquoise gasped. "God, you startled me, Chief."

"Hey, Barb, Jenny. I sure hope to see Joe at the public health committee meeting Wednesday night."

Barb turned pink and laughed. "Well, I guess he's safe now that the Chief of Police has heard me! I wouldn't dare touch him."

All things considered, Caleb thought, the women of this village seemed to threaten to kill their husbands on a fairly regular basis. First Rose—at least according to Ned—and now Barb.

For love or vengeance?

— • • • —

Alone on the screen porch that evening, Caleb stretched out on the sofa, hoping that a little meditation session might help him manage his stress level.

Hey, the Hindus have been doing this for centuries. They must know something. And they must have had a few unexplained deaths to deal with, to say nothing of a few Earls of their own.

Rachel had gone off with Zoe and Tenley to help Elliot pack up Mary Jane's clothes to give to the women's shelter, He was left alone with his thoughts in the empty house.

The high-pitched humming of cicadas filled the searing late summer air, rising in pitch like a surfer's wave, then falling quickly to quiet. Harmonizing with their song was the distant hum of turnpike traffic and the lowing of cows. A memory of boyhood summers flashed in his mind. His mother sat on the terrace, a book in one hand and a tall glass of ice-cold lemonade on the table at her side. He and Tenley whacked a shuttlecock back and forth over a net they had erected in the backyard. His mother poured lemonade for them, placed the glasses on a tray, and brought them across the lawn toward the net. Caleb was lifting one to his lips when he drifted off.

His father's barking orders jarred him. Still in the netherworld between waking and sleep, the thought Caleb had lost in the office suddenly reappeared. If indeed there was a killer, did that person know that Elliot would be out of town and plan the crime around his absence? With Elliot gone, there would be one less chance of getting caught. If so, who would have had that information aside from Mary Jane and their friends? Office mates? Clients?

Caleb jumped up off the sofa, ran to his cruiser, and raced up Swift Road to the intersection with Wildflower Road. He took a fast, sharp turn into the driveway of Harriet Jablow's cottage, hoping she'd be home. And sure enough, she was standing among the wildflowers, the lowering sun's rays backlighting her as she poured fresh nectar into a hummingbird feeder.

"Back again so soon, Chief?" Harriet said with a chuckle. "I'm beginning to think you come here just for the cake." She indicated with lifted chin a plate of pastry on the patio table.

"Yes, I'm back, and of course your cake is enticing. But that's not why I'm here. I have a few more questions."

When the two had settled into their seats on the patio, Caleb began. "Harriet, what do you know about Sandy True's brother?"

"Hollis? Oh, my. How did his name come up?"

"He's back in town. Sandy referred to him as the prodigal son."

Harriet closed her eyes and lowered her head. "I did hear that. Except that, unlike the prodigal son, Hollis didn't waste a fortune. He wasted his life."

"How?"

"He went through a pretty rough patch. Drugs, booze, petty theft, fights. What a shame, too. He was a very bright, sensitive kid when I had him."

Fights. Interesting.

"Did he straighten out?"

"I heard he did several stints in rehab. I hope that's what the prodigal son reference is about."

"So, what happened? What made him go off the rails?"

"Sandy's accident. Justin Blakely was his best friend."

"And Sandy's boyfriend."

Harriet blew out a breath. "Yep."

The two sat quietly, picking at the cake. Caleb pondered this new information.

"Thanks, Harriet. I've gotta go now."

"That was fast."

"Yep." He grabbed another blueberry muffin, winked, and left.

The second Caleb got into the cruiser, he dialed his cell phone. "Scott, first thing tomorrow I want you to get Hollis True's complete criminal record. And don't tell Sandy."

— • • • —

Next day, Caleb shut the conference room door behind him and took a seat at the table. Scott Cruz opened the manila folder lying in front of him.

"True has a long sheet, including over a dozen fights, mostly bar brawls." He pushed the folder toward the Chief.

After looking it over, Caleb pulled his shoulders back and did a few neck rotations. "It appears he has a very short fuse."

"But he's been clean for a while," Scott said. "What was he like before all his troubles?"

"Harriet says he was a bright and sensitive student."

Jack slapped at a mosquito. "When was his last arrest?"

Scott shuffled through the file. "He hasn't been in trouble of any kind for six years."

"I like him for it," Jack said. "Like you always say, Chief, there's no such thing as a coincidence, and True's being here the very same weekend Mary Jane died is, well . . ."

Caleb looked up from the file he had been staring at and nodded. "I didn't want Sandy to overhear this conversation. And you two are not going to tell her we had it, okay? Not unless, or until, there's something to tell."

The officers looked at each other and in unison said, "Got it, Chief."

Sandy was absorbed in her computer when Caleb walked through to the front of the station. Only when she felt him approach her desk did she look up.

"Hey, Chief," she said. "How was your interview with Harriet Jablow?"

"Interesting," he said. He wondered how to approach Sandy with the information Harriet had given him.

Sandy raised her eyebrows at his curt response.

Caleb decided to approach the subject head-on. "Sandy, will you come into my office?"

"Please close the door," he said once she'd rolled in.

"What's up, Chief? You seem a little distracted."

"Harriet told me that you and Mary Jane had a falling out in high school. Were you planning to tell me about that?"

"Oh, my God, Chief. Is that what this is about? That water went under the bridge so long ago I didn't even think to mention it."

"So, mention it now. Please."

Sandy collected her thoughts. "I know you and she were really good friends, but Mary Jane had a little of the mean girl in her when she was young. In retrospect, and as an adult, I can see that started after her mother died. It must have been really rough on her."

Again, somebody talking about Mary Jane as a mean girl.

"And . . ."

"And she used to go around acting as if she was so superior to everybody else in school. She made fun of regular, average kids like me as well as the popular kids. She didn't care who she offended."

"How did she offend you?"

"Oh, gosh, how can I count the ways? Mostly, she made fun of my wanting to enlist in the Army, but she did it by starting a rumor that I was gay. At least, I always assumed it was Mary Jane who started it. Back then it was a much bigger problem than it would be now."

"Didn't she know that you had a boyfriend?"

"Justin and I didn't get together until my sophomore year," she said. "Harriet told you about Justin?"

"Yeah, she did. I'm really sorry about what happened. Why didn't you ever tell me?"

"It's just not something that's come up in conversation. The accident happened so long ago." Sandy paused for a moment, her eyes misting. "Besides, it's still painful to talk about."

Caleb crossed the room and sat down next to Sandy. "Harriet said that Mary Jane stayed in Queensbridge so that she could be close to her father."

Sandy shook her head. "I have a different theory. Mary Jane was accepted to Yale, but then suddenly changed her mind. I always suspected that she went to UMass 'cause she felt some guilt for having been so mean to me."

"What makes you say that?"

"Because after the accident, she came to visit me in the hospital and in rehab—at least twice a month. Mary Jane actually visited me more often than my friends did."

"So, did you and Mary Jane mend fences?"

"More than that. I'd say we became friends. You know how Mary Jane loved to travel, right? Well, she would bring me a souvenir from every place she went and then tell me all about it, complete with pictures and funny stories. She did that up until the day she died." She paused and shook her head. "Funny how things turned out."

"What's funny?" Caleb asked.

"Maybe my accident helped Mary Jane grow up. She became a really good person."

— • • —

On his way home, Caleb decided to stop at Elliot's house. He walked up the driveway toward the front door. "Hey, Ell, open up!" he called.

Elliot came out onto the screen porch. "Hey. What's up? The girls, er, women just left with another pile of Mary Jane's stuff."

"I just thought I'd stop in and say hi."

"Thanks, Caleb. I know I haven't been too sociable lately. I'm trying, but . . ."

The two men sat down in the Adirondack chairs.

"Everybody cares about you, Ell."

"I know."

They fell into a comfortable silence, listening to a chorus of birdsong.

Caleb broke the quiet. "Tell me how're you really doing, Ell."

"How am I doing? I'm sad. I'm angry. And I'm really frustrated. During the day, work keeps me busy, but nights are tough. I keep thinking about how she died all alone, how she was murdered. She must have been terrified."

"She never said anything to you about somebody bothering her? Threatening her?"

"Come on, Caleb. If I'd had any inkling, don't you think I would've told you?"

"There may be something that, at the time, you didn't think much of, but could be important."

Elliot shook his head.

"El, why don't you come for supper? Rachel would love to see you."

"Nah. Thanks, but I think I'll take a rain check."

"You sure?"

"When you catch the SOB that did this, I'll make dinner."

Caleb left his friend on the porch and headed home.

CHAPTER TWENTY-SIX

Caleb was driving up Swift Road the next day when the radio crackled in his cruiser.

"Chief, Jonas Summers just called to say there's somebody else in the cemetery," Sandy announced. "He said the guy is waving his arms around like he's talking to somebody, but nobody's there with him."

"Jonas Summers ought to get out more. He calls 911 way too often."

Caleb made a quick U-turn in the middle of the road and hit the accelerator, but just as he turned onto Mountainview Road, he came up against a big yellow school bus with its "Stop" sign extended. He screeched to a stop. The kids getting off the bus were taking their time, probably making plans to talk on the phone—or did they all text now?—as soon as they got home. He drummed his hands on the steering wheel, willing them to hurry up.

After an excruciatingly slow minute, the kids were all safely across the road. Caleb passed the bus, gunned the engine, and tore off toward the cemetery. He pulled onto the grass in front of the low stone wall that bordered the burial ground and leapt out. Racing through the open gate, he couldn't see anything. He stopped to appraise the area, then spied a figure hunched over in the southwest corner of the graveyard. He headed in that direction. The person looked up. It was Hollis True.

"Is visiting the cemetery a crime all of a sudden?" he asked, a sad smile creasing his young face already craggy from years of sea and sun exposure.

"We got a call that somebody was in the cemetery, so I came up to see."

"Don't people usually come to a cemetery to pay their respects?"

"Sure, but we've had reports of some odd things going on here, so I thought it would be a good idea to check it out."

Hollis pulled a cigarette out of its pack and lit it with a yellow plastic lighter.

Gauloises. The same kind of cigarette that was in Mary Jane's yard. Now Caleb knew that at least two people in town smoked that brand.

"Well, I'm not here to vandalize anything, if that's what you're worried about. I came to see my friend." He got up and wiped blades of grass from his jeans.

Caleb looked him over. "I'm curious. What made you come back to Queensbridge this summer?"

Hollis picked a stray piece of tobacco from his lip and grimaced. "I know it's been a long time, but Queensbridge is home. Now that I'm clean, sober, and employed, I thought it'd be nice to see the folks here and show them I've straightened out. Before now I've been too ashamed to come. Especially for Sandy. I couldn't impose on her when I was strung out. She's suffered enough."

True fell silent. His answer had the ring of truth, but Caleb sensed something else running beneath the surface.

"And?" he prodded.

He met Caleb's eyes, then rubbed his hand over his face and sighed. "Our dad told Sandy he didn't want her riding on that bike. I was the one who convinced him to let her go."

Caleb cringed. It had been his idea to go for a beer the night Manny was shot and killed. That knowledge ate at him every waking moment. He could understand True's reaction. Except that he had support, from Rachel. True had turned to drugs and alcohol.

"So, you blame yourself for the accident?"

"Wouldn't you?" True asked, shaking his head.

"But it was Justin driving recklessly. Not you."

"Right."

"Maybe it's time to forgive yourself."

Hollis took a drag on the cigarette and blew out a long trail of smoke as he sighed. "That's what rehab was supposed to be all about."

"Has it worked?"

"To some extent, yeah. I'm a lot better now than I was."

"Tell me, what's this about the Gauloises? I see you and Ned Reese both smoke them."

Hollis gave a soft laugh. "Yeah, that's on me. When we were in high school, we saw this old French movie. The hero was smoking them, so of course we had to. We all thought we were so cool."

So, the cigarette at Mary Jane's could have been dropped by either man.

"Thanks, Hollis. I hope you find some peace."

"Thanks, Chief. I'm working on it."

Caleb returned to the station and found Sandy in his office ready to pounce.

"So, you couldn't tell me you're investigating Hollis?"

Caleb's heart clutched. He didn't respond. How did she find out that he was looking into True's background?

"Did you think I wouldn't be able to handle it? Did you think that I couldn't be objective?"

Caleb pulled a chair over and sat down facing Sandy. "Sandy, I'm sorry you feel excluded, but you have to admit that you would've had a conflict of interest here. I have to go by the book on this."

She glared at him before speaking. "And you don't have a conflict investigating your own friends?"

Touché. She doesn't know how right she is.

Sandy took a deep breath and seemed to calm down a little. "I wouldn't have talked with Hollis. You know that, right?"

Caleb was silent. He placed his elbows on his knees and ran his hands through his hair, then raised his head with another thought.

"Why do you think your brother returned to town? Why now, of all times?"

"Hollis has turned his life around. Do you know about Twelve Step programs? He needs to make amends with his family, ya know?" Sandy's steel gray eyes were flashing, whether with anger or grief, Caleb couldn't tell.

Could I have handled this better? I can't risk losing Sandy. She's a major asset to my team. She may not be a cop, but she often has better instincts than Jack.

"I hope you're right, Sandy. I can't apologize for keeping you in the dark, but I do for any intimation that I don't trust you. Because I do."

Sandy nodded but her eyes were dark. And sad.

209

"He blames himself for my situation. Or he did until he went through tons of rehab."

"Does Hollis know that you and Mary Jane became friends?"

Sandy tipped her head to one side in thought. "I don't think so. He left town right after graduation to join the Merchant Marine."

Revenge?

CHAPTER TWENTY-SEVEN

The foliage was at the last of its green lushness, but restless from lack of sleep and frustration, Caleb barely noticed it during his morning tour of the village's streets and parks. So consumed was he with the case, he felt as if a heavy net had been thrown over his body and he couldn't seem to fight his way out of it. Bits and pieces of Mary Jane's story were visible through the holes in the net, but not the whole picture.

Now seated at his desk, Caleb drank his coffee, hoping that the caffeine jolt would stir up some of the myriad facts swirling in his head and put them into place. He scanned the morning paper. Drought and wildfires down south, unemployment among the young, and yet another bomb blast halfway around the world dominated the headlines. In the classified ads at the back of the paper, a small item asking for all manner of household items caught his eye. "Old and new wanted," it stated in bold letters.

Caleb bolted upright with sudden clarity. Harriet had said the words "old and new" in referring to the people Mary Jane had befriended. He had taken that to mean people of all ages, but in retrospect he realized that she hadn't said "old and young." She was referring to natives and newcomers. Old and new. Mary Jane had been open to everybody. Had one of the transplants had reason enough to kill her? Earl's rant came back to him. Did he have a reason for hating one particular New Yorker? He jumped out of his chair and headed toward the door.

Before he had made it halfway there, Earl Bennett stormed into his office, causing the door to bang against the wall. The man stomped toward Caleb and stood mere inches from his face. Earl's breath was stale, his eyes red. Feeling his space violated, Caleb reminded himself to breathe.

"I was just on my way out to see you, Earl. You seem to be in a big hurry."

"You bet I am, but you certainly aren't. Why are you sitting here on your butt and not out trying to find Mary Jane's killer? How much time do you need?"

"Please, Earl, have a seat," Caleb said, and went to the sideboard to pour water into two glasses. He wanted to avoid an argument with the angry man.

Caleb handed a glass to Earl then returned to his desk. He immediately began rubbing his hand along the arm of his chair. He reminded himself that Earl was hurting. He wanted to be sympathetic, but the man was a sledgehammer.

Earl dropped into the opposite chair and launched into the purpose of his visit.

"Did you ever think Freund might have hired somebody to do the job for him, and that he planned it for when he would be away?"

Caleb's clutched the chair arms, turning his fingers white. He had indeed thought of this horrific possibility. No way was he going to share that with Earl.

"A hitman? Earl, you've been watching too much television. Where would Elliot go about hiring a hitman?"

Sandy's comment about Elliot not being in Queensbridge came back to him. She had said, "couldn't have been here," not that he couldn't have been responsible. Elliot had an iron-clad alibi. But could he have hired somebody to kill Mary Jane? Would he have the ability to plan a murder in cold blood, hire a hit man, appear calm and collected in Chicago, and then seem stunned at the news here? Absurd. But everything about this case was bizarre.

And what would his motive be? Anger over the baby? It was no secret that Elliot had been unhappy to learn of Mary Jane's pregnancy. But had he been enraged enough to have her killed? And, if Elliot had hired somebody, wouldn't he have wanted it to look as if there *had* been a break-in?

Unless, of course, the hired hand made a big mistake.

His stomach began to roil again.

So, if Elliott hadn't done it, and if he hadn't hired somebody to do it, then what?

Earl continued his rant. "He works for Legal Aid, for Chrissake. He probably comes across all kinds of shady characters."

"Earl, just because somebody's poor doesn't mean he's a criminal."

"So, you're saying that somebody with money could just as easily have done it. In fact, I'll bet hiring out for murder is a very lucrative business."

Caleb took a big gulp of water, in the hope it would lubricate his parched throat. He decided to change the subject and ask the question that had caused him to seek out the man before he was stopped.

"Earl, you're constantly going on about New Yorkers. Why? Is there a particular New Yorker who's bothered you or Mary Jane?"

Earl seemed taken aback by the question. "Nah. New Yorker is just my way of referring to outsiders. I don't want any of 'em here. And I especially don't want any of 'em sleeping with my daughter."

Caleb wasn't sure whether to be relieved or annoyed. "Earl, you can show yourself out."

Earl stood, then turned on his heel and exited, slamming the door. The rank scent of the man's body was still in the air when the phone rang. It was Tom Gorham. Dispensing with small talk, he got right down to business.

"The Select Board is meeting tomorrow night."

"That's not news, Tom. They always meet on Tuesday."

"They're not happy. They want you to drop your investigation."

"I don't really care if they're happy. I'm not dropping anything. My job is to investigate what I'm convinced is a murder, and I mean to find out who did it."

"Do you have any evidence to back up your theory?"

"Tom, you know I can't discuss the details of an investigation. But trust me, we're getting evidence, and I won't stop until I can wrap it up."

"So, you're sure?"

"Sure that I won't drop it or sure that it's a murder?"

"Both, I guess."

"Then both. And if the Select Board wants to fire me, then let 'em. I'm not gonna back down on this."

It was quiet on the line. Except for the distinct sound of Gorham's breathing,

"Good for you, Caleb. I'll support you."

"Thanks, Tom," Caleb said, the knot in the chief's gut loosening.

I'd better make sure to be at that meeting.

He picked up the phone and dialed the head of the Select Board.

— • • • —

Caleb took a deep breath to steady himself before entering the Select Board's room at the town hall. He had been seeing red since talking with Tom Gorham, and he wanted them to know that it wasn't their call.

The meeting was already under way when he entered the room, so he took a seat in a folding chair on the aisle in the back row. After a lengthy discussion about whether to build a dog park, the board chairman, Jim Greeley, called for a vote. Then he recognized Caleb.

"Chief Crane? You asked to be on the agenda tonight?"

Caleb stood. "Yes, I did, Jim." He strode to the front of the room.

"Folks, I understand you want me to stop investigating Mary Jane Bennett's death."

"That's right, Chief," said Sally Quinn, a transplant from Boston. "You have to understand. People come here for beauty and culture. They don't want to hear about murder—"

Brett Collier broke in. "And we don't want our property values to suffer if it gets out."

"So, what you're saying is that money means more to you than justice for a woman who grew up in this village?"

215

"We just don't want word getting out about this," Greeley said.

"Oh, it'll get out. And when it does, everybody will know just what kind of town we have. And they'll stay away in droves."

Collier rose from his seat. "Are you threatening us?"

"No. I'm just telling you what will happen. Queensbridge is a tiny town. Nothing can be kept secret for long. Do you want it to look as if you're hiding something?"

"Chief, we just want what's best for the village."

"Then please let me do my job."

"Or?" Sally Quinn asked.

Caleb's spine stiffened. "Or you can get yourself a new chief of police."

The room went silent for a long moment before the board members turned their backs to huddle. Caleb caught only a few snatches of their conversation: "son of a bitch," "reputation," and "Earl."

When they had finished talking, Greeley looked up and said, "Well, I guess all that Boston Brahmin 'please and thank you' pedigree hides a tough negotiator. We'll stay out of your way."

"Thank you," Caleb said. He turned and left the room, hoping the group didn't see his smile.

CHAPTER TWENTY-EIGHT

The next morning, Officer Scott Cruz sat in his SUV in a pull-off on the side of Swift Road. He balanced a radar gun on the ledge of the open driver's side window. Speeding had become a problem along this stretch of road. A lot of the blame could be placed on the tourists who, on breaking free of the city, wanted to spread their wings and fly in the country. Well, they might be in the country, but so were walkers, joggers, and bicyclists, all at risk of being mowed down by a careless driver. And what about the occasional tractor lumbering along?

Most cars and trucks instinctively slowed down if they caught sight of a police cruiser, so he'd only had to issue a couple of tickets that day. Then the roar of a motorcycle whipping past snapped him to attention. Cruz clocked him at sixty miles an hour, a good thirty over the speed limit, so he laid the radar gun aside, turned on the siren, and hit the accelerator. A minute later, he pulled over to the grassy shoulder behind the biker.

He sauntered over to the Harley.

"License and registration, please."

"Yes, officer. I'm sorry. I didn't realize how fast I was going."

"Sure you didn't."

He checked the license. Hollis True. So this was Sandy's brother. On closer look, he could see the resemblance.

"Have you been drinking, Mr. True?"

"No, sir."

Cruz went through the routine and administered a Breathalyzer test. He was surprised that it came back clean. Too bad the department didn't have one of those new marijuana testers, although he had to admit the guy didn't smell like weed.

"May I have your permission to look in your bag?" he asked, pointing to the back of the bike.

"Sure, no problem. I've got nothing to hide."

Cruz removed the sissy bar bag and brought it over to the hood of the cruiser. He unzipped it and raised the cover. He reached inside and pulled out a water bottle, a flashlight, and two protein bars, and set each item aside. He put his hand in one more time and found a leather pouch at the bottom of the bag. He pulled it out and unzipped it.

"What's this?" he asked, holding up a hand over which a few necklaces and bracelets were draped.

Hollis True stared at the jewelry. "I've never seen this before in my life. I swear."

"Why don't you come down to the station with me? We'll sort it all out there."

— • • • —

Through the one-way mirror, Caleb and Scott observed Hollis True, his knee bouncing rapidly and his fingers tapping out a melody on an invisible keyboard on the table.

"What d'ya think, Chief?" Scott asked.

"Did you give him a breathalyzer?"

"Yep. He's clean. He had no drugs on him, either."

"Well, let's go in and see what he has to say for himself," Caleb said as he turned to enter the interrogation room. He pulled out a chair and sat down opposite True. He turned on the recorder and slapped a manila folder and a lined pad onto the table. He decided to start slow and easy with the speeding ticket. He needed to know more about the man seated across from him.

Caleb put his elbows on the table. "Hollis, I don't get it. Tell me, why in God's name you would ride a motorcycle knowing that your best friend was killed, and your own sister paralyzed while riding?"

True looked down at his hands resting on the table and said nothing.

"Didn't you think it would upset Sandy?"

True blew out air before speaking. "Sandy thinks it's great. Sure, she worries about me, but she wants me to have a life. Not to be afraid of what might happen."

"Tell me more about what happened with you after Sandy's accident."

True didn't blink at the sudden turn the conversation had taken. "Justin Blakely was my best friend and because of him my sister is a cripple."

"So, you were angry."

"Damn straight I was angry. The cops said it was Justin's fault. He was driving over the center line. The truck driver didn't see them coming around the curve. But I couldn't take it out on Justin. He was dead. And I couldn't blame Sandy. She was lying in a hospital bed, paralyzed."

Survivor's guilt?

As if he had heard Caleb's thoughts, he said, "Yeah. I was the one who came out without a scratch."

"Where were you that night?"

Hollis squinted. "I was at the prom."

"I'm a little confused. What were you doing at the senior prom?"

"Justin and I were both seniors. Sandy was a sophomore, but she was dating Justin."

"Did you have a car?"

"Not my own. I had to drive my mother's minivan."

Caleb winced with empathy. "That must have been embarrassing for an eighteen- year-old."

"You know it. It even had a bumper sticker that said: 'My kid is an honor student.' Oh, man." Hollis shook his head with a short exhalation that might have been a laugh.

"Why didn't Sandy and Justin drive with you?"

"Justin had this bike he'd restored." His eyes misted over as he gazed into space. "It was a real beauty, that Indian. It was the senior prom, and it was a really nice summer night. He just had to ride that bike after all the work he'd put into it."

"So, after the accident?"

True grimaced and drummed his fingers on the table. "I went on a real bender. For years. Anything to make the pain go away." He coughed, a husky smoker's bark. "It took me a long time and a lot of rehab to get back on track."

Caleb decided to change directions again.

"What about Mary Jane?"

True's head pulled back, frown lines deepening on his forehead. "Mary Jane? Mary Jane Bennett? What does she have to do with this?"

Now Caleb was again confused. True seemed to be totally clueless. Was he playing mind games with him? "I heard she gave Sandy a hard time."

"Oh, yeah. She was a real bitch, that one."

"What exactly did she do?"

"You know, typical mean girl stuff. Sandy was really independent. She didn't hang out with a bunch of giggling girls. So, Mary Jane must have figured she could make fun of Sandy 'cause she didn't fit into her idea of what a girl should be. Maybe 'cause she wore her hair short. Or 'cause she wanted to go into the army. Yeah, Mary Jane was a real piece of work back then."

It's time to switch gears again.

"Okay, so how is Sandy going to react to hearing her brother has been picked up for burglary?" He knew the charge probably wouldn't rise to the level of grand larceny, but it was theft, and it certainly couldn't help his status with the Merchant Marine.

"I told you. I didn't steal anything. You've gotta believe me. I haven't even been in town for years. How would I have known where to find jewelry?"

"Every woman has jewelry, Hollis. And they usually keep it in their bedrooms. Do you actually expect me to believe that you don't know that?"

True sighed and dropped his head to the tabletop for a moment, then raised it and directed his gaze at the police chief. "Listen, if I did come here to steal jewelry, wouldn't I have scoped out rich women with the real deal? That stuff you found in my bag is just costume jewelry, right? Not worth that much."

True had a point. In fact, he had made several good ones. And the same thought process came back to him: why would he risk getting caught, in a speed trap of all places, when he had finally gotten himself clean and employed as a productive member of society again?

"So, Hollis, you want to tell me what you were doing with that jewelry in your bag?"

Tears sprang to Hollis' eyes. "You've gotta believe me. I didn't steal anything. I don't know how that stuff got in my bag. I swear."

Isn't that what they always say? Officer, I don't know how that got there. Give me a break. But I have to admit that True's protest sounds real. Or he's a great actor.

"I want to believe you, especially since you're Sandy's brother, but—"

True jumped in. "Why would I give the guy permission to search my bag if I had something to hide?"

Another good point.

Caleb shrugged. "We're going to keep the jewelry here. Somebody's bound to be looking for it."

"Can I go now?"

"For now, but don't leave town."

"I wasn't planning to. I've got a long vacation and I plan to spend it here."

"Good."

Caleb stood and showed Hollis out the door. Then he went to the observation room. "Scott, please catalogue the jewelry, and Jack, call other departments to see if they've reported any burglaries."

"What? You're just gonna let him go?" Jack sputtered.

"We can't hold him unless, or until, somebody reports her jewelry's missing."

— • • • —

Caleb and Scott were in the conference room, coffee cups and an empty donut box pushed to the side. A lone ant feasted on the sugary crumbs, and a slight breeze from an open window ruffled the papers on the desk. Scott had laid out the jewelry confiscated from Hollis True onto a long side table and was busy cataloguing every item.

Voices emanating from the vicinity of Sandy's desk floated through to the men. Conversation in a decidedly female register was punctuated by occasional laughter. Not a minute later, Rachel and Zoe floated into the room.

"We're here to stage an abduction. We're taking you to lunch," Rachel announced.

Caleb looked up and smiled. "I could use a break," he said, slapping his hands on the desktop. "Scott, you know how to find me." He turned in his chair, grabbed his keys and his phone, and stood up.

As he rounded the table, he looked back. Zoe was standing before the carefully laid out array of jewelry, frowning.

"Zoe? Is there a problem?" he asked.

She began to tremble. "Um, C-Caleb, where did you get this jewelry?"

Rachel turned to where Zoe was pointing and gasped. "Oh, my God. Caleb, where did you get these?"

"We confiscated them from a guy Scott Cruz stopped for speeding. It looked suspicious that he'd be carrying women's jewelry. Why?"

"These are Mary Jane's things."

A bolt of electricity shot up Caleb's spine.

"I'm sure of it," Rachel said. She began to lean over the table, finger pointing.

Scott held out an arm to stop her. He handed her a pencil, cautioning her not to touch anything with her hands.

Rachel slid the pencil point under a necklace of jasper beads and lifted it. "I gave her this for her birthday a couple of years ago."

"And I was with her the day she bought these," Zoe said, pointing to a pair of delicate silver filigree earrings. "We were at the Berkshire Arts Festival last summer and she fell in love with them."

"Didn't you two help Elliot clean out Mary Jane's closet at the house?"

"Yes, but we only did clothes and shoes," Zoe said. "I didn't even think about the jewelry."

"Did Mary Jane mention that anything was missing before she died?"

"No, but remember, she wasn't wearing much jewelry this summer. It was so hot, and she'd been retaining fluid," Rachel said. "Her fingers were so swollen she couldn't wear any rings at all."

"So, we don't actually know when the stuff was taken," Caleb said.

Zoe suddenly became agitated. "Wait a minute," she cried, pointing. "These two are my rings. They must have been taken that day my house was broken into. Oh my God, he could have killed me, too, if I'd been home!" Her eyes widened, the whites stark against her dark mahogany irises.

Rachel wrapped her arms around Zoe and rubbed her back.

"Could he have gotten into Mary Jane's the day we were helping her paint? We had every single door and window open to help air out the house. A burglar could have gotten in then. Maybe while we were downstairs having tea and cookies?"

Scott punched the air. "I think we've got our guy. Chief, should I go pick up True?"

Caleb shot him a look. No need to rile people up.

"Sandy's brother Hollis? I can't believe it." Rachel said, her voice quivering.

Zoe fell into a chair along the wall and leaned forward, elbows on her thighs. "Hollis True? My God, he must have taken my jewelry when we were meeting at my house."

"How could he have done that, Zoe?" Scott asked.

"He asked to use the bathroom. It's right down the hall from my bedroom. He must have snuck in there and taken the stuff."

Caleb and Scott exchanged glances.

"And to think I wanted to go into business with him. To think that I actually flirted with him!" Zoe cried.

Caleb stood by the table, bouncing on his feet. Rachel got the message. "No lunch, right?"

"Right. I need to be here. And, guys, please not a word to anybody about this."

"Of course not," Zoe said.

After Rachel and Zoe left the station, Caleb returned to his desk, leaned back in his chair, and tried to make sense of the crime. Was True back on drugs and looking for a way to score? Even if high, he had to have known that Mary Jane's costume jewelry wasn't worth much. So, why take such a big risk for such a small pay-off?

And what about practical matters? When could True have taken Mary Jane's jewelry? It would have been an incredible coincidence that he was near the house at the same time doors and windows were open. The three women were in the bedroom painting. They most certainly would have seen him. Or did he take advantage of the fact that everybody in town would be at the funeral and try his luck then? But if so, how did he get into a locked house?

There was a third—much worse—scenario. Did True take the jewelry after strangling Mary Jane? But again, if he did, how did he get into the house that night? He didn't have a key. And he couldn't have gotten one from Sandy since she didn't have one, either. The doors and windows would have been closed by then.

Except for the second-floor bedroom windows. The screens were intact when he checked them, but the killer could have replaced them before he left, then walked right out the front door.

But how would he have gotten into the house in the first place?

And why take just those two rings from Zoe? Did he have only enough time to take them when he met with her to discuss doing business together?

"Scott," he called. "Get Hollis True back here. Now."

"Yes, sir."

An hour later, Caleb was back in the interrogation room with Hollis True.

"So, Hollis, what made you come back to Queensbridge that weekend?"

"What weekend?"

"The weekend Mary Jane Bennett died."

True popped up in his seat as if a puppeteer had yanked his strings. "I already told you." His voice had a pleading quality to it. "I wanted to see Sandy and show her how I've changed my life."

"It's a pretty big coincidence you were in town—after such a long absence—at the very time that Mary Jane Bennett died." Caleb waited a beat before adding, "Especially since it was her jewelry we found in your bag."

True was silent, his eyes wide and bulging, his mouth open in a perfect circle.

"Where were you the Friday night she died?"

"I was at an AA meeting. I go to three a week, no matter where I am."

"Those meetings end early. Where were you in the middle of the night, like around 1 a.m.?"

True paused.

Thinking up a story?

He emitted a low bleat. "I was with one of the women from the group. I spent the night."

"You think she likes you enough to lie for you?"

He sagged in his chair. All the air seemed to have leaked out of him.

"She doesn't have to lie. It's true."

Caleb stood and went to the door, leaned out and called, "Jack, come and read Mr. True his rights."

"Charge?" Jack asked.

"Breaking and entering, and burglary."

"Not murder?"

"Murder?" True shouted. His face had turned gray.

"We don't have any evidence of that yet. But Mr. True can think about that while he's awaiting his arraignment."

As Caleb handed True over to the officer, Rachel's mantra, that things aren't always as they seem, reverberated in his mind.

This investigation isn't over yet.

Sandy had been waiting at her desk for the Chief to come out of the interrogation room. When he stopped on his way back to his office to refill his coffee cup, she confronted him.

"Chief, I need to talk with you about Hollis."

"Okay, come into my office."

She didn't waste any time after shutting the door. "Chief, I've been through enough with him that I know what Hollis is capable of, and what he's not. My brother is a tortured soul, but he's getting better. He's been through therapy to deal with his guilt about my accident. He's off the drugs and liquor. He's got a good job. A career."

"Guilt? What's he got to feel guilty about?"

I've heard about this guilt from both Harriet and Hollis. What does Sandy have to say about it?

"Hollis was Justin's best friend. He encouraged our relationship, and he feels responsible for urging our father to let me ride on the motorcycle that night."

"I hope you're right, Sandy. I really do. But the fact is that he had a substantial load of women's jewelry in his bag. What am I to make of that?"

Sandy looked down, drumming her fingers. Caleb noted the mannerism that the two siblings shared.

"I admit it, I don't know," she said. "Look, Chief, I know this looks bad, but Hollis has changed. He came here to make amends. He wants to settle down. Why would he do something stupid and jeopardize it all? And Hollis is not stupid."

"So, what are you saying?"

Sandy closed her eyes and took a deep breath. "This may sound paranoid, but I think Hollis was set up."

Caleb was silent for a moment before speaking. "If that's true, Sandy, it leaves us with a big question. Who would want to set him up?"

CHAPTER TWENTY-NINE

Saturday morning was warm as Caleb and Elliot drove through town to their favorite fishing hole.

"We haven't done this in a while. Rachel will be thrilled to get some nice trout," Caleb said. And I'm happy that you're actually interested in doing something."

"Yeah, as long as you clean it." Elliot's attention was suddenly diverted. "Hey, isn't that Harriet Jablow walking there?" He indicated with lifted chin a woman walking at the side of the road. Her signature curls—once a deep carrot orange and now rust-like and streaked with silver—cascaded down her back over a purple and pink tie-dyed tunic. Over her arm she carried a woven basket.

"Sure looks like her." Caleb honked the horn and pulled the car over to the side of the road.

"Hey, Harriet. What're you up to today?" Caleb asked.

"I've been gathering wild chicory root." She showed them the contents of the basket, stuffed to overflowing with the roots. The green handle of a garden spade stuck out at an angle.

"What do you do with it?"

"I roast and grind it to put into my coffee, New Orleans style."

"Where do you pick it? You don't take it from the side of the road, do you?

"Oh, no. That stuff probably has all kinds of road salt and other toxins in it. I like to forage all over the mountain. I can walk for miles harvesting the stuff."

"The neighbors are okay with that?" Caleb asked.

"Oh, I offer to share the harvest, although not that many people really want wild plants. I think they're afraid." Harriet tut-tutted. "Silly, really. Anyway, everybody is very nice. Most of them know me. They probably just think I'm eccentric."

"I'll bet they're sure of it," Elliot said.

"Touché!"

— • • • —

After cleaning the fish, Caleb and Elliot sat down with Rachel and Tenley at the farm table and dug right in, tearing off hunks of a crusty peasant bread to dip into the buttery sauce that covered the fish. The three ate quietly for a few minutes, until they had taken the edge off their hunger.

Caleb broke the silence. "So, what have you two been up to today?"

"We went pumpkin picking with Zoe and then had a quick lunch at the Bee."

"You couldn't just get a pumpkin at the farmers market?"

"That wouldn't have been nearly as much fun. Plus, we got in a good hike and some fresh air and sun," Tenley said. "Remember, this city girl needs a good dose of country."

"So, where are the pumpkins?" Caleb asked.

"They're at Zoe's. She got an urgent call from a client," Rachel said. "We're going over later to decorate them. We have some great ideas for the festival."

"An interior design emergency?" Elliot tried not too hard to hide a smirk.

"It's a different world, El," Tenley said, and patted him on the shoulder.

Rachel got up and went to the refrigerator to retrieve a bowl of fruit salad for dessert, and Caleb took the opportunity to whisper to his sister.

"Thanks for getting Rachel out of the house to do something fun. She's been so sad."

"I know. She's gotten so thin and pale, but today she's starting to look a little better. The sun and fresh air did her a world of good."

"Good. And I think the fishing expedition helped Elliot."

After lunch, Caleb drove to the station. He made himself a cup of coffee and sat drinking it while looking out his office window. Couples strolled along Main Street in the bright sunlight of a perfect mid-September day. They stopped to look in the display windows of boutiques, antique shops, the florist, and the greengrocer. They bought the *New York Times* and the *Boston Globe* at the general store. They ate sandwiches and sipped iced tea under umbrellas on the patio of the Trattoria. The soft murmur of their voices broken by an occasional staccato laugh made their way across the street and through the windows open to a warm breeze that caressed his arms.

What an ad for a peaceful getaway. I should take a picture to put on that postcard Zoe always talks about.

He looked at the cars parked along the street, belonging to tourists from so many different places. They came in greater and greater numbers every summer for music, theater, and dance, then in the fall for the foliage. Soon they would be coming to view the magnificent fall display. Lots of New Yorkers and Bostonians had homes in the Berkshires.

"But how many of them knew Mary Jane?" Caleb asked aloud. Local villagers may have known her from childhood, but some of the transplants most certainly did, too, especially if they had kids in the school system. His mind started churning as he tried to put his ideas into a logical progression. He jumped up and went to the conference room, picked up a black marker, and stood before the whiteboard. He needed to get organized. He began to jot down some thoughts.

First: Most locals only left their homes to go to New York or Boston occasionally, for pleasure. Second: A few had business that took them on the road more frequently. Third: A significant number of snowbirds traveled back and forth between Queensbridge and wherever. All three groups would have had access to adult video stores from which they could purchase a DVD anonymously, and with cash. The internet would not provide the same protection since credit card records can be traced.

But again, how many of these people had anything to do with Mary Jane?

He sketched out a chart with the names of people who fit into each of the categories. After two hours of going through his files and moving things around, he copied his findings into a notebook to take home and study. He glanced at the clock on the wall and was surprised at how much time had passed. Just as he stood to leave, Jack knocked on the doorjamb.

"Chief?" he said.

Caleb looked up. "Yeah, Jack, what is it?"

"True's alibi is solid. He was at an AA meeting that Friday night, and then went dancing with a bunch of the members."

"How late did that go?"

Jack flipped through his notebook. "Late. After midnight. And then he went home with one of the ladies."

"And?"

"She saw enough of him to report about a birthmark on his left thigh. Shaped like a dolphin."

Caleb nodded.

"Well, we got him for the burglary," Jack said.

"Yeah, sure." Caleb murmured. He wasn't so sure he had the right guy for that, either. True had seemed truly surprised by the jewelry found on his bike. Something didn't fit.

"It sure wasn't easy getting his friends to admit that any of them had been at the meeting. They have some sort of confidentiality pledge in AA."

"But you got confirmation? From more than one person?"

"Yeah."

"What about from somebody who isn't a friend?"

"Yeah. The club manager also saw him."

"Then that's that. Let's call it a day."

Caleb locked the conference room door, noting his obsession on keeping away prying eyes. Somebody in his beautiful little community was a killer.

— • • • —

Back at home, Caleb lay down on the screen porch sofa, letting the magnificent sounds of Mahler's First Symphony flow through him as a gentle breeze wafted through the screens and attempted to cool him. His thoughts went to summer Tanglewood picnics. They'd pull a wagon laden with coolers and blankets to set up on the lawn overlooking Stockbridge Bowl. Until Mary Jane died. Was murdered. Would the friends ever attend a concert together again, without her?

Caleb shook his head to rid his mind of bad thoughts and focus on the virtuosity of the orchestra's playing. But soon enough his mind began to wander in a different direction, thinking back to his own piano lessons as a child when he had no patience for the seemingly endless hours of scales and theory homework. He would race through practice, then run outside to play ball. What kind of childhood had these musicians had? Did they ever play ball, or were they afraid to break their fingers?

Caleb envied the talent of every performer he pictured on the stage. He felt a tiny pang of regret that he had never continued with his music studies. "Patience is a virtue, Caleb," Mrs. Aleksandrov had said over and over in her thick Russian accent. "Patience and persistence are what you need to accomplish your goals."

Patience. Persistence. He had patience and persistence all right, just not for piano practice.

Mary Jane's death had been no accident. Of this, he was sure. And it wasn't a crime of passion. It had been too carefully planned. A serial killer? He doubted, and prayed, that it wasn't. But then, there were those threatening letters. Threatening more death.

Yes, this was premeditated murder. There had to be some relationship between the killer and the victim. He reminded himself that eighty percent of murder victims are killed by people they know—friends or family. But who, among all the people who knew Mary Jane, had wanted to murder her?

It had been well over a month since Mary Jane had been found dead in her bed. Caleb and his team had interviewed everybody who had ever known her and followed up every story. Unless he could find a crack in somebody's alibi, he would never solve this case.

Yes, patience and meticulous planning. That's exactly what the killer must have had to conduct what amounted to the execution of Mary Jane Bennett. He had to have known that Elliot would be out of town. He had to have had easy access to the house.

As the music played, all the tension of the previous weeks slowly lifted from Caleb's shoulders, and he began to drift off. Then, as the fourth movement and its spectacular finale began, his eyes popped open.

A set-up? Could Sandy be right?

CHAPTER THIRTY

When Caleb brought his breakfast out to the porch on Monday morning, he was surprised to see a dusting of silvery frost on the backyard lawn. If summer was truly over, he'd better think about bringing in the outdoor furniture. And about helping Elliot. It wasn't a job for one person.

Rachel poked her head out the door and said, "Brr, forget it," and hustled back inside.

"It'll warm up!" he called after her.

An hour later, Caleb found himself back in Elliot's basement, helping him set a picnic table down in a far corner. Three more trips back-and-forth brought in the benches and a croquet set. Just as they came in with the last chair, the phone rang.

Elliot took the stairs two at a time to answer it, shouting, "Keep the grill outside. I might want to make a steak or two before it gets really cold."

While waiting for him to return, Caleb went to the open doorway, enjoying the last of the season and idly running his hand up and down the door's edge. Suddenly something sticky on his fingers woke him from his reverie. He ran his fingers over the spot again and bent over to get a better look. He pulled a flashlight from his duty belt and aimed it at the tacky spot, exposing a faint rectangular outline.

Caleb looked up as Elliot came down the stairs carrying two bottles of Sam Adams lager. "Ell, is there a reason that you would have taped the lock open?"

"Huh?"

"Come here." Caleb beckoned Elliot who removed his eyeglasses and bent over to take a closer look.

"I have no idea what that is. It looks sticky."

Caleb was quiet. No key had been needed to gain entrance to the house. He pulled his phone out and dialed the station, having decided to use his cell phone exclusively during the investigation. He didn't want anybody with a police scanner listening in on his conversations.

Sandy True answered.

"Sandy, is Jack there?"

"No, he just went out to get some lunch, Chief."

"Okay, I'm coming in. We'll meet in the conference room."

Caleb then called Jack's cell phone number.

"Hey, Chief, what's up?" answered Jack.

"When you looked at Elliot and Mary Jane's place after she died, did you look carefully at the doors?"

"Yeah, of course, Chief. I told you. There was no evidence of a break-in."

"Did you happen to look at the edges of the doors?"

"The edges?"

"Yeah. I'm here in the basement and I just found a sticky, adhesive-like substance on the edge of the door, right where the latch and lock bolts are."

"What are you saying?"

"What I'm saying, Jack, is that somebody may have taped it over at some point, making it very easy to gain access to the house without a key."

Jack interrupted him. "And making it look as if there had been no break-in."

"And that leaves us with the question: Who could have had access to the house to do that without raising suspicion?"

"That's not such a long list of people, Chief."

"Exactly."

"Come down to the station. We're definitely dealing with a murder."

So maybe Hollis True did happen by when the doors were open, and set the stage for a late-night break-in.

As he started the car, another thought popped into Caleb's mind. He pressed down harder on the gas pedal.

— • • • —

In the conference room, Caleb led off the discussion. "An intruder had to bet that Elliot and Mary Jane wouldn't be using the cellar door between the time he placed the tape on the lock and the murder."

"I'm curious about one thing, though," Sandy said.

Caleb looked up from his notebook. "What's that?"

"Somebody went to a lot of trouble to stage this murder masquerading as a kinky sex game gone bad. Why leave the adhesive?"

Caleb gazed into space and said, "The killer may not have realized it was there. Remember, it was the middle of the night. It would've been hard to see."

"What if he deliberately left the adhesive marks on the door?" Sandy asked.

"Why would he do that? Where's the motive?" Jack asked.

"To confuse us. To send us off in a dozen directions," Sandy said.

Caleb considered the possibility. "That would be one hell of a red herring. And it indicates that we're dealing with one very smart, very obsessive killer."

"And, what about opportunity?" Sandy asked. "Only somebody with access to the house could have taped the lock."

"Elliot's smart enough to know that the spouse is always the first suspect," Scott said. "And his best friend is the Chief of Police. Unless Elliot is a total sociopath, I can't see him doing it."

"But would he have hired somebody to do it for him?" Jack asked.

"I don't think so," Sandy said. "He seems genuinely broken up over her death."

Caleb wanted to agree, but the thought continued to plague him.

"Zoe told me that all the doors and windows were open the day she, Mary Jane, and Rachel were painting," Caleb said. "So, anybody happening by would have had access."

"It would be a huge coincidence that a person with evil intent just happened by at that time," Sandy said, "especially since the house is set back in the woods."

"But Ned Reese goes by regularly. Ned Reese smokes Gauloises. And Ned Reese has a key," Caleb said.

So, why use tape?

"Maybe Sandy's right, Chief," Scott said. "This is just a devious plan to divert attention from the real killer.

Frustrated, Caleb ran his fingers through his hair. "There's no such thing as a perfect crime," he muttered.

"How 'bout when we catch the bastard, we ask him?" Jack said.

CHAPTER THIRTY-ONE

At Rachel's insistence, Caleb lay in the backyard after lunch with a book in his lap. Leaves rustled in the breeze and fluffy white clouds scudded across an azure sky, so at odds with his gray state of mind. After a half hour of staring at its pages, he realized that he had read the same paragraph at least five times. He rolled out of the hammock and walked the length and breadth of his property, trying to shake loose the sticky cobwebs forming in his brain.

He remembered the day they found this house. Set on a hill overlooking the village green on one side and facing east on another, the Craftsman style house had a large, flat backyard that Rachel had envisioned filled with a swing set, sandbox, and kids. Lots of kids. He shrugged his shoulders, sighed, and turned toward the vegetable garden.

The leaves on the tomato and zucchini vines were turning yellow. Amazing, he thought. It's hard to believe that these now-withering stalks once produced the most delicious vegetables. Now only a few small, hard green tomatoes remained.

And here we go again. Once again something that appears to be one thing is entirely different. Rachel's Sunday school project is really getting into my head. It's almost taunting me. What am I not seeing? What, or who, is behind the mask?

He hauled himself out of his chair and called out, "Rachel, I'll be back in a while!"

The station was quiet, with no calls for help or to report a crime, so he was finally able to focus on his backlog of paperwork. The only sound in the office was an occasional burst from the printer. Just as he was thinking of calling it a day, the telephone rang, startling him out of his focus.

The Caller ID displayed Dr. Butler's name.

A phone call from the ME? Not a good sign. Caleb pressed the button to connect to the right line. "Dr. Butler, how are you?"

"I'm fine, thanks, Chief. How are you doing?"

Caleb thought he detected a tone of concern in the medical examiner's voice. "Doc, what can I do for you?"

"Is it true you're conducting a murder investigation into the death of Mary Jane Bennett?"

"Where did you hear that?"

"It doesn't matter where I heard it. I want to know why you're doing it. Wasn't my ruling good enough for you?"

"Doc, I respect you and the work you do. But I knew Mary Jane Bennett. She was a close friend. I just can't believe that she died the way you think she did."

"Personal feelings should not get in the way of your professional duties, Chief." Now Caleb wasn't sure if the tone he heard in Butler's voice was concern or defensiveness.

Caleb took a deep breath and gripped the edge of his desk. "This is more than personal, Doc. My gut—my professional gut—tells me that something is off here, and I want to pursue it."

"Well then, do what you have to do. I'd just hate to see you ignore more pressing things in your village while you're chasing after wild geese."

Caleb sat frozen in his chair, rubbing the edge of the desk. The second person within days was urging him off the investigation. What should he make of that? And what could possibly be more pressing than solving a murder of one of his own neighbors?

His conversation reminded him that he hadn't heard back about the DNA on the cigarette butt. He called Scott into his office.

"Have you heard anything about the cigarette butt yet?"

"Actually, the lab just called me, Chief. The lab found nothing. No fingerprints, no DNA."

"How could that be?"

"Well, maybe all the rain we've had degraded it."

"But it was in good condition. Didn't you find it under the eaves?"

"Right. It was damp, but in one piece."

Caleb blew out air. He began to wonder if the killer was teasing him. There were no fingerprints and no DNA on the DVD. Or the cigarette. Or anywhere in the bedroom.

Back to square one. Damn it.

He stood and went back to the conference room. Standing before the whiteboard, he picked up a marker and began to rock on his feet, rolling it between his hands, the cylinder clinking against his gold wedding band with each pass. After a minute, he popped the top off the marker and began to write.

1: Not everybody who knew Mary Jane from childhood loved her. Had she done something so horrible that time had not healed the wound?

2. Not everybody in town knew Mary Jane from childhood. There were plenty of transplants and second

homeowners in the village, many of whom were involved in village life. Could one of them have had it in for Mary Jane? For what reason?

3. Could somebody begrudge her success as an adult?

Caleb stopped writing and sat down at the conference table to thumb through his notes. Of the dozens of interviews he'd conducted over the past few weeks, one point kept coming up. The village had many newcomers.

He stared into space, trying to put together the pieces of evidence. It's as if they're all from different jigsaw puzzles. He realized he needed to think like the killer. His reflections returned to Hollis True. If behavioral history was any predictor, then Hollis wasn't his man. His entire sheet manifested an impulsive personality, and even a hair trigger temper at times. This wasn't a person who could plan a murder and leave no evidence. Perhaps Hollis True's appearance in town really was just a coincidence.

So, if Hollis wasn't his man, he had to think again about how the real killer got access to the cellar door in the first place. Ned Reese had a key, as did several other people. But why use tape if they had a key? And whoever it was had to have had entree to the cellar in order to place the tape over the deadbolt. Who had that?

Another possibility flitted through Caleb's mind, but he lost it. He frowned, trying to force it, but had no luck. His head began to throb, so he got up to pour himself a cup of coffee, his fourth of the day, hoping the caffeine would help him retrieve the thought.

I really need to cut down on my coffee consumption.

He and his team had gathered statements from everybody who knew Mary Jane, followed every lead. And yet, having sorted through his notes and set everything back onto the white board along a timeline, he still had nothing.

Everybody had an ironclad alibi.

But somebody had gained entry to her house. Somebody had murdered her. That he knew. He began to pace the length and breadth of the room. Back and forth, then around and around the conference table. His father's cold, aloof voice rang in his head, telling him that he had chosen the wrong career. He should come back to corporate law, back to the family firm. That was where Crane belonged. A cop? Bad choice. Bad reflection on the family.

Maybe Father was right. Maybe I have chosen the wrong career. No, I can do this. I just need to focus.

Grabbing his keys, he headed for the door. He jumped into the cruiser for the quick ride to October Mountain State Forest. There was still plenty of daylight left.

— • • • —

Caleb breathed in the scent of deep woods as he hiked, hoping that the exertion would make his heart pump the oxygen-rich blood he needed to think creatively, the way a murderer might think.

When he reached the Washington Mountain Marsh Loop, he stopped and sat down on a fallen log. Sifting through the evidence again, he tried to make some sense of it. Somebody had entered Mary Jane's house in the middle of the night through a door whose latch had been taped open. Therefore, that somebody must have been in the house at some point prior to the fateful Friday night. But, Caleb considered, he had to have been there close enough to the time of the murder so as not to risk the tape being discovered by either Mary Jane or Elliot.

Elliot. Was it just a coincidence that Elliot was out of town when Mary Jane was murdered? Despite the law enforcement truism that the intimate partner is usually the first suspect, Caleb just couldn't see Elliot as a killer, or as an employer of one. And so far, he had no evidence to the contrary. Anybody could have entered the house unseen through the cellar while Rachel and Zoe were helping Mary Jane move furniture and paint the second-floor bedroom.

He bent over to pick up a large pinecone, thinking that Rachel would love a basket of these. She loved to do crafts of all kinds. Maybe she could use them in school. He took off his jacket and began to gather the cones in it before noticing the sticky sap rubbing off on the cloth.

What we do for those we love. I'll have to throw this into the wash as soon as I get home.

"For those we love." The thought that had eluded him for so long suddenly appeared. Could somebody have wanted to get Mary Jane out of the way while at the same time giving Elliot an alibi? Who would want to protect Elliot?

Caleb's head spun with facts, suppositions, and the heady fragrance of pine. So consumed was he with his thoughts that he didn't notice the sky slowly turning gray. But when the wind began to whip up pine needles and pebbles, he decided to hike back down the mountain. He barely made it to the cruiser before black clouds released a torrent of rain.

Back in his own driveway, Caleb ran from the Explorer in a futile attempt to stay dry in the heavy downpour. He yanked open the back door and wiped his wet, dirty boots on the doormat. He bent down to unlace them and placed the pair next to the radiator in the mudroom.

After changing his clothes, Caleb sauntered into the kitchen and found a note on the farm table, tucked under a plate of peanut butter cookies, informing him that Rachel was at Zoe's working with the Pumpkin Festival committee. It also asked him to bring Elliot along. They'd all have supper there.

He sat down to enjoy his snack while sorting through the stack of mail Rachel had left there. Midway through the pile and halfway through the cookies he saw an envelope of heavy, ivory-colored stock addressed to him in a familiar, meticulous hand. His chest aching, he turned it over and confirmed by the return address that it was from his father. Who else would have engraved stationery? His hand went to the table's edge and began running back and forth as he stared at the envelope. He put it aside for later. He would need a stiff drink to read it. Leave it to his father to send him a formal letter rather than pick up a phone and call. He'd be surprised if the letter hadn't been typed from dictation by his secretary. Or written by her.

Pushing himself up from the table, he said aloud, "The Pumpkin Festival planning committee sounds like a place I need to be." Snagging another cookie, he left the house and headed toward Zoe's house.

Twenty minutes later, he followed the sounds of chatter to Zoe's kitchen. At the round table sat Rachel, Tenley, and Dennis. Between them were four orange pumpkins and one large white one, and scattered around them were toys, pipe cleaners, miniature dolls, glitter, and other assorted craft items.

"Glitter again for supper? Didn't we just have that on Tuesday?" Caleb said.

"Is it dinner time already?" Tenley said. "We've been so wrapped up in this project that time just flew."

"Where's Elliot?" Zoe asked.

"He's not up for it."

"Even with us? We have to do something."

"Give him time." Caleb turned to look at the squashes on the table. "What are you all making?"

"I've made pumpkin pie," Dennis said, turning his gourd around to show the Greek letter *pi* carved into the flesh.

"Very clever, Dennis. I guess that math major in college is finally paying off."

"I have a Cinderella coach. See?" Zoe turned a fat white pumpkin around and pointed out some horses, a driver, footmen, and a couple of mice who apparently hadn't yet been magically converted into footmen. "But I'm having some trouble getting the wheels attached to the pumpkin. Elliot's good with tools. Maybe I can get him to help me."

"That's a good idea. Put him to work on something. But I'm famished. Feed me."

Yes, I know I just ate a plate full of peanut butter cookies.

"It's a deal," Zoe said. "I have a nice pot of lentil soup on the stove, a crusty baguette, and a really fine block of Black Diamond cheddar."

"Good. No glitter," Caleb said. "So, why are you doing these now? The festival isn't for another few weeks."

"We're using them as publicity. We'll place them in high-traffic spots in the village," Zoe said. "My pumpkin will go into the library surrounded by Cinderella books."

"I'm putting mine in the bakery." Dennis said. "Get it? Pi? Bakery?"

How can they all be so cheerful? Our good friend is dead. Even Rachel seems happy.

As if in answer to his unspoken question, Rachel said, "We're billing the festival as a tribute to Mary Jane. It was Zoe's idea."

Zoe nodded. "Mary Jane loved the pumpkin festival. We're going to post colorful fliers with pictures of our creations all over the village. We'll get people really pumped up for the fair."

Caleb tried to focus on the upbeat conversation. "That's terrific. You'll get a record crowd this year."

"All right. Go wash up. We'll have to eat in the dining room," Zoe said.

Rachel squeezed Caleb's arm on her way to the bathroom.

Thank God for Rachel. But why am I wasting time here when I have a murder to solve?

CHAPTER THIRTY-TWO

Sunday dawned bright and sunny, with more than a hint of chill in the morning air. Caleb, Rachel, and Tenley hiked to the top of the hill at the Windy Hill Orchard, crunching over a thin layer of frost, and looked out over the valley that showed the beginnings of its annual crazy quilt of orange, rust, red, and yellow foliage. A stiff breeze kicked up, causing them to zip up their fleece jackets.

"It's so nice to have you with us for our annual trek," Rachel said.

Tenley smiled, her cheeks flushed pink from both the chill and the exertion of the hike. "But it's really not the same without the whole group, is it?"

"Elliot just couldn't face it yet. And Zoe's afraid to strain her foot." Rachel's eyes filled with tears. "And Mary Jane will never be with us again. Zoe was right. This was absolutely her favorite time of year. She loved the colors of the foliage, and she even looked forward to the winter solstice because then, she said, the days would start getting longer again."

"That was Mary Jane. The glass was always half full," Tenley said.

Tenley decided to change the mood. "First one to get a box wins!" she shouted, then ran toward the regimented rows of trees.

Twenty minutes later, they had filled three large cardboard trays with just as many varieties of apples. Caleb hefted them onto a low wooden wagon whose red paint had been flaking off for years, and the trio ambled back to the parking lot. Caleb paid for their harvest at a little green shack that offered a variety of apple products, including fruit for those not inclined to pick their own. He loaded the hatch of Rachel's car and the three drove home.

After a hearty lunch of grilled cheese sandwiches and a steaming hot tomato soup, Rachel and Tenley cleared the table. Caleb set up a special tool that would peel, core, and slice the apples, and tightened the clamp onto the farm table. Then he lifted the trays onto the counter and tipped them into the sink, where Rachel washed, and Tenley dried the fruit. Just as they finished, they heard a knock at the back door.

"Anybody home?" Zoe called.

Caleb went to the door to let her in.

"Just in time," he said. "We're about to start making everything apple."

"Great! I'm so sorry I had to miss out on the apple picking." Zoe stepped into the kitchen, tripping on the threshold and falling forward. Caleb caught her by the arm as a glossy purple gift bag flew across the room. Rachel caught it.

"Good catch," Tenley said. "Zoe, another trip like that and you'll end back up on crutches."

"I hope you moved that treacherous basket," Rachel said.

251

Zoe smiled. "I brought something that will go perfectly with an apple dessert. Open it but be careful in case I broke it.

Rachel removed lavender tissue paper and lifted a cube-shaped box out of the bag. She opened it to reveal a set of vintage Sandwich glass bowls.

"Oh, Zoe, these are great, but you shouldn't have," Rachel said.

"I was in the Design Center with a client, and I thought of you immediately."

Zoe took a seat at the table and picked up an apple. She said, "These apples are perfect."

"We worked hard this morning," Tenley said. "Only the best for us."

"But even wild apples are fine once you take the brown spots off," Rachel said.

"Not for me they aren't," Zoe said. "I could never eat them."

"That's why God made insecticide," Tenley said.

"And makeup," Zoe added.

Tenley raised an apple in toast. "Here's to keeping up the image."

"Well, you've both eaten our wild applesauce before and neither of you have complained," Caleb said.

"Or perished," Rachel said.

"Ugh, really?" Tenley said and made a face.

Zoe changed the subject. "So, this is a treat, Tenley, that you've been able to spend so much time up here. I'm so glad we're getting a chance to know each other. Despite the circumstances, of course."

"Of course, we could've met up in New York."

"If you weren't so busy with your Manhattan lifestyle, and always on the arm of New York's most eligible men." Rachel turned serious. "There's nobody special, out of all the guys you date?"

Tenley went quiet as she contemplated the apples. After a minute she said, "No. And, frankly, after my marriage to the toxic Clayton, being single isn't so bad." She turned to face Caleb. "You know, in retrospect, Clayton was just like Father. A saint in public, but in the house an arrogant, controlling son of a bitch. I should have learned my lesson from watching what Mom went through."

Caleb's memory flashed to an image of his former brother-in-law and his father playing tennis, both frowning in intense competitive concentration. And not particularly gracious losers, smiling through clenched teeth.

He wondered if they even enjoyed the game, or had they just cared about besting their opponent?

"Tenley, there are some wonderful guys out there," Rachel said. "Your own brother is one of them. And Elliot."

"You're probably right. Maybe I should go after him."

Zoe's eyes widened. "Don't you think it's a little early for that? I mean, Mary Jane just died."

Caleb rescued his sister. "Zoe, when you get to know Tenley a little better," he said, "you'll see she can be a bit on the facetious side."

Zoe shook her head. "Anyway, I came over to let you all know that I'm going to have a housewarming dinner party, and you're all invited. It'll be quiet, just the six of us. But it's time for Elliot to get back into life."

"Good idea, Zoe. Make sure to seat me next to him," Tenley said with a grin.

Zoe pulled a face.

— • • • —

A little after seven o'clock on Saturday evening, a dark green Subaru Forester pulled into Zoe's driveway. Caleb, Rachel, and Tenley got out, followed immediately by Dennis in his BMW. As the three approached the front door, Elliot's Ford F150 pickup drove up.

Zoe came to the door to greet everyone, drying her hands on a towel. "Come on in and make yourselves at home. I just have a few last-minute things to do, and then I'll join you." She turned to Elliot and placed a hand on his arm. "I'm so glad Caleb convinced you to come. It's so important to surround yourself with the people who love you."

"Yeah. I'm sure he's right."

"And you've never been here before."

Elliot shrugged.

Rachel and Dennis wandered over to the Yamaha baby grand in the great room. Arranged on the glossy black surface was an array of family photographs. Zoe's cat perched on the piano bench.

"I love these photos," Rachel said. "And not an ugly one in the bunch. This little girl with pigtails is adorable."

"It figures. Even her cat is gorgeous. Aren't you, Truffles?" Dennis said and ran his hand through the pet's soft fur.

Caleb and Elliot joined them. "Meow. What are you two being so catty about?" Elliot asked.

Rachel groaned and rolled her eyes.

Is Elliot getting back to his old self, bad puns and all?

"We're just expressing our envy of Zoe's stunningly good-looking family," Dennis said.

"These are like my family's pictures," said Rachel. "Just holidays and vacations. It seems we never use the camera any other time."

Caleb peered at the array. "Hmm. Palm trees on sandy beaches. Snow-capped mountains. Could be any beach or mountain in the world. I can't place them. Ell. What d'ya think?"

An avid traveler and photographer, Elliot enjoyed trying to determine where pictures had been taken. His eyes moved from one photo to the next and back again.

"Nope. Haven't a clue. Could be anywhere."

Elliot stood facing them and frowned in concentration. "There's something about these pictures that's different. They're not your usual family photos at the beach, but I can't put my finger on it."

"You'll figure it out," Caleb said.

Rachel elbowed Caleb in the ribs. "It must be the happy family."

Caleb snorted. No wide grins in Crane family photos. He thought about his mother, a wan smile on her face. His father, erect and arrogant. And his sister, Tenley, always with a rebellious smirk on her face.

But always in the most elegant of places: Paris, London, Vienna. Only the best for Matthew Crane. And, oh yes, his family.

Elliot put his hand on Caleb's shoulder. "Your pics with Rachel are happy, right?"

"Right," Caleb said.

"So, things are okay."

Zoe reappeared and, after setting a soup tureen onto the table, joined the group.

"I see Truffles is finally warming up to you," she said. "It only took, what, seven years?"

"She's beautiful and she knows it," Rachel said. "Why be nice to us unless we can do something for her?"

"And worship at her feet," Dennis said. "We give dogs food and shelter and play with them, and they think we're gods. Cats get the same treatment and conclude that they're the gods."

"So there!" Zoe said with a laugh.

"Speaking of which, where is that most wonderful dog?" Dennis asked.

"He's out back," Zoe said. "Guarding the house."

Caleb pointed to a studio portrait of a handsome man with a full head of black hair threaded with silver. "Is this your husband?"

Zoe's body stiffened as she managed to croak out a response. "Yes, that's Evan."

"I'm so sorry," Rachel said. She put her arm around Zoe's shoulder.

"Thank you. He was a wonderful guy. I miss him every day. I know I'll never find anyone like him."

The clock sounded the half hour, breaking the melancholy mood, and Zoe invited everybody into the dining room. A Mexican-themed decor was laid out, complete with a sombrero-shaped bowl filled with an arrangement of crimson poppies, scarlet ranunculus, and giant sunshine yellow gerbera daisies in a bed of delicate ferns. She set to ladling out bowls of a fresh gazpacho that smelled like summer, with cucumber, tomato, onion, parsley, cilantro, and garlic.

As she passed a bowl to Caleb, Tenley said, "Zoe, this is really something. You went to such trouble."

"It's so nice to have somebody to cook for. Plus, it was the perfect excuse to buy the sombrero," she said with a laugh, pointing to the centerpiece.

At that, everybody dug in, enjoying the cool and crunchy vegetables with just a zip of hot pepper.

The meal continued on the Mexican theme, with a chopped salad with honey lime dressing, seven-layer tortilla pie, and corn bread, all washed down with Dos Equis.

Elliot said, "I feel like a pig in clover. Mexican is my favorite food."

"I'm so glad you like it. It was such fun putting it together." She turned to her right. "Do you cook, Tenley?"

"Never!"

Caleb laughed. "Believe me, Zoe, you wouldn't want to eat what Tenley cooks. I've been there."

"It's not like I poisoned you, brother."

"Close enough."

"Then Rachel and I will do the cooking," Zoe said. "The guys are safe with us."

— • • —

Later, as they walked to their cars, Caleb said, "That was fun."

"It was, and I'm glad you insisted I go," Elliot said. "But I can't stop thinking about those photos. There was something about them . . ."

"You're the expert photographer. It probably has to do with something technical that we mere mortals can't see."

"Yeah, maybe. Goodnight all," Elliot said.

Before he climbed into his truck, Rachel gave Elliot a big hug, then got into the Subaru with Caleb and Tenley.

"That Zoe is a funny one," Tenley said. "She was so over-the-top in the décor tonight. Did you catch that sombrero vase?"

"I loved it. Remember, it's her business, and she probably couldn't imagine doing it any other way," Rachel said.

"You're right. I'm probably being judgmental. It's hard starting out again as a single woman after being married. And to have to support herself in New York City? That's not easy. I was lucky to have a nice trust fund to depend on."

"Well, I'm glad she's found Dennis to work with," Rachel said.

"They've really developed a special friendship. Did you know that she goes as his date when he has to meet with his more conservative clients?" Caleb asked.

"I did. Zoe really believes that she needs to protect him from homophobes, and that pretending to be his girlfriend projects the right image," Rachel said.

"She has his back. That's wonderful," Tenley said.

"We really need to help her find somebody special," Rachel said. "Zoe can't spend her life as a beard for Dennis."

"What about for you, sis?" Caleb asked.

"Here? Thanks, bro, but I'm not a candidate for village life."

"Zoe told me she wants Dennis to find you a house, or even a condo, here," Rachel said.

"She's deluded. Queensbridge is a beautiful place with lots of culture, but it's definitely not for me. I need a big city with lots of noise and lots of people."

When they got home, Rachel and Caleb settled into the den to watch the late news while Tenley went to sleep. Rachel worked at the knitting in her lap, but Caleb had already zoned out, thinking about the murder investigation. The talking heads simply served as background noise to his thought process.

"Somebody's asleep at the switch," Rachel said.

Caleb's head snapped up, Rachel's voice bringing him back to earth. "Huh? What do you mean?"

"Just look at the newsreader. See how he's looking away from us? I'm pretty sure a light is supposed to be on the camera he looks at, but somebody forgot to change it."

"Huh," he said with a grunt. He sat up and focused his attention on the news, but an odd feeling began to worm its way into his gut. Why? The story being reported wasn't upsetting. In fact, it was a rather heart-warming tale of a dog saving his master. So, why was it bothering him? He took a sip of his chamomile tea and tried to concentrate on the television.

After about three minutes of news, a commercial for a digital camera came on. The celebrity spokesman demonstrating it had zoomed in on a bevy of beach beauties with a mischievous look in his eyes, only to be swatted by his girlfriend.

"But I'm taking a picture of the waves!" the spokesman cried.

Rachel laughed, but a little bell was ringing in Caleb's head. What was it about the news that was bothering him? He shook his head, as if to re-organize the puzzle pieces jumbling around in his brain.

CHAPTER THIRTY-THREE

The next day, the sky was made darker by heavy gray clouds rolling in from the west as Caleb entered the brightly lit post office to retrieve the day's mail. Nobody was behind the service counter, so he headed directly to his box, rifling through his key chain to find the right key. He opened the gray metal door, ruing the day the Postal Service pulled the old boxes from use. He loved the elegant, chased-brass antiques that reminded him of his summers in Maine, and of Dottie the postmistress who gave him a home-baked cookie every time he picked up the family's mail.

He reached his hand into the long compartment, and pulled out a thick wad of envelopes, a magazine, and the weekly *Shopper's Guide*. He brought the pile over to one of the two high tables placed on either side of the front door just as Dennis came in. They greeted each other, and Dennis went to claim his own mail.

"Look at this mountain of paper, Dennis. Why is the police department getting toy catalogs? Do you think there're any real mail in here?"

"You mean, like a letter? Written by a person you know?" Dennis chuckled and took his bundle to the other table, and the two friends sorted through their mail side by side.

Halfway through his stack, Caleb flipped through several envelopes that had been put into his box by mistake. Harriet Jablow. Sam Saget. Zelda Bootes.

"Hmm, that's a name I don't recognize. She must be new in town Caleb muttered.

"They must be training a new person," he said. "I've got mail for other people." He went over to the service window and hit the bell on the counter. He waited a minute, then called out, "Jan? Are you there?"

Nobody answered.

He shrugged and slid the envelopes through the mail slot next to the service window. "I'm sure these will eventually find their way to the right person."

"I'd better hustle," Dennis said, checking his watch, "I'd better get home to let Henry out before I go up to your house."

"Henry?"

"Formerly known as Zoe's rescue dog. That experiment didn't last long. When Empress Truffles started hissing and spitting at him, I took him. That is one jealous cat. And one really sweet dog."

"That was good of you to take him in."

"I couldn't see sending him back to the shelter. Those dogs need love."

"Don't we all? You know, I've meant to say something. It was really lucky that you were there to bring Zoe to the hospital."

"Zoe's my best friend. I'd do anything to help her. And she knows I stay up late, not like you old married folks. She was in a little bit of shock. When I got to her house, she was shaking and really scratched up. I gave her a big glass of bourbon and carried her to the car."

261

"You're a good friend, Dennis."

"No big deal. Anyway, the club scene in Albany wasn't all that great."

"Well, I'll see you in a few."

"Oh, damn, it's raining again."

Caleb gathered up his mail and tucked it inside his jacket before dashing to the car.

He found Rachel standing at the stove when he came through the back door into the mudroom, followed immediately by Elliot. He dropped the pile of mail on top of the washing machine and they both removed their wet shoes before entering the kitchen.

"I got him," he said.

"Yep, he got me," Elliot said. "He said you'd feed me."

Rachel crossed the room and put her arms around Elliot and kissed his cheek. "I'm so glad you came." She pulled back suddenly and said, "Elliot, you're soaking wet!"

"There's some serious rain coming down out there."

"At least it's not snow. How about some hot spiced mead to warm you up?"

"Sounds perfect. Thanks." Elliot looked over Rachel's shoulder and said, "Hey, there are six place settings on the table. Who else is coming?"

"Zoe and Dennis."

"Is this another intervention?"

Caleb exchanged glances with his wife, then clapped Elliot on the back and said, "No, it's friends getting together."

"You guys go into the den while I finish up here in the kitchen," Rachel said. "And, Caleb, would you get some warm slippers for everybody, so they don't have to go barefoot?"

At that moment, the back door opened, and Zoe and Dennis came in.

Dennis emitted a load moan. "My brand-new boots are ruined. Damn this rain."

"Oh, don't be such a baby, Dennis," Zoe said. "They'll dry and you'll polish them."

"I'm not a baby. These are expensive boots."

"Then you shouldn't have worn them in the rain."

Caleb came into the kitchen with an armful of slippers and distributed them to his friends.

"Thanks, Caleb. Now quick, get me to the fireplace," Dennis said, scuttling over to the ceiling-high stone hearth.

Caleb poured more glasses of mead and handed them out.

"Yes! Give us some honey wine," Elliot said.

"Thank you, Caleb. This is just what the doctor ordered," Zoe said.

After dinner in the kitchen, the friends picked up their mugs of tea and moved toward the den. On their way through the dining room, Elliot lifted his chin and pointed toward the table, piled high with papers.

"What's that you've got going on there, Rachel? Another school project?"

"Yes! My sixth graders are going to love this one. I'm doing a lesson on names next week. What do they mean and where do they come from."

"First names?" Zoe asked.

"Actually, I'm focusing on last names for this lesson, but I may do first names another time."

"That's cool. I know that Hendrikson is Dutch for Henry's son," Dennis said, "but my father's name is Robert, and his father's name is Paul!"

"So, tell me, is Crane a bird or a big piece of machinery?" Elliot asked.

Caleb laughed. "Maybe it's a piece of machinery that looks like a bird."

"Actually, the name Crane stems from the one of the ancient clans of the Scottish-English border area. It was a nickname for a person who's tall with long legs," Rachel said.

"So a perfect description for Caleb," Zoe said with a laugh.

"And my name, Honig, means honey."

"And that's why we drank mead tonight," Caleb said. "Rachel gets a royalty check every time somebody drinks it."

"My name means friend," Elliot said.

"Aptly named," Rachel said.

"Zoe, what does Bouvier mean?" Dennis asked.

"I don't know. I've never actually thought about it before."

"It's obviously French," Rachel said. "Caleb, didn't you take French at Andover?"

"I did, a million years ago." He paused gazing into space. "I think it means ploughman, or maybe huntsman."

Zoe stiffened. "What a terrible thought."

"Not at all. There's a constellation with another form of that name," Elliot said.

"What's it called?" asked Dennis.

"It's pronounced Bo-owe-teez but spelled like boots with an 'e' at the end," said Elliot. "So, Zoe, you're a star. Actually, a bunch of them."

Zoe laughed and said, "I've always wanted to be a star. Elliot, do you know how to find it?"

"If I remember my Astronomy 101 correctly, it's right below Ursa Major, so it should be visible here."

"I never knew my name had anything to do with the night sky," Zoe said. "I'd love to see it. Would you show it to me?"

"Sure, but we'll have to wait for a clear night. We can't see anything tonight with all this rain."

"I'd like to see it, too," Dennis said.

"Sure. The more the merrier," Elliot said. "Let's aim for tomorrow night."

"Aren't you afraid you'll ruin your boots?" Zoe asked.

"They were expensive!" Dennis cried. "Besides, I'd wear something appropriate."

"Good that you learned your lesson," Zoe said.

"Well then, let's drink to our ancestors," Caleb said.

They all raised their glasses and drank.

— • • • —

Rachel was propped up on her pillows, reading, when Caleb came out of the bathroom.

"Ready for sleep?" he asked.

"Not yet. I'm still a little wired from having company, so I thought I'd read a little." She put a bookmark between the pages of the novel in her hands and looked up at Caleb. "It was nice to have everybody here with us tonight, wasn't it?"

"Yeah, it really was. Even if Elliot thinks of it as an intervention, it was fun."

"And I think it was good for you, too. You needed to get your mind off this investigation. If only for one night."

"You're probably right."

"By the way, do you know where your first name comes from?"

"Caleb is an old family name. Is it biblical?"

"Yes, but there are actually two possible derivations. One is *kol lev*, or full heart, and the other is *kelev*, or dog. They're both perfect descriptors for you."

Caleb snorted. "Dog?"

"Yes! You do your job with a full heart, you're loyal, and you're dogged in your pursuit of truth and justice—"

"Like Superman?"

Rachel laughed. "How about cute and cuddly?" She pulled the covers aside and patted the space beside her. "Hurry up and get in. I'm freezing."

Caleb leaned over to kiss his wife. "I think I'll read for a little while, too, until my eyes get tired." Within minutes, his eyes were closed, the book slipping down on his chest.

CHAPTER THIRTY-FOUR

Caleb found Elliot in the bar at the Moonlight Diner, his head propped up on one hand and his eyes rimmed in red. He was wearing a denim jacket over a wrinkled olive t-shirt that had a mustard stain on it. Elliot had never been more than a two-beer kind of guy, but it was apparent that he had been into the hard stuff all evening.

"Hey," Caleb said.

"He-ey." The word came out in two syllables.

"How long've you been here?"

"Since four."

"Ell, it's eight now. That's four hours."

"Yep. The man sure knows his arithmetic."

"Listen Ell, I know you're depressed about Mary Jane. We all are, but —"

"You don't know what I'm feeling," Elliot snapped, his eyes blazing.

"True, but I know that Mary Jane would never want you to drink yourself into oblivion."

"So, Rachel must be feeling sad? Or relieved?"

Caleb started. "What's that supposed to mean?"

"With Mary Jane dead, neither of them can have babies."

Caleb felt a stab in his chest but took a deep breath and tried to attribute the venom coming from Elliot to grief magnified by liquor. He leaned over and put his hand on Elliot's arm. "Okay, you've had enough. Put the glass down. I'm driving you home."

He put his arm around his best friend and escorted him to the cruiser. As he strapped him into the seatbelt, he remembered the day they found Mary Jane's dead body. He had held Elliot up then, too.

That night, Caleb couldn't sleep, going over and over Elliot's allegation about Rachel. He had to acknowledge that Rachel was envious of her best friend's pregnancy. After all, it was only human nature to want a baby, and it must have been very hard for her to watch another person get it so easily—supposedly without even trying. But Elliot had made it sound as if Rachel were nothing but a jealous viper. He just couldn't wrap his mind around him saying such a hateful thing.

After a lot of tossing and turning, Caleb finally fell into a fitful sleep, but woke a few hours later. The glowing red numbers on the digital clock read 5:15. He got out of bed as quietly as possible and went downstairs to make coffee and retrieve the newspapers from the box at the end of the driveway. He was finishing his first cup and was halfway through the *Eagle* when the telephone rang. He looked at the caller ID. Elliot's number. He took a deep breath and answered.

"You must have a hell of a hangover this morning."

"Yeah, I do. Can you come to the house?"

Caleb wondered if Elliot remembered the previous evening's conversation, or if he remembered anything at all. But he decided to give him the benefit of the doubt, so he got dressed and headed toward Pine Mountain Road. As he pulled into the driveway, he saw Elliot standing on the front porch. Even through the screens, he could see that Elliot looked pale, and he immediately felt sad for his friend.

"You have coffee for me?" Caleb asked.

"Plenty. I'm on my third cup already."

"You really tied one on last night."

"I did." Elliot poured coffee as Caleb grabbed a chair. "I also think I may have said some pretty nasty things last night."

"You really crossed the line, Ell, but I'm gonna chalk it up to grief compounded by alcohol."

"Caleb, I'm so sorry about what I said last night. I don't know what came over me. This whole thing is just making me crazy. You know I think the world of Rachel."

Caleb sighed. He caught himself running his hand along the chair's arm and stopped himself by picking up his mug. He took a big gulp of the hot liquid.

"Ell, have you thought about talking with somebody?"

"What am I doing right now?" His voice shook.

"I mean a professional. That might help you sort through your feelings. It's gotta be better than self-medicating."

"You may be right. I'll think about it." Elliot turned the mug in his hands a few times as if he were examining the ceramicist's workmanship. Then he cleared his throat twice before continuing.

"There's something else."

"What's that?"

Elliot took a long swallow of coffee and set the mug down, keeping his eyes on his hands. After a long pause, he sighed, looked up and said, "I had a moment."

Caleb drew in a breath. "A moment?" He imagined this is what a priest felt like in the confessional.

"The other night Dennis, Zoe, and I went to look at the constellations. We were just sitting out there looking at the stars. We were talking and laughing. It felt so good to laugh."

"Did anything happen?"

"No! But I found myself getting aroused."

"Where was Dennis?"

"He got a call from a client, so he moved away to talk to him."

"Elliot," Caleb said, putting his hand on Elliot's forearm, "you're human. You have needs. You drank half a bottle of wine."

"A third."

"And Zoe is a very beautiful woman."

"Yeah, I know all that." Elliot twisted the napkin in his hands. "But . . ."

Caleb raised an eyebrow.

"I don't want to be with anybody yet. I don't know if I'll ever be ready." He shuddered. "And I don't want her thinking that anything can happen."

"Hey, Zoe's been a friend for a long time, especially of Mary Jane's. And frankly, given that Dennis was right there and it was dark, she probably didn't even notice anything."

"Yeah, you're probably right. We were just two stargazers."

No wonder he got so drunk last night. He's suffering from a bad case of the guilts.

Caleb laid a hand on Elliot's shoulder, and the two sat that way without speaking until the trembling stopped. The only sound was the distant lowing of cattle.

Bad timing. A year from now, Elliot might have been able to move on and pursue a relationship. Really bad timing.

— • • • —

The sky had turned gray in the afternoon and gotten darker by the minute, ultimately unleashing yet another enormous downpour during the dinner hour. With water from the rainstorm still dripping from the eaves, Caleb and Rachel sat side-by-side on the sofa in the den. The *Times* crossword puzzle was in Rachel's lap, and big mugs of cocoa sat on the vintage steamer trunk that functioned as a coffee table.

"A nine-letter word starting with a 'p' ending in 'e' meaning 'keep going,'" Rachel said.

"Persevere?"

"Perfect. We're done." With a contented sigh, Rachel flattened out the paper and placed it in the pile destined for the recycling bin. "That was the fastest we've ever done it."

"I like crossword puzzles," Caleb said. "No word stands alone. Each one is dependent on another."

"That's a perceptive look at a seemingly simple game," Rachel said. Then she gave an impish grin and said, "We deserve a reward. Frozen treat, two words, eight letters?"

"Sounds good to me."

They went into the kitchen where Rachel scooped black raspberry ice cream into glass bowls. They sat at the farm table to enjoy it.

"These are the bowls Zoe brought us from New York," Rachel said. "They're real Sandwich glass. Wasn't that so sweet of her?"

"Very thoughtful. I guess she knows who likes ice cream."

"That's what friends are for," she said popping a spoonful of the purple treat into her mouth.

"So, how's the planning for your Purim program coming?"

"Really well. You know, the more I read about it, the more I appreciate Esther. Every person in the story has a role. There are no extras that just walk on, as in a movie. Even the minor characters have a part to play in how the story unfolds. They either move the action or support it."

"For example?"

"For example, at the beginning of the story, the king urges his queen, Vashti, to parade before them, wearing her royal crown. Just the crown. When she balks, his cronies urge him to punish her. The weak-willed king assents and banishes her. Once that scene is over, the cronies are gone, but their influence has set the story in motion."

Caleb pondered what Rachel said. He spooned up some ice cream, enjoying the sensation of its melting on his tongue. Everybody has a role to play, whether as an actor or supporter.

"It's sort of like the crossword puzzle," Caleb said. "I wonder if that's the situation I have here with the murder."

"That's a real-life puzzle."

"It is," he said grimly. "The question is: Are some people, knowingly or unknowingly, supporting the killer?"

CHAPTER THIRTY-FIVE

Caleb took a sip of hot cocoa, then placed the insulated mug in the cup holder in anticipation of a chilly start to his morning rounds. He turned the key in the ignition, put the cruiser in gear, and backed out of the driveway.

In the few days since their apple-picking, the landscape had turned into a riot of bright colors with scattered notes of green spruce and fir. Soon, without their summer foliage or dazzling autumn colors, their essential selves would be open to the world for inspection and evaluation, and he found himself noting various configurations of branches. Some were cheering, their branches straight up and waving in the wind. Others were shouting hallelujah, their arms stretched outward to the heavens. Still others were bent downward as if carrying bags laden with heavy goods. If only we could strip people to their essentials, he thought. Find out what's beneath their fancy dress.

He drove down Main Street and saw a few merchants already preparing for the day, sweeping debris from the sidewalks in front of their shops. Although the trellis at the flower shop was now bare of roses, Hallie Cartwright had hooked pots of yellow, orange, and red mums over the lattice and was busy arranging gourds in varying shapes and sizes on the ground before it. Caleb dreaded the loss of the full shade trees lining the summer streets and the coming of the cold that would be there in short order. Just the thought of the naked, gray branches made him shiver. He tightened his hands on the steering wheel, frustrated. It had been too long since Mary Jane was found dead, and he still hadn't found her killer. He had interviewed everybody who had known his friend, but still made no arrest.

What am I missing?

Morning rounds completed, Caleb headed to the Queen Bee, newspaper tucked under his arm. He looked around to see who was there, spotted Elliot, and joined him. Sally came over to pour coffee.

"Morning, Chief," she said. "Ready to order?"

"Yeah. I'll have the blueberry pancakes."

"You just missed all the excitement, Chief."

"Why? What happened?"

"We were all talking about these crazy storms all over the country, and of course that started us on the topic of climate change. Earl got into it and, well, let's just say he was being himself. He was practically apoplectic. I actually had to ask him to leave."

"That bad, huh?"

What is the matter with that man? I warned him.

"That bad. And, of course, Elliot here got the brunt of it. What is it with those two?"

"Don't ask," Caleb said with a rueful shake of the head.

"I'm sitting right here, folks! I can hear you talking about me," Elliot said.

Sally grunted and left to bring the order slip to the kitchen.

"I'm glad you're here," Elliot said. "I took your advice and made an appointment with a therapist."

"I'm glad, Ell. It's good to talk out your problems and get an objective point of view."

"Yeah. The doctor's helping me sort through stuff." Elliot poked his fork around the omelet on his plate but didn't take a bite. "And she gave me some tools for dealing with Earl."

"Maybe you can teach me some of those."

Elliot coughed out a laugh, then turned serious again. "But I won't be able to settle down 'til you find Mary Jane's killer."

"That's understandable, Ell. Just be sure I won't rest 'til we find out who did this."

Elliot flinched.

"What?" said Caleb.

"Zoe just came in."

"Haven't you come to terms with that yet?"

"I still feel kinda awkward around her."

Zoe made her way over to the booth and gave a big smile. "Hi, guys. Have you seen Dennis?"

"No. Are you expecting him?" Caleb asked.

"Yes. We have an important meeting today and he was supposed to meet me here to go over our presentation." She laid a hand on Caleb's shoulder. "I haven't seen you in here for breakfast in a while. Everything all right?"

"Sure. Just needed some of Sally's blueberry pancakes."

"No crime at the Queen Bee today," Elliot said, trying for lightheartedness.

"The only crime in this place is the sheer number of calories in one of Sally's cinnamon rolls," she said.

Caleb laughed.

Elliot sat straight-backed.

Just then, Dennis hustled in, face flushed and breathing heavily.

"Sorry I'm late," he said. "I couldn't find my keys. They were on the coffee table, Zoe."

"Oops. I'm sorry. I must have put them there yesterday when I moved your car to get out of the driveway." She smiled and gave him a peck on the cheek. "I'm forgiven, right?"

Dennis grimaced and said, "Do I have a choice? Come on, let's get to work."

Again, keys, Caleb thought. Could there be a connection? Hollis True and Ned Reese grew up together in Queensbridge. Could True have been one of the friends who came up with the secret coding system? Could he have taken the key to Mary Jane's house from the pegboard in the Reese kitchen? And what about those Gauloises?

"I'm outta here, too," Caleb said, sliding out of the booth. "I've gotta earn my pay. I'll see you guys later."

When Caleb reached the door, he patted his pockets, pretending to have lost something, and returned to the booth.

"How're you doing? You were sitting up so straight I thought you had rebar up your butt."

Elliot snorted. "Still feeling guilty. Like I've betrayed Mary Jane."

"But nothing happened. You're human. You'd been drinking. You're vulnerable right now. Give yourself a break, Ell. Besides, Zoe doesn't act as if she noticed anything." Caleb stood, slapped his friend on the shoulder, and said goodbye. "And do those exercises the doctor gave you."

— • • • —

He crossed the street to the station, but instead of going inside, got into his cruiser and headed straight for Sandy True's house where her brother, wearing an electronic ankle monitoring bracelet, was awaiting trial on the burglary charge.

"Tell me about your secret code."

"Huh?"

"The one you and your friends had in middle school. You wrote notes with it."

True laughed. "That was a million years ago, Chief! It was pretty tame stuff. Any teacher wanting to figure it out would've been able to do it easily."

"So, what was it?"

True squinted his eyes in thought. "I think we just moved two letters to the right. Or maybe was it three? Stupid, kid stuff. We acted like we were James Bond. Why do you need to know? Are you thinking of becoming a spy?"

"You're in no position to be a wise ass, Hollis."

"You're right, Chief. It's my weakness. But know this, I am not a burglar. And I am definitely not a killer."

So, Caleb thought, Hollis True did know the code. He had a solid alibi for the night of the murder, but not for the burglary. Did he take Zoe's jewelry when they met at her house? But when could he have taken Mary Jane's jewelry?

Caleb's head began to spin again.

He went back to his office and dialed the phone. Ned Reese picked up.

"Hey, Chief. What's up?"

"Has Hollis True been to your house since he came back to town?"

"Yeah. We had him to supper right after he got here."

"When was that, exactly?"

Caleb heard what sounded like the pages of a paper calendar flipping.

"Here it is. He was here on August 22nd. It was a Thursday night."

The night before Mary Jane's murder.

"Has he been back?"

Ned laughed. "Nah. I don't think Hollis really got into the whole baby, pets, noise thing we've got goin' on here. But we have met up at the VFW a few times."

"Was he drinking?"

"Just ginger ale. He doesn't drink liquor anymore."

"Did he go into the kitchen at all that night?"

"At the VFW?"

"No. When he came to your house."

The line was silent while Ned thought.

"Yeah. We were eating on the patio, and he helped us clear the dishes."

"Was he ever alone in the kitchen?"

"I don't remember."

"One more question. How did your secret code work?"

"Back in middle school? We added two letters to each letter we wanted to write. So, an A would be a C."

"Do you still use it?"

"Actually, yeah. For the keys."

"Can you check and see if the key to Elliot's house is on the board?"

"Sure."

Caleb heard footsteps and jingling. A moment later Ned was back on the phone.

"It's right here where it's supposed to be, Chief."

"One more thing. Have you been to Elliot's house since then?"

"No. Not since last winter, when I worked on the boiler."

"Right. You did tell me that. Thanks, Ned."

Caleb closed his eyes in an attempt at sorting through the facts.

There were a lot of keys on that board. Hollis couldn't have had enough time to sort through them all and then puzzle out the codes on them, all while people were moving around him. Somebody would have noticed something.

What if the killer didn't have a key?

CHAPTER THIRTY-SIX

The growl of a refrigerator truck rolling down Main Street toward the market derailed whatever train of thought Caleb was on. He reached for his mug, only to find that the coffee had turned cold. He slapped his hands on the desk and pushed himself up from his chair. Hoping to get some inspiration, he decided to take a drive. Back to the scene of the crime.

Not in the mood for either news or commentary, Caleb tuned the radio to the classical jazz program. Herbie Hancock's "Maiden Voyage" was playing, and he tapped his fingers along with it against the steering wheel.

In about five minutes, he arrived at Elliot's house and climbed out of the SUV. A bright sun had warmed the air a bit as the day had progressed, and a strong breeze immediately whipped his hair into a wild mess. Caleb didn't care; the brisk air was a pleasant contrast to the stale indoors of the police station. Besides, maybe the wind might just jog something loose in his mind.

Caleb pulled on a pair of tall boots and started up the driveway toward the back of the log cabin, his breathing becoming labored with the effort of slogging through the deep mud made deeper by the incessant rain. It felt more like March than September and he was happy that he had thought to keep a pair of Wellies in the cruiser. True fall would be here soon enough, followed quickly by winter, and he made a mental note to put his snowshoes back into the SUV. He didn't like the ones he had. They didn't distribute weight nearly as well as his grandfather's antique wood and animal hide model. Maybe he could find out if Granddad's old pair was still stored in the basement of his parents' townhouse in Louisburg Square. But that would require calling his father. On second thought, maybe he could find a pair in an antique shop. Thoughts of his father reminded him of the unopened letter on his desk. He would have to suck it up and read it sooner or later.

The smell of burning wood from a nearby fireplace tickled his nostrils and he breathed deeply to enjoy the moment. Although there wasn't a house around for at least a quarter mile, he realized he wasn't alone on the mountain. He counted half a dozen different animal tracks and their owners' scat deposited on the soft, rain-soaked, packed-earth driveway. Fox, coyote, bobcat, deer, wild turkey, and porcupine had all left their calling cards, but oddly, not a single tweet or howl betrayed their presence.

After a few seconds of near-total silence, his ears detected the hum of the distant turnpike. Then a dog began barking from somewhere on the mountain, followed by a chorus of honking geese flying overhead.

He neared the edge of the property at the back of the house, where it began to fall away down a steep hill. "What am I missing?" he said out loud as he gazed westward toward the sun beginning its early descent behind the hills.

Caleb started to hum the song he had been listening to in the car. Then, he grunted as he acknowledged that his own maiden voyage investigating a homicide was not smooth sailing.

A dull roar interrupted his reverie, followed by a speck appearing in the corner of his eye. What was that? A moose? No, it was a person. On an ATV. He let the dark figure approach closer before he realized it was Ned Reese. Ned pulled up and turned off the motor.

"Hey, Chief."

"Hi, Ned. What're you doing here?"

"Remember? I'm the caretaker for some second homeowners. I wanted to make sure that everything was okay after that crazy storm we had."

"Sure, but Elliot isn't a second homeowner."

"No, but some of the people around here are. I usually take the truck from house to house, but it's gotten so nice that I thought a little fresh air would do me some good. I can go for miles from field to field without touching a surface road."

"Aren't the woods treacherous for the ATV, with all kinds of branches and roots to get caught up on?" Caleb asked.

Ned turned to face west, "Yeah, but isn't it just amazing up here? After all these years, I still get a thrill looking out over this view. It's so beautiful."

But not peaceful. And not everything is as it appears. That damn Sunday school project has really wormed itself into my head.

"Chief? You okay?" Ned's voice penetrated Caleb's daze.

"Yeah, sure," Caleb said, snapping alert.

Ned picked up on Caleb's need to be alone. "I'd better be heading out. I've gotta pick up Michael from his after-school program."

"Well, you don't want to be late for Michael," Caleb said, grateful that Ned was getting the hint to leave him to his thinking.

He watched Ned ride away down the mountain and continued his meditation, trying to calm himself. He to searched his memory slowly and methodically, going over the dozens of interviews he had conducted and conversations he had had since the discovery of Mary Jane's body. "Picture postcard." "Colorful fliers." "I could've killed him." "Rose'll kill me." "Field to field." These phrases came roaring into his head one after the other. He had heard all of them in different contexts. The, his heart jumped as a thought occurred to him. Sandy had said something about the tape having been a decoy. A well-planned tactic to divert suspicion from somebody with a key. He ticked off the names of those who held keys to the house. Earl, Rachel, Zoe, and Ned Reese. And, of course, Elliot. Then there were people with access to those with keys: Rose Reese, Dennis, Luisa, Zoe, and even Tenley. At least he could eliminate his sister; she hadn't arrived in Queensbridge until after Mary Jane's death. That left seven people. One of whom was his own wife.

Feeling suddenly drained, Caleb headed back to his cruiser. He pulled his seat all the way back, stretched out his legs, and closed his eyes. He began slow breathing, hoping for an energizing power nap. He was out in a matter of seconds.

Twenty minutes later, his eyes snapped open, his heart flapping against his chest wall. What had wakened him? All was silent except for the drip-drip of water from an overhead branch. He lay still, trying to retrieve the thought that had brought him out of a dead sleep. More snatches of another conversation bounced around his brain like marbles in a pinball machine. Mead. Honey. Honig. French class. Names. Names!

He bolted upright and immediately turned on the ignition. He raced down the mountain to the station and went straight to his desk. He logged onto the computer and began a search, alternately praying and cursing the village's slow Internet service. He rubbed a hand over the nubby fabric of the chair's arm. Back and forth, back and forth. Come on, come on, hurry up.

And there it was. Exactly what he had feared. He didn't get up but sat staring at the screen. After a long moment, he got up and went to the conference room, pulled out a marker, and attacked the white board, writing in a frenzy, ideas coming thick and fast and bumping into each other.

He sprinted out to the front desk. "Sandy, have Scott go to the Board of Assessors and bring me some maps of the west side. Focus on Swift Road and Pine Mountain Road. I want to see those lots."

"You don't need to wait. You can get the maps online. "I'll pull it up from their website and print it out. It'll just take a minute."

— • • • —

While Sandy typed, Caleb paced. Her task only took a few minutes, but from the look on his face, it could have been hours. After pulling it from the printer, she laid out on the Chief's desk the map of every property in the area of town he had requested. Each lot was numbered, but no names or addresses were attached to them.

"Sandy, I'm not even sure which one of these lots is Elliot's. Would you please get the names of the property owners that abut his land?"

"No problem, Chief. I'll have that for you right away." She picked up the map and took it with her.

He walked over to his office window and watched as the gaslights flickered on along Main Street. He rued that sunset was coming earlier with each passing day. Before he knew it, full-on winter would be here. Then Christmas. It would be a sad one this year, and probably for many more to come.

Sandy knocked on the doorjamb rousing him from his thoughts. "Chief," she said, "I've got those names for you."

He jumped up. "Good, thanks. Let's take a look."

He could see that Sandy had marked in neat block letters the names of every landowner.

"Elliot Freund's lot number is 108. Five properties abut it."

Caleb nodded. "You do good research."

"This is as close to police work as I get," she said quietly.

"This is police work, Sandy."

She smiled.

Caleb bent over the map to look more closely. There. Elliot's property on Pine Mountain Road. He ran his finger from one lot to the next. Immediately north was conservation land. To the south was an undeveloped lot purchased last year by a New Jersey couple named Pryor. The western border of Elliot's lot was wider than the eastern end fronting Pine Mountain Road, and three lots with addresses on Swift Road made contact with it. The southwest lot was owned by the Jordans, a musician and his artist wife. Directly west of Elliot's lot were the Crafts, summer people who occasionally

285

came up on winter weekends. Straddling two edges of the northwest corner of Elliot's property were a lot and house belonging to an elderly couple, the Turners. These were not topographic maps, but Caleb knew that heavy woods ran between the Pine Mountain Road and Swift Road lots. Treacherous terrain.

He stood quietly, staring at the map. And at the annotation on one of the lots.

"Chief?"

At first, Caleb didn't answer. He seemed to be lost in thought. Bits of conversations over the past few weeks came crashing into one another like so many giant jigsaw pieces: Harriet Jablow walking for miles between fields to pick her blueberries and chicory root. Ned Reese going from house to house to do his security checks. The Jackson kid climbing over the wall in the cemetery.

"Chief? Are you okay?"

Caleb shook his head. "I'm fine, Sandy. I'm fine."

He didn't feel fine. He felt sick to his stomach.

— • • • —

Alone in his office after everybody else had left for the day, Caleb pulled out his phone and searched through his photos. There. The six smiling friends, standing together at the village farmers market. His stomach churned.

He riffled through the cards on his desk and, locating the number he wanted, picked up the phone and dialed.

"Hi. Is this Mike?"

"Yeah, it's me."

"This is Police Chief Caleb Crane."

"Hey, Chief. I remember you."

"I'd like to send you a picture to the store's email address. Can you tell me if you recognize anybody in it?"

"Sure. Send away. Nothin's goin' on here anyway."

Caleb hit "send" and waited. Phone receiver tucked under his ear, he ran a hand over the edge of the desk. He could picture Mike squinting at the screen as his fingers ran over the keyboard.

"Yeah, I remember her," he said.

"Which one?"

"The one in the middle."

"Are you sure?"

"Absolutely. I remember 'cause she was one hot babe. And most of our customers are men."

Caleb thanked the clerk and hung up. Acid rose in his throat. The fear that had dogged him for weeks finally formed into a concrete image. He closed his eyes and gulped air. How could she have done it? Why?

He checked his watch. After five. Rachel should be home, making supper. He picked up the phone and dialed. Ring. Ring. *Hurry up, answer.* Ring. Ring. When the voice mail picked up, he slammed the receiver down and dialed her cell phone. Again, no answer. Where the hell was she? What was she up to?

He grabbed his keys, and within moments, he was in the Explorer. He peeled out of the parking lot, heading home. His hands were like vises on the steering wheel as he raced up the hill.

He pulled into the driveway and jumped out, the car still rocking. He ran to the back door and let himself into the kitchen.

"Rachel!" he called. No answer. "Rachel!" He called out repeatedly, running through the house from room to room, up the stairs to the second floor, and then down to the cellar. Nobody. His heart pounding, he checked the kitchen table, their customary note-leaving place. Nothing.

He stopped in the middle of the floor. Close your eyes and take a deep breath. Cleansing breath. One, two, three, four. Slow down and think.

After about thirty seconds, Caleb opened his eyes and slowly began to scan the room. There, practically hidden underneath a bowl of fruit in the middle of the table, sat a piece of notepaper. He bent over to retrieve it.

His stomach roiled. Rachel had written that she had gone to bring soup to an ailing Zoe.

Oh, God.

CHAPTER THIRTY-SEVEN

Caleb ran to his cruiser and pulled out of the driveway while calling the station.

"Sandy, I need back-up at Zoe's house. Send Jack and Scott."

"There's a huge car crash and fire in the valley. They're both there."

Caleb blew out air. "See if one of them can handle it alone. Send Scott and tell him to come around to the back of Zoe Bouvier's house on Swift Road."

"Is she in trouble?"

"Just do it."

As he pulled up to Zoe's house, he saw that Rachel's car wasn't there. *Thank God.* But if she wasn't here and she wasn't at home, where could she be? Was Zoe at home? Her car wasn't visible either, but lights were on in the house. He eased into the driveway, gravel crunching under the tires, and waited a few seconds before getting out, rehearsing again in his mind how he would approach Zoe. Finally, steeling himself, he got out of the cruiser and approached the front door. He lifted the moose head knocker, banging on the heavy wooden door three times, noting the heft of the metal in his hand.

Zoe opened the door. Her voice was husky, her nose red, the whites of her eyes threaded with red squiggles. "Caleb, this is a surprise! Come on in. Would you like some tea? I just made some."

"No, thanks Zoe." Entering the warm house, he looked around. "Rachel left a note that she was coming here. I was hoping to catch her."

"She was here. She brought me some wonderful chicken soup for my cold. Between the soup and all the tea I'm drinking, every germ in my body should wash right out." She smiled and turned toward the kitchen. "The tea is steeping. I'll bring a cup for you in case you change your mind."

While she was in the kitchen, Caleb walked over to the piano to look at the photos arranged there.

"As long as I'm here I'd like to ask you some more questions about Mary Jane. Maybe working together we can retrieve something from your memory that will help find her killer."

"Sure, Caleb."

Zoe returned with a serving tray laden with a teapot, cups, saucers, and a plate of ginger snaps. She set the tray down on the coffee table and took her own seat on an overstuffed armchair.

"Where's Truffles? I don't see her," Caleb said.

"Oh, probably sleeping on the sofa in the den. That's her favorite place."

"Dennis tells me she didn't get along with the dog."

"That's the understatement of the year. Truffles is a real princess. I guess she didn't like the competition."

Neither did you.

Caleb began his careful approach. "Y'know, Zoe, I don't think I've told you how much Rachel and I have treasured your friendship. Especially since Mary Jane died, you've been a great support to us, and especially to Elliot. I know he appreciates it, even if he isn't quite up to knowing it yet."

Zoe smiled. "Elliot needs us more than ever right now. I'm happy to be there for him. And Rachel and I have a special bond, both of us being childless."

He switched topics. "A while back I got an envelope in my post office box addressed to a Zelda Bootes. Why didn't you ever mention that you changed your name?"

Zoe made a face of disgust. "I changed my name for business. I've told you before that interior design is all about image. Nobody would hire a Zelda Bootes. And there's nothing illegal about it. People do it all the time. Look at Hollywood," she said with a laugh.

She didn't hesitate at all. Rehearsed?

"Rachel was so worried about you when you couldn't talk about Evan without breaking down. So, I did a little surfing on the Internet, thinking I could help her understand what happened that hurt you so badly. And guess what I discovered?"

Zoe clenched her teeth. "What did you find? Have you been snooping around about me?"

"Evan Bootes. Your late husband, alive and well and living in Silicon Valley. Zoe, why did you think you had to lie to us? We're your friends."

Zoe twisted the tissues in her hands, then looked up at him with tears in her eyes. "I *am* all about image, Caleb. I'm not proud of it but being divorced in my family is a tragedy. They're very old fashioned and they loved Evan. More than

291

they ever loved me." She dabbed at her eyes and blew her nose, then continued. "Haven't you ever wondered why my family doesn't come to visit? I'm an embarrassment to them."

She certainly seems to have answers at the ready. Could I be on the wrong track?

"Yeah, about your family. Y'know, I thought Dennis and Rachel were just being a little catty when they said your family photos were too perfect. Elliot was the one who noticed something off about those pictures. The poses were natural enough. Certainly not fashion models, but real people. But just a bit wrong. It took me a while, but I finally figured it out. They weren't looking directly at you holding the camera, but at something else."

"What are you talking about?"

"Did you use a long lens to take those pictures of somebody else's happy family? Or did you just print these photos from the web?"

Zoe was silent, twisting the tissue in her hands.

Caleb continued. "It was somebody else's family, wasn't it?"

"Those are my nieces and nephews!"

"But you told us you were an only child. Was that also a lie?"

"What about Evan? Isn't he allowed to have siblings?"

"Sure, he is, but their kids are still in their cribs. I spoke with him."

Zoe sighed and threw her hands into the air. "Honestly? Evan was a moron. He didn't know what he had. I made him who he is today. If it hadn't been for me, he would never have met the people who made him so successful."

"But he left you and moved to California. That's where the photos were taken, right? He threatened you with a restraining order to stop you stalking him, didn't he?"

"No comment."

"And that so-called break-in here? I'm trying to wrap my head around it. You took the jewelry, but you had to chuck the stuff somewhere to make it look like a burglary."

"Hollis True stole it! You saw the stuff from his bag." She took in a quick huff of air.

She just realized she's tipped her hand.

"I've gotta say, Zoe. Implicating Hollis was a real stroke of genius. Too bad you made some pretty big mistakes."

She picked up her cup and chugged it. "Mistakes? What mistakes?" Her words began to slur.

"You wanted sympathy for the break-in. But then you realized you had the opportunity to make the story even better. So, you made an appointment with Hollis to talk business at your house. And you did it while I was right there with you at the Queen Bee. That was ballsy, Zoe."

Zoe scowled. "If I took the jewelry, how did it get on Hollis True's motorcycle?"

"At some point—you went by Sandy's house, maybe?— you planted the stuff on his bike. How else would you know the jewelry was in his bag? So, there it is. Your first really big mistake, Zoe, trying to pin it all on Hollis True."

Zoe looked at him through slitted eyes.

I know I'm pushing her, but I can't stop. I have to know the whole story.

"Hollis wouldn't have known about the hidden cabinets. The jewelry was behind the front panel." He paused. "Nobody would've known. Except you."

"Rachel knew." Zoe said with a sneer. "You knew, too. Even Dennis knew about the built-ins."

Grasping at straws?

Caleb pressed on. "You and Rachel were the only ones who ever actually saw the cabinet. Dennis knew about it, but Hollis wouldn't have known that the closet even existed."

Before Zoe could respond, Caleb changed the subject again. "How's your ankle? Has it healed completely?"

"Oh, it's fine now. That happened ages ago. Now I just have to deal with this cold."

"The scratches on your face and arms have faded, too."

"Thank goodness." Zoe blew her nose into a tissue. Just then, Truffles padded into the room and jumped into Zoe's lap. She smiled and ran her fingers through her pet's soft fur.

Zoe was one cool customer. Where should he go next? Caleb decided to mix things up and try to keep her off balance.

"It was so good of Dennis to come back from Albany to drive you to the hospital."

"Dennis is a good friend. Of course, he would help me."

In a soft voice he said, "But you didn't sprain your ankle in the house that Friday night, did you?"

"What do you mean, Caleb? You saw me on crutches."

"I mean, you didn't do it in the house."

"I told you I tripped in the hallway."

"Those scratches were big and nasty. They weren't from falling into a basket of pinecones. In fact, there was no basket of anything in your hallway. Actually, I think you got scratched when you tripped in the woods. Running away after killing Mary Jane. The Turner property abuts hers."

Treacherous terrain.

Zoe walked over to the sideboard in the dining room.

"I have to say I'm impressed, Caleb. You have quite the imagination."

Above the crackling of the burning wood in the grate, Caleb heard a noise off to his right. Before he had a chance to consider the source, Rachel came through the front door into the living room, carrying a bag with a drug store logo. He jumped up from the chair and headed toward her.

"Caleb! What a surprise! I didn't expect to see you here."

She turned toward Zoe. "I picked up some more cough medicine for you, and a little treat." She waved a package of gummy bears. Suddenly, her eyes widened with fright.

Caleb turned to see Zoe aiming a pistol directly at his chest. A Sig Sauer P250. Small, but with its thirteen-round magazine, powerful enough to rip a hole in his heart many times over.

Caleb's heart began to gallop. He knew he needed to stay in control and use his brain. His greatest strength had always been his ability to keep calm under pressure. But this was his wife, the love of his life, standing not ten feet away from a murderer. A murderer holding a lethal weapon.

Caleb turned to Rachel and raised his chin in an attempt to signal her to back out slowly.

"Don't even think of moving, Rachel," Zoe said.

Caleb knew he had to keep Zoe talking. He folded his arms and shook his head, hoping to look nonthreatening.

"Well, I guess you decided to buy a gun anyway, even after we all tried to talk you out of it." His right hand inched toward the holster strapped under his left arm. He prayed he wouldn't have to use it.

"You know how afraid I've been since Mary Jane died."

"Except that you knew that Mary Jane wasn't shot."

Zoe's eyes narrowed. "I got the gun for protection after the dog didn't work out."

"That's one hell of a weapon, Zoe. You must have dropped a lot of money on it."

"Yep, and it will be worth every penny." Zoe's hand shook as she clutched the pistol.

"I know you didn't apply for a license to carry here in Queensbridge. Did you get it in New York?"

"Yes," she said. "I'm still a resident there. All perfectly legal."

She sneezed suddenly. As she reached into her pocket to get a tissue, Caleb used the distraction to try to signal Rachel to escape, but he couldn't catch her eye. She was staring open-mouthed at Zoe.

"To get a license, you would have to have taken a gun safety class, right? You know you should never point a gun at somebody unless you plan to fire it."

"Yes, Caleb. I do remember that lesson," Zoe said, a beatific smile on her face.

The muscles in his neck tightened.

"And here I didn't think such a small-town cop could figure it out. After all, you were so proud of the fact that this little village had never had a murder." Her voice was so soft and raspy he had trouble hearing her.

Caleb switched directions again. "So, you moved here and fixed your sights on Elliot. Planned to start a new life."

Zoe got a dreamy look in her eyes. "Yes, with Elliot. Tenley was never going to have him if I had anything to say about it. I saw her flirt with him. Shameless."

Rachel gasped. Her already pale face had turned ashen. "But Tenley's not interested in him. That's just the way she and Elliot interact."

"Were you planning to kill her, too?" Caleb asked.

"Gotta eliminate the competition."

He took a breath, then continued. "I've gotta hand it to you, Zoe, you really had this planned out right down to the tiniest details, just like a client's home decor. You even made sure that Elliot would be out of town when the murder went down."

"Of course. I didn't want anybody casting suspicion on him."

"And telling me that Mary Jane lent the scarf to you? Did you get a kick out of dangling the murder weapon right in front of me?"

Zoe barked out a laugh.

"When did you first think this little ruse up?"

"When I was in her bedroom to see the famous closet. She got a phone call and left the room. And that's when the idea came to me. I knew she wouldn't be wearing scarves in the summer. She never even noticed it was gone."

Caleb tried to absorb the reality that their friend was a cold-blooded killer.

"You really had us on a wild goose chase there, looking for a stalker, what with those notes you wrote to yourself and Rachel."

"The *coup de grace!*" Zoe's smile was getting to Caleb.

Rachel stiffened, her eyes dark and flashing. "Oh my God, Zoe! It was you who sent the letters?"

Caleb continued. "Printing the Pumpkin Festival fliers on your high-end printer might not have been such a good idea."

"You're probably right, but I figured there are lots of good printers around. You'd never connect the dots."

Caleb changed the subject. "When exactly did you put the tape over the lock in the basement?"

Zoe laughed. "Oh, that was easy. The day Rachel and I went to help Mary Jane paint her bedroom, I offered to go down to the cellar to get some drop cloths. Easy. I have a key. Just had to unlock the door from the inside, tape the lock, and then come back later. Pretty good, huh?" Zoe's eyes were glazed, whether from fever or hysteria he couldn't be sure.

"And nobody was the wiser. Until now."

For a moment, Caleb thought he saw Zoe puff up with pride at her accomplishment. Hoping to divert her attention from Rachel, he began to pace back and forth. Every time he turned, his back to Zoe, he tried to catch his wife's eye. He mouthed "Run!" But she was frozen in place with a deer-in-the-headlights look on her face.

Zoe waved the gun. "Stop moving!"

He stopped halfway between himself and Rachel, blocking Zoe's view of her.

"You even left your fingerprints all over the bedroom. Quite the bold statement."

"The night of the dirty deed, I wore gloves. Didn't want my DNA on her body, but I needed some prints to be there. Rachel and I had both been in the room that day."

"And you sanitized Mary Jane's hands and arms. Very thorough."

"You know me. I'm always very thorough."

"You really got just about every detail right. Even down to the cigarette smoke in Mary Jane's house. Another way to direct attention toward Hollis, one of two people on our list

298

who smoked Gauloises. But that's where you made another mistake."

"How do you figure that? I thought it was a brilliant move." Zoe pushed a stray hair from her forehead.

Caleb caught a glimpse of Rachel. Pale and trembling, she propped herself up against the doorjamb.

He felt sick to his stomach, wondering how he had ever trusted Zoe. But he had to get to the truth.

"You wore gloves, right? So, no fingerprints. No DNA. If you'd been smart, you would've taken one that Hollis had dropped on the ground."

Zoe shrugged.

"Did she struggle at all, Zoe?"

"Mary Jane was out cold. Remember, Elliot himself said that nothing short of an earthquake could wake her. That baby she said she wanted so badly? Elliot would've had to get up at night with it. She'd never hear it."

Acid rose in Caleb's throat.

I was wrong. Mary Jane's death did have something to do with her being pregnant. Maybe everything.

Zoe laughed. "When we had our girls-only weekend at Canyon Ranch last year, the fire alarm went off. Rachel and I practically had to carry her out of the room she was so out of it."

"So, you had it all figured out."

Zoe ignored the question. "I've been in love with Elliot for years, ever since the first time I saw him. Why else do you think I kept coming back to Queensbridge every summer? For the music?" She snorted.

Caleb continued pressing her. "The whole time you pretended to be the great, supportive friend you were actually plotting to get close to Elliot. But Mary Jane was an inconvenient obstacle."

"Yes." Zoe nodded in agreement. "She was exactly that. An obstacle."

"But why kill her?"

"Mary Jane always got everything. She monopolized Rachel, flaunting their friendship from childhood."

"But Mary Jane loved you!" Rachel cried. "We both loved you. We trusted you with our secrets. We were best friends." She shuddered. "How could you kill her?"

Zoe snorted. "You and she were best friends. I wanted to be yours, but I was always only a third wheel. She just tolerated me. She had Elliot. She didn't deserve him. And she didn't deserve to have his child. Mary Jane was the only thing preventing me from having him and you. Once I learned she was pregnant, I knew I had to act before she screwed everything up."

Zoe suddenly whirled around, waving her arms. "Mary Jane, Mary Jane," she sang in a high-pitched, nursery school-teacher voice. Her eyes were wide open and glassy. "Such a little girl's name for a grown woman. Elliot needed me. I could give him the life he deserves. Not that log cabin mountain man thing."

She's completely unhinged. I've got to keep her talking while I figure out how to get that gun out of her hand. I really don't want to have to shoot her.

"Elliot loves that house. He built it himself," he said.

"He would have learned to love the good life."

"Zoe, put the gun down."

"I don't think so." She laughed.

Shivers ran up Caleb's spine. "What do you plan to do with the gun, Zoe?"

"I plan to kill you with it, of course."

Rachel moaned. Her face was even whiter than before.

"Why do you think you need to do that?"

"Because you want to arrest me, but I don't want to go to prison. I can't go to prison. The dirt. The noise. The kind of people you find there."

Caleb continued to press her. "What kind of people do you find there, Zoe?"

"You know. Low-class types. Burglars, drug dealers."

"Murderers?"

As he inched toward her, Caleb detected a whiff of alcohol. "You've had a lot to drink, haven't you?"

"I've had a couple. For medicinal reasons. And don't come any closer. I will shoot you."

"I can see that. But Zoe, if you've been taking cold medicine on top of the liquor, your judgment is impaired. You don't want to do something you'll regret. Please put the gun down on the coffee table."

Zoe thrust her arm forward, the gunmetal catching the light from the fireplace.

Caleb stood still, looking straight into her eyes. Zoe took a step forward, but Caleb remained where he was.

The cat entered the room, purred, and jumped onto the console table against the far wall. Zoe turned toward it, murmuring, "Good girl, Truffles."

Seizing the opening, Rachel snapped to attention and made a dash for the front door.

"Get back here, Rachel, or I'll shoot him right now."

"Run, Rachel, run!" Caleb shouted, but his wife returned to her post by the doorway.

"I can't leave you."

Zoe rasped out a laugh. "You'll never catch me where I'm going, Caleb. You're a nice guy for a local, but you're not smart enough."

"Zoe, I've already caught you."

She sniffled, her eyes blazing now. "Move over to the chair and sit down, Caleb."

"No, I don't think so." He calculated the distance between himself and Zoe. Was there anything he could use as protection without having to resort to his service revolver? His eyes swept the room. A set of andirons stood by the fireplace. Could he get clear across the room?

"Zoe, let's calm down and talk this out."

"I am calm. Perfectly calm. You know me. I'm always in control."

"Yes, and never a hair out of place."

"Are you making fun of me?"

"I wouldn't do that Zoe. I just know that you like everything to be just right. That's why your house is picture perfect."

"Yes, it is!" she said. "That's why I picked this village. It's picture perfect. That's what I always say."

"Yes, you do. But not everything is the way it appears, is it? Like those bowls that you gave to Rachel."

"Those are real Sandwich glass!"

"Yes but meant to show what a kind and generous friend you are. And you brought them from New York. How convenient that you go there so frequently. You must know all the antique stores. And the adult video stores."

Zoe's eyes widened.

"Did you buy the porn video on one of your trips to New York?"

"Porn? Me? That's just insulting. I would never buy anything so disgusting."

"No? Funny how the clerk at the video store recognized you from a photo."

Zoe let out a sigh. "Well, well, you've really done your homework, Mr. Chief of Police."

He spied a heavy glass bust set on a pedestal, but Zoe was standing right next to it. What could he use to subdue her?

"I've gotta hand it to you, Zoe. Other than those two big boo-boos, this was a really well-planned murder."

The three remained motionless as the clock on the mantel ticked the seconds.

The cat purred again and jumped off her perch.

"That's right, Truffles," Zoe said, her gaze sweeping between Caleb and Rachel. "It's almost over. Mummy will be with you soon."

Caleb felt the Glock in the shoulder holster under his jacket, cold and hard against his ribs, a contrast to the sweat dripping down his back, soaking his uniform shirt. He slid his eyes to the side to check on Rachel and saw terror in her eyes.

Suddenly he felt something soft and warm on his leg. He looked down to see that Truffles had padded up and was rubbing against him. Caleb took his chance. He bent over, scooped up the cat, and threw it toward Zoe. Startled, she put her up hands to catch it, but the gun in her hand prevented her from doing so. The cat landed on all fours and scampered out of the room. Caleb lunged toward Zoe and grabbed her wrist and, twisting it, forced the gun from her hand. He pushed her to her knees, grabbed the handcuffs from his belt, and snapped them onto her wrists. She squirmed feverishly, trying to wrench her body away from him. Spittle sprayed from her mouth as she screamed.

"Just you wait! You'll see. Elliot will bail me out and defend me. He will love me! And you and your Rachel can go to hell. I don't need you!"

He pulled zip ties from his pocket and secured Zoe's legs at the ankles while Rachel ran over and pushed the pistol away with her foot. Caleb picked it up using a handkerchief and set it aside to be bagged.

"Oh my God," said Rachel. "How did you know?" Her knees began to shake, and she collapsed into the nearest chair.

Before he had a chance to answer, they both heard a noise coming from the back door. Caleb drew his weapon from its holster and edged along the wall of the great room until he reached the kitchen. The back door's knob was jiggling but it was too dark outside to see anything. He pulled his flashlight from his belt and shined it at the window. Scott was working at jimmying the lock. Caleb yanked the door open. Scott's face was covered with perspiration and his uniform smelled of gasoline.

"I got here as fast as I could, Chief," he said.

"It's okay. It's all over. Take Zoe in and book her. I need to take care of Rachel."

"Book her? For what?"

"Murder."

— • • • —

Hours later, Caleb returned home, his face drawn and gray. Rachel, Tenley, and Dennis got up from their seats at the farm table and went to him. Elliot went to the sideboard and poured himself and Caleb a glass of bourbon.

Caleb finished the liquor in one gulp and poured himself another. He then sat down at the table and the friends gathered around him. They listened with mouths agape as he listed Zoe's actions that had brought them to this terrible point. He described how she had planned the murder, the jewelry theft, and the framing of Hollis True. And he told of her depraved plot to snare Elliot that had started the entire mess.

When he finished, Dennis stood and began to pace. He looked for something to punch but had to settle for his open palm.

"How could she use us all like that? I feel so dirty. And really pissed. She was supposed to be our friend. I can't believe I did business with her."

Elliot hunched over, elbows on the table. He shook his head as if to rid it of unwanted images, then ran his hands over his face.

"I can't believe I couldn't see what she was. I'm supposed to be a good lawyer, able to see who's lying and who's telling the truth. How did I miss all the signs?" He groaned.

"She was wearing a mask the whole time we've known her," Rachel said.

"And what about Hollis True? I hope you've set him free," Tenley said.

"It's in the works, and with sincere apologies," Caleb said. "Sandy was right. The poor guy's been working so hard to get his life back on track, and Zoe almost destroyed him."

"How's Sandy?" Dennis asked. "It must've been really hard to see her brother hauled off."

"Sandy's a professional. She saw the evidence and knew the procedure we had to follow," Caleb said.

"That doesn't mean she liked it," Dennis said.

"No, and I think she's still a little pissed off at me."

Caleb turned to see Rachel sitting quietly, eyes glazed. She stared into space as silent tears ran down her cheeks. He wondered if she was mourning the loss of yet another close friend—or perhaps of her own open and generous heart. His own heart ached for her.

CHAPTER THIRTY-EIGHT

Caleb woke late the following Sunday morning to the distant sound of shovels scraping and snow blowers roaring. The neighborhood was cleaning up after a monster storm that had surprised everybody both for its ferocity and for how early it had come in the season. He lay in bed and savored the softness and warmth of the covers, enjoying a feeling of calm for the first time in many months. It had been over a week since the confrontation with Zoe, but it had taken all that time for the tension to leach from his tightly wound body. He also felt vindicated, whether or not his father ever knew about his successful conclusion of a murder investigation. It had taken a while, but he had used his skills to solve a serious crime. He was a cop. And a good one. He thought about calling his father to tell him, then dismissed it. Too needy, he would be told. Let him read about it in the newspaper. But that unopened envelope still sat on his desk.

He rolled over and inhaled the scent of Rachel's shampoo on her unoccupied pillow. He could hear her working in the kitchen, the opening and shutting of cabinets and drawers, and the clink of plates and flatware. The aroma of freshly brewing coffee and the sputter of pancake batter on the griddle finally pried him from the bed. After putting on his robe and slippers, he raised the eastern-facing shades to a blindingly bright morning. He placed his hands on the window frame and leaned forward to gaze out at the scene before him. The village lay covered in a heavy marshmallow blanket. Icicles glinted in the sunlight, and snow-covered roofs sparkled. Evergreen trees sported fluffy white frosting like so many conical cakes.

Caleb considered the edging of crystals that bejeweled the windowpanes and leaned his forehead against the ice-cold glass. His home. His village. He took a deep breath and turned to join Rachel in the kitchen.

Rachel looked up from the kitchen counter, her eyes moist. He started.

"Are you crying? Did you cut yourself?"

"No, I didn't cut myself." She smiled, her eyes glinting through the prism of her tears.

Please, not another period. But is that a smile?

"Okay, I'll bite," he said. "What's up?"

"What makes you think something's up?"

"Because I know you." Caleb felt a tickle in his chest. "What is it?"

"I'm pregnant."

Caleb's jaw dropped open and he bounded across the room. He wrapped his arms around his wife, lifted her and spun her around. When he set her down, he held Rachel's face in his hands and gazed at her, not uttering a word.

"Are you okay?" she asked.

"I'm better than okay. I thought we would never have this conversation. I'm amazed."

More tears cascaded down Rachel's cheeks. She lowered her head and whispered, "Frankly, you're a lot happier than I thought you'd be. What happened?"

"I've thought a lot about what you said. About how we are not my parents. About how there are no guarantees in life. About how we would be great parents. I realized that nobody could be a better mother, and you'll help me to be a good father."

"Maybe I should go to law school. I'm pretty persuasive," Rachel said.

"Sure, why not?" Caleb grinned. "How far along are you? Do you feel all right?"

"I'm fifteen weeks along, and I still feel pretty awful in the morning, but that's fine with me. It's a good sign."

"Why did you wait so long to tell me?"

"I wanted to be sure this one would take."

"Yeah, I can understand that. I'm amazed that I didn't notice you were sick."

Rachel scrunched up her nose. "You've been a little distracted lately, sir."

"True enough. But I promise to make it up to you. We'll take that trip and relax. Just the two of us."

Rachel cleared her throat and looked up into Caleb's eyes. "If it's a girl, I'd like to name her after both your mother and Mary Jane. How do you like Mary Elizabeth?"

"I like it a lot."

He drew Rachel to him and closed his eyes. He could feel two heartbeats where their chests met.

That evening, Caleb retrieved the ivory envelope from under the blotter on his desk. He stared at his father's handwriting for a long minute, wondering if he had the desire—or the courage—to call him. What could he say to this man who had demeaned his mother and derided every choice he'd made?

Then again, he had important news to share. He had solved a horrific crime, proving he had what it took to be a good cop. Even better, Rachel was pregnant. Now he could show his father that he had made excellent choices—although he probably wouldn't tell him about the gun Zoe had aimed at them.

Taking a deep breath, he leaned across the desk and picked up the silver letter opener that had belonged to his mother. He carefully slit open the envelope and pulled out a single sheet of the heavy stock. He unfolded the paper and read.

After a few minutes, he reached for the telephone and dialed.

"Father?"

Thank you so much for reading THE FIRST MURDER. If you've enjoyed the book, we would be grateful if you would post a review on the bookseller's website. Just a few words is all it takes!

Acknowledgements

This book would not be in the shape it's in without the input of so many people. West Stockbridge Police Chief Tom Rubino, Worcester Police Officer John Doucimo, and Zorran Atanasovski of the Massachusetts Firearms Records Bureau explained police procedure and gun licensing law. Dr. Lara Goldfeder, Office of the Chief Medical Examiner for the City of New York took time out of her very busy day to help me understand what a medical examiner does. Thank you all. Any errors are unintentional and totally due to my own ignorance.

A very deep thanks to my fairy godmother, Sharon Healy-Yang, for encouraging me to submit my book to her publisher. And to Sheri Williams and Kim Coghlan, who welcomed me so warmly into the TouchPoint Press family. To Eleonora Masala, my very patient editor, thank you. To my critique group ladies, Ruth McCarty, Sharon Daynard, Janet Raye Stevens, Carol Perry, and Donna Ricci: Thank you for taking in this green fiction writer and teaching me so much. To my children Seth, Avi, and Elana, who saw early drafts and made valuable suggestions, thank you. I love you sooo much. To Barb and Artie Dean, Ellen Weingart, and Lorrin Krouss, thank you for indulging me.

And to Joel, who brought me to tears—of laughter—while pointing out gaps in the story. You are my rock.

Made in the USA
Middletown, DE
30 March 2024